I0546245

SINGLE JEOPARDY

A Peter Sharp Legal Mystery

By Gene Grossman

From Magic Lamp Press
Venice, California

Press ™

www.legalmystery.com

This is a work of fiction. Any resemblance to actual persons, living or dead is entirely coincidental.

SINGLE JEOPARDY
Peter Sharp Legal Mystery #1

Peter Sharp Legal Mystery Series
http://www.petersharpbooks.com

ISBN: 1-882629-19-1

The Complete
Peter Sharp Legal Mystery Series

www.legalmystery.com

Single Jeopardy

By Reason of Sanity

A Class Action

Conspiracy of Innocence

...Until Proven Innocent

The Common Law

The Magician's Legacy

The Reluctant Jurist

The Final Case

An Element of Peril

A Good Alibi

Legally Dead

```
If a shipbuilder build a boat for some one,
    and do not make it tight, and if during
  that same year that boat is sent away and
suffers injury, the ship-builder shall take
the boat apart and put it together tight at
   his own expense. The tight boat he shall
                      give to the boat owner.
```

Number 235, from Hammurabi' s Code of 282 Laws

1

Boating can be a great sport, but not in a back yard – which is where I'm presently doing my yachting, as the result of several swift moves choreographed by my soon-to-be ex-wife and her beady-eyed divorce lawyer, whose cheap business card should be changed to read 'Gary Koontz, Schmuck at Law.'

My sleeping quarters were involuntarily changed from the bedroom, to the living room couch, and then out to this 1956 classic forty-foot Chris Craft Constellation, a bull-nosed cabin cruiser I've been restoring out here in the yard for the past seven years. Having been told to take the rest of my life off by the law firm I was formerly employed by, I'm sitting here in the cabin of my boat/office talking on the phone to my San Fernando Valley friend Stuart.

One good thing about Stuart is that no matter how bad off you might think you're doing, Stuart can convince you he's doing worse... and he usually is. His cause de jour is suing the United States Government and some large corporations for poisoning him: he claims to be suffering from mesothelioma, a form of asbestos damage to the lining of his lungs that he claims was a result of spending four years working in the Navy as a ship's boiler room engineer.

To humor him, I prepared and filed a lawsuit last month so that he wouldn't blow the Statute of Limitations, and now he wants to go ahead with it by having the U.S. Marshall's office serve the lawsuit on all the defendants.

Wonderful. A federal case. Just what I need at this low point in my life. I tell him now that I'm semi-retired I don't have the office staff, but I'll try to associate another attorney in on the case who is much better equipped to handle this type of case.

My involuntary retirement may not be such a bad thing after all, considering the fact that there'll be no boat restoration distractions from clients like Stuart. For the past few years, every time he calls it's to either file another lawsuit or go with him to meet his uncle Label, who's supposed to own a boat in the Marina.

When I was a kid, growing up in Chicago on North Kedzie Avenue, one of my favorite Saturday afternoon pastimes was packing a lunch and hopping on my bike for a long bike ride down Lawrence Avenue, and then south along Sheridan Road, to Belmont Harbor. I would spend all afternoon there sitting on the concrete seawall, daydreaming, my legs dangling over the edge. I used to rest my arms on the middle rung of the guard rail – the rail that kept the have-nots without boats away from the privileged few 'haves' who not only had boats, but also had the political pull to get a mooring in the city's most popular Marina. The daydream was usually the same... someday I'd have one of those big, shiny, varnished wood cabin cruisers, complete with an ornament that so many of them seemed to be displaying on their foreward decks – a beautiful redheaded wife.

It took almost thirty years, before fate was kind to me - but with a string attached: I was allowed to achieve my dream, but found out you aren't allowed to enjoy both the boat and the wife at the same time.

There's a tragic procedure that takes place in many marriages, all brought about by a conflict of goals. A woman will view a prospective husband as a work in progress... a project... an acquisition she can transform into something respectable who is safe to bring to boring social functions. On the other hand, a man looks at a woman, likes what he sees, and hopes that she stays just like that forever - without ever changing.

Unfortunately, the opposite of what they each hoped for usually takes place. The woman fails in all her attempts to change the man, whose traits are usually etched in stone. And on the other side of the equation, the woman goes through all the personality and cosmetic changes, winding up being nothing like what the husband thought he would spend the rest of his life with. Some states have a six-month waiting period before a divorce becomes final, but it might be a better idea to put the waiting period in front, making it a six-month wait and then a trial period before the marriage is a locked-in deal.

Neither going through changes nor staying the same is necessarily a bad thing, but either case can cause disappointment and strain on a marriage. That's what happened in our case. My wife Myra is still beautiful, but she progressed from being a gorgeous demure redheaded receptionist, to a legal secretary, to a paralegal, on to law school, passed the Bar exam and now is a ball-busting brunette prosecuting attorney with the local District Attorney's office. On the other hand, I have remained a completely unchanged, dedicated, poor, defense attorney representing the downtrodden (but in most cases guilty) people who have been charged with crimes by her office.

The philosophical difference between prosecution and defense attitudes can be enough to break up a marriage. This strain on the relationship is never brought out clearer than when the mind-sets collide head on at a social gathering. Most prosecuting attorneys eventually assume the zeal of people on a crusade to 'put away the bad guys,' who are all assumed to be guilty just because they've been arrested. Even the smallest file on a misdemeanor theft is no longer a case... it's a crusade, with the defense attorney looked upon as being a troublesome barrier between the D.A.'s office and justice.

The calendar clerks never put Myra and I up against each other in the courtroom, but our being on different sides of the fence has created a Marcia Clark versus F. Lee Bailey type of atmosphere, as displayed on television every day some years back during the O.J. Simpson criminal trial. I'll never be able to figure out how that republican-democrat marriage of Mary Matalin and James Carville seems to have flourished so well unless they finally figured out how to do what my soon-to-be-ex and I never mastered: leaving all of our philosophical differences behind at the office.

Things got worse when we tried to bring our circle of friends together, because hard-nosed right-wing district attorneys with that prosecutorial badge-heavy swagger don't mix well with left-wing defenders of drug-dealers, pornographers and child molesters. But that wasn't all: when it looked like my boat restoring project was within a year of completion, we went boating with some friends and discovered that my beloved wife has a very low tolerance for motion. She can get terribly seasick at any distance more than 10 feet from the dock. Seasickness is quite common with self-centered people who have difficulty taking into consideration the boat, motion, other people around them, and a lot of other factors that contribute to the illness.

Our differences didn't stop just with the enjoyment of boating. I had to work my way through high school, college and law school by playing piano in saloons. Once we could afford a nice living-room piano, I discovered that my wife was tone-deaf and didn't like the way I played. This was definitely a marriage-counselor's nightmare, so I guess that's why while I'm out here in the back yard sitting in an old boat, my wife and her lawyer are inside that nice Brentwood home, scheming. Looking over there occasionally I notice his beady eyes peering out at my boat through the house's mini-blinds. He spends a lot of time ogling my wife and my boat... but it'll be over my dead body before he gets his hands on my boat.

I'm hoping that Stuart will tire of talking soon so I can get back to trying to fix an electrical short in the boat's wiring system before it burns the boat, and my wife's house with it. She owned the house before we were married, so she'll no doubt stay in at after I'm gone.

Fixing things on the boat are harder than I expected – mainly because I don't know what the hell I'm doing. Boat wiring is a lot different than house wiring: you can't just connect things with supermarket extension cords, because they're not heavy-duty enough to withstand the extremely harsh elements of a saltwater environment. Humans don't belong in the ocean, and the ocean keeps telling us that by trying to invade our territory just like we're invading its. An electrician friend of mine told me that I've done a nice job of cosmetically restoring this old tub, but without a complete re-wiring job it won't last too long after it's put in the water. Without a steady source of income, I'll have to cross that bridge when I come to it.

2

Not having handled any personal injury cases for a couple of years since my tow-truck driving friend lost his job and my paralegal Ricky Hansel disappeared, it was a pleasant surprise last year to receive a phone call from one of the alcoholic insurance adjusters I used to do business with. Whenever an adjuster calls it's usually because he's got some money to offer you. I thought that this call was for one of the old cases I'd filed and forgotten, so I agreed to meet with him at a local eatery.

Quite often when there are multiple plaintiffs in the same damaged vehicle, the adjuster will be given authority to dispose of all the cases at one time, for some maximum total amount of settlement money. In cases where one plaintiff attorney is handling everyone in the car, the attorney and adjuster usually get together to calculate how the distribution of funds will be made between the plaintiffs... and if the meeting is in an establishment where alcohol is served, there's always a possibility that the settlement amount might increase towards the maximum as the successive rounds are served. Our meeting started out cordially enough, but one small thing bothered me. I only had one drink, but I didn't recognize the names of the people involved in the case. I told him I didn't represent these people. The adjustor must have thought I was either trying out a new settlement tactic or experiencing the onset of Alzheimer's. When my denials of representation became more adamant and he realized I wasn't kidding, he produced some recent correspondence he received from my office, listed at "Peter Sharp & Associates" and signed by my wannabe 'associate,' Ricky Hansel, who in reality, was a former law clerk of mine.

I pointed out to him that the Ventura Boulevard business office address and telephone number printed on the letterhead weren't accurate, and showed him my present business card. He admitted that he didn't use the phone number on the letterhead because due to our previous dealings my number was still in the speed dial of his phone. The only way to get to the bottom of this situation was to visit the address on the letterhead and meet with 'attorney' Hansel.

I kept thinking that this is unbelievable. Ricky was the nicest guy you could ever want to meet... and a hard worker. One time I had a case where title to a classic car was illegally transferred. Ricky worked on it almost full time for over a month until all the paperwork was properly filled out and we were able to repossess the vehicle for the client. Everyone liked him and there was no doubt that when he finished law school he'd quickly build a successful practice. Little did I know that he didn't want to wait until finishing school – or becoming a lawyer to start building his law practice. We both drove over to the business address printed on the correspondence and saw that it was one of those storefront private Mail Box places whose customers use their box numbers as 'suite' number on stationery. We were told that pasted on the clerk's side of the box was the directory label 'Peter Sharp & Associates.'

After a convincing argument from me plus a twenty-dollar bill, we convinced Jack Bibberman, the store's mail clerk, to reveal who rented that box. My suspicions were confirmed when he named my former paralegal Ricky. Jack told us that he never met the guy... the box rental transaction was all done by mail and the guy only came in once to pick up a UPS package delivery... probably stationary. All mail pickups from the box were probably done at night after the counter closed.

The adjustor finally seemed to believe me and I thought the matter was closed. Our local legal newspaper, The Los Angeles Daily Journal, carried the story several months later: Ricky was arrested, convicted, fined and sentenced to several years of probation for the misdemeanor of practicing law without a license. Needless to say, his chances of ever being allowed to take the California Bar exam were greatly diminished, if not gone forever. What I didn't expect was what the insurance company did next... they turned the matter over to the State Bar for a full investigation... of me.

The State Bar filed charges against me for 'negligent supervision of an employee' and 'aiding in the unauthorized practice of law.' Usually those types of charges don't result in a serious disciplinary sentence. In fact, I thought my hearing was actually going quite well... until they brought out their files from the past fifteen years and the State Bar's prosecutor told the hearing judges about my alleged previous 'attitude' towards the Bar's investigation attempts.

The first recital was about when I began my practice in a Van Nuys storefront office on Sylvan Street, a block away from the Van Nuys courthouse. The small coffee shop next door to my office was going out of business, so I bought and re-named it "Peter Sharp's Division 86." At the time, there were eighty-five divisions in the Los Angeles Municipal Court system, ergo our name and the double intendre of being "86'd." In those days, the Bar didn't allow attorneys to do any type of advertising: They considered it to be conduct described as 'unprofessional.'

Most people got a kick out of the place's name, but some jerky attorneys in the neighborhood (are there any other kind?) complained to the Bar that because my name was on it, that I was unethically advertising. When the complaint letter from the State Bar came in, I informed them that I heard Ralph Williams (the largest auto dealer in the San Fernando Valley at that time, with more than twelve dealerships on Ventura Boulevard) was going to attend law school and then open up an office in the Valley. I requested that we hold off on my hearing until Ralph opens his law office, so we can see how well the Bar does in getting him to remove his name from all twelve of those car dealerships.

The Bar didn't care for that response, but it must have struck a proper chord, because I didn't hear from again them for another two years. This time it was another nasty letter telling me that I was once again being accused wrongly advertising because of my personalized license plate – "PS ESQ."

I did some quick research with our state's Department of Motor Vehicles and informed the State Bar that they finally caught me, and I would be looking forward to my hearing, assuming they would be holding it in the downtown sports arena, so that the other three thousand two hundred fifty one California lawyers with "ESQ" in their license plates could also attend with their attorneys and defend themselves.

Once again they backed down. I never had any problems with the State Bar again over unethical advertising – but they finally got their pound of flesh: any other attorney in the same situation would probably have gotten a slap on the wrist and a severe warning to straighten out his act. I was expecting a suspended sentence and maybe a fine, but it's not a perfect world.

In view of my past experiences with our revered State Bar Association, along with the fact that Ricky appeared as a witness for the State Bar and blamed everything on me, testifying that I set him up with the mail box and shared the fees, the prosecutors took Ricky, the convicted criminal's word over mine. Several years before my hearing the State Bar lifted its ban on advertising; the judges didn't care – they admitted the recitations anyway, as evidence of my lack of respect for them. The Bar must have decided that it was time to make an example of another attorney, so I wound up with a two-year suspension and probation. Go figure. An immediate appeal might have delayed the suspension for a while, but considering all that was happening in my life at the time, I thought a break from the active practice of defending scumbags for a while might be a good thing... an appeal could always be done later... and that's why I'm sitting in a back yard on Waterford Street in Brentwood Glen, trying to talk my friend Stuart out of going ahead with a suit against the Federal Government. I've had enough of going up against the establishment for a while.

The suspension was bad enough, but it had a profound effect on my prosecutor wife and her mad dog associates. I was now looked upon as a common criminal... because for the next two years I would be reduced to doing legal research, private investigating and process serving for other attorneys. In their eyes there were only two types of criminal defense attorneys: those who had been suspended for unethical behavior and those who hadn't been caught yet... and neither category met with their approval.

With the help of her associates, my beloved wife finally came out of the ether and decided that I was a social liability that had to be cut loose, so she decided to downsize the household. Therefore, I am now sitting on the aft deck of my liveaboard yacht enjoying the surrounding sea of grass, while she conspires with Gary Koontz, her beady-eyed divorce attorney... a former classmate of mine. I never liked him back then in law school, and still can't stand him.

Amazingly, our divorce proceedings went quite smoothly, in spite of our respective attorneys' efforts to screw up the case and build up their fees. My attorney specializes in representing male members of the Bar, so having only lawyers as clients, he didn't think it was too big an oversight to miss a court appearance. In my case, he didn't show up the day of the hearing, so the judge filled in for him by asking me the stock questions off of a prepared sheet that contain the ones that judges usually ask unrepresented women who come in for their default divorce hearings. Everything went fine. I knew the judge from past appearances in other court matters, so as a courtesy he even offered to give me back my maiden name. Everyone wants to be comedian.

The Property Settlement Agreement was quite simple: she owned the house we lived in before the marriage, so she kept it afterwards. There were no kids involved. In a community property state like California, the courts can treat appreciation in real estate value during the marriage as a joint asset, so we decided to forgo that argument and in exchange I'd keep clear title to my old back-yard Chris Craft.

As any married man knows, there are times when the absolute truth just doesn't apply. One instance is the classic situation of when the wife turns around in front of you and asks if the dress she's wearing makes her look fat. The problem is that in most other cases a little fabrication can usually come back and bite you in the ass.

Before having that old wood Chris Craft lifted by crane off the truck and dropped into our yard, I may have mentioned to my wife that even if she doesn't particularly like boats, this one will be worth at least fifty thousand when I'm finished fixing it up, so it's really a good investment, considering the fact that I got it for only eight thousand.

That came back to bite me when her lawyer was making up our 'simple' property settlement agreement. In order for me to keep the boat for myself, he took that 'future value' into consideration, and in order to keep the boat and not look like a liar, I had to give up my entire interest in the appreciation of the house while we were married. The matter of alimony was settled by my promising to give her fifty percent of the net profits from my law practice for two years. This provision was added just before my suspension took effect and was another reason she was pissed off. Now she might have to wait several years before I started earning money again as an attorney – and then it would be a slow curve to build up a new practice. But that's the way the cookie crumbles.

I never handled a divorce case past the property settlement agreement stage... a decision made out of fear. Several years ago an associate in my former law firm asked me to fill in for him late one evening. A divorcing couple had worked out the division of their property and wanted to come to the office after work hours, to have it finalized on paper. They were both deputy sheriffs. Everything went fine until we got to the stereo, which she claimed was supposed to belong solely to her. The husband immediately jumped up and declared "over my dead body!" to which she replied" that can be arranged!" At that time they both made gestures towards their respective holsters. This type of experience was not exactly what I expected when starting law school. I managed to calm them both down before the office became the OK Corral and haven't handled a domestic relations case since then.

But enough of what should only be minimally interesting to Dr. Phil, because another problem needing urgent solving just popped up. With our divorce coming to a close, I knew the back yard would no longer be available as a place to dock my boat for too much longer. Gary Koontz, schmuck at law, snidely relayed the eviction notice to me. This meant that a slip in some Marina must be gotten, because they frown on live-aboard boaters in the public park - which brings me to the reason why I'm now looking down at my law school alumni directory and trying to get up the nerve to call Melvin Braunstein – one of the most disliked persons in our old law school class... the other was Koontz.

Some people are born with traits that become more pronounced as they get older. Melvin Braunstein was a putz all the way through high school and college and seventeen years ago he achieved the uppermost level of putzdom... he became an attorney.

When my wife and I first started dating she was a naïve legal receptionist. The first time she heard me refer to another attorney as a schmuck, she was shocked... not by the word, but by the denigration of a professional attorney! I tried to explain that if a schmuck goes to law school, the education he gets doesn't remove the schmuck part of his personality - all it does is add the knowledge of the law, and you wind up with a *schmuck attorney*. If you look up that phrase in the dictionary, you should see pictures of Gary Koontz and Melvin Braunstein, along with numerous other members of the bench and bar.

But Melvin is no longer Melvin: he has now become Marcel Bradley, a very nice gentile-sounding name that he thinks killed two birds with one stone: it changed his religion and still allowed him to use his embroidered shirts and hankies... which doesn't really help much, because no-one with an ounce of class would ever be seen with him. Melvin only developed one people-skill: he had the unique ability to make everyone he met detest him because of his rude sense of non-deserved superiority and antagonistic views about society – and women, in particular. You can tell how out of touch with people Melvin was when you realize he thought that making people think he was *French* would mean they'd like him more.

I went to law school with Melvin in the Los Angeles San Fernando Valley, at a non-accredited 4-year evening school we affectionately nicknamed Betty Crocker College of Law, on Sepulveda Boulevard in Van Nuys. During those four years of evening classes I learned to tolerate him because twice a year he ran the school's bookstore, and by working for him a week each semester I received my casebooks and textbooks free of charge, saving me hundreds of dollars. I was working my way through school by being a process server during the day and playing piano in saloons at night, so the free books were a great help and I felt I owed him something for that.

During our second year of law school Melvin thought it would be cute to have a bumper sticker that said, "Let's give Apartheid a chance!" The sticker only had a bumper-life of about three minutes after his car was parked. That evening after class, Mel saw the remains of the sticker, still pasted onto the bumper. Unfortunately, what he didn't see was the rest of the car. It was gone. Melvin called the police to report the theft and then smugly smiled, claiming that he was right: "if there were Apartheid, no one 'of them' would have stolen my car."

Melvin was never wrong. He was right and the rest of the world was wrong. The only clients he seemed to be able to attract were chauvinistic men hiding their assets while going through nasty divorces. Maybe it's because they appreciated Melvin's philosophy that the Saudis got at least some things right: their women aren't allowed to vote or drive.

As a result of his sterling personality, his law practice spiraled downward to the level of doing collection work and serving papers on deadbeats. He hired lawyers to appear on his behalf, because no judge in the district liked Melvin's obnoxious personality.

And now almost twenty years later, I find myself once again about to go into Melvin's debt. The word among the alumni is that Melvin finally snagged a steady client, one for which he could utilize the attributes of his personality: he's doing all of the tenant eviction and collection work for our large local Marina. They wouldn't pay him the exorbitant amount he thought he was worth, but they do allow him to live rent-free on one of the square box houseboats that the Marina owns and rents out... sort of a floating trailer. It wouldn't look so bad if it wasn't parked in a slip that faces directly into the fifty-foot slips, where right in front of Melvin's box-boat is an almost new fifty-foot fiberglass Grand Banks trawler – one of the most beautiful luxurious cruisers in the world, and the exact same model I've always dreamed of having, complete with the four-person Asian crew that's always cleaning it and touching up the varnished teak rails.

Melvin hands me a drink as we sit on the front deck (porch) of his houseboat, which is a strange thing to see: Mel is a mess – fat as ever, sloppily dressed and half drunk, but his boat is immaculate. None of the people walking by on the dock dare to acknowledge his presence – much like convicts in a prison won't nod to the hangman; he might be called upon to evict any one of his neighbors at any time and they know he won't hesitate.

After the usual complaining about women that men usually do while going through a divorce, I tell him about my cabin cruiser and he immediately jumps on what he sees as an opportunity to advance his own agenda. He knows about my suspension and isn't bothered by it. He even goes so far as to offer me employment in drawing up some pleadings, doing investigative work, legal research and serving papers on people. I tell him that everything depends on me being close to his location, and he realizes what I'm hinting at... I need a slip. He says he'll look into it and let me know what can be done. I also spot an opportunity, and to make my services more desirable to him, I offer to cut him in on what could be a huge case... Stuart's. Melvin sounds interested. He's heard about asbestosis litigation and wouldn't mind getting involved in it – but the only way he'll take it is if I agree to do the trial work, which will probably be enough years away for my suspension to have expired.

The meeting goes better for me than anything else has for the past few months. Not only will I probably be getting a slip for my boat, but I also succeeded in dumping Stuart's case. As I'm driving out of the Marina I see a most amazing sight... one of those rounded off four-seat electric vehicles with no side doors is being driven down the street by a huge St. Bernard dog. By the time I have a chance to turn around to get a better look, it disappears down a small access road leading to the boats, and I lose sight of it. I make a mental note to look for that thing again, if it really existed, but in the meantime I won't be mentioning it to anyone. Enough people already have their doubts about my sanity.

An old saying suggests that 'when life gives you lemons, make lemonade.' Looking around, I realize the wisdom of that adage: my lemons were the suspension, divorce and eviction, and the lemonade I'll be making is the possibility of a new life without client responsibilities, and living on my boat in the Marina, surrounded by millionaire yacht owners – and some peasants on houseboats. Life is good.

Melvin knows absolutely nothing about boats, but because he's slightly connected to the Marina's management, he's been able to get my name moved up on the empty slip waiting list. When my wife's lawyer informed me that if the boat isn't moved in five days it'll be used as firewood, I'm lucky to have had good old Melvin come through for me. My boat doesn't have engines yet, but I'm not planning on going anywhere, so it doesn't matter. For now, I'm just happy it floats

When moving day arrives, they put slings under its bottom and the old Chris Craft gets lifted up and put onto a large truck by a huge, two hundred dollar-an-hour crane. After being gently loaded onto a specially built truck, it's now being driven down the San Diego Freeway to the Marina Freeway and will be off-loaded at the boat yard. After the bottom gets a fresh coat of anti-fouling paint, it'll get lowered into the water and Vessel Assist boat-towing service will pull it over to its empty slip, which fortunately is the at least nine spaces out from the seawall, and behind Melvin's big boxy houseboat. This is good, because the Dockmaster lives in an apartment overlooking the boat slips and now she may not be able to notice that I'm illegally living aboard.

There are twenty-one boat slips on our dock: ten forty-five footers on our side, face-to-face with fifty-footers on the other side of the walkway. There's also one long end tie that must be more than a hundred feet long, and docked on that end tie is the biggest mega-yacht I've ever seen close up. It not only covers the entire end tie dock, but overhangs at least another five feet on each side, making it about a hundred and twenty feet long, and worth mucho million dollars. Melvin tells me that George Clooney owns it, and the dock neighbors say he's a pretty nice guy. I figure it's just a matter of time before we bump into each other and become friends, giving me a great reason to send out e-mails to everyone I know, bragging about my new social status.

So far everything is going smooth. I have a place to stay, my wife and her prosecutor friends are very far out of hearing distance, her beady-eyed attorney won't be ogling my boat, I don't need any malpractice insurance or secretary, and because Melvin is picking up the slip rent as my monthly minimum retainer, no rent or payments to worry about. The work from Mr. Braunstein should keep me fed and clothed nicely. The only downside is the proximity to my boss Melvin's boat... and the remote possibility that Stuart and his boat-owning uncle Label might discover my location and decide to drop in without calling.

After getting settled in I walk over to the local market to get some victuals for the boat and see that sight once again... the driving dog! This time I'm able to get a closer look, and to my surprise and relief discover that the dog isn't driving. Instead, the most adorable little Asian girl I've ever seen is behind the wheel, wearing a floppy little sunhat and seriously steering. The large dog is sitting up on the seat next to her.

I watch for a minute or so until they drive down the small driveway near the boats. She pulls into a parking space, speaks a command to the dog in some Asian-sounding language, and the two of them march down the gangway towards the boats. Suddenly the dog stops, turns around, and whines back towards the electric car, where a small cat is sleeping on the back seat. Hearing the dog's call, it jumps up and runs down the gangway towards the boat. The trio then walks down the dock, turns, and steps aboard Melvin's houseboat.

The next couple of weeks are spent getting used to my new environment and waiting for neighbor George Clooney or one of his celebrity friends to walk by. Being on the boat isn't anything new, but sleeping on it in the water is definitely a new experience. There's nothing like being awakened by a noise that you're positive is someone walking on the deck right over your head - and then discovering it's only a person who boarded a boat nearby, causing a slight wave that rocks your boat. Footsteps are conducted through the water like sound from one Dixie cup to the other through a piece of string. There are also the halyards, ropes and other lines that flop in the wind against sailboat masts – to say nothing of the gnawing noises heard from below the water that some people believe are small undersea creatures eating at the bottoms of the boats.

The next morning I comment to a dock neighbor about the flopping halyards I heard the night before and ask him if the noise bothers him. "What noise?" he asks. It seems that after a while living aboard, the noises disappear into the environment and you don't even hear them anymore. When I was a kid in Chicago my parents used to take me along in the car to a family vacation spot. On the way, we passed through Gary, Indiana and nearby there was an area that had quite a few oil refinery plants. I'll never forget trying to hold my breath as long as I could while we passed through that area. When I asked my parents how the people who live there stand the smell, their answer was almost the same as the one my dock neighbor gave me - "after a while you don't notice it." The flopping halyards I'll probably get used to in a while. The stinking refineries were something else.

Underwater creatures are only part of the environment. Above-the-water creatures that inhabit our dock are much more interesting. Aside from Melvin, who manages to keep himself drunk enough to stay out of sight most of the time, there are two females – one being the cute little Asian girl with the giant dog, and the other a burned-out woman I heard someone address as "Laverne," who lives on another one of the Marina's boxy houseboats several slips down from me. Laverne looks like she's some mid-forties low maintenance broad with plenty of miles on her speedometer. After three weeks, I only know one thing about her: she gets picked up at seven thirty each morning by a husky guy who also brings her back each evening at five forty-five. I couldn't help notice that the garbage bag she dumps each morning by the gangway gate trash can usually includes at least one empty booze container. I've only spoken to her once, and that was to excuse myself for bumping into her, at which time she smiled, welcomed me to the dock and looked at me like I was something on the menu.

The local Chamber of Commerce boasts that our Marina is home to more than seven thousand boats – and from what I've seen, it looks like ninety nine percent of them do as much traveling as my engine-less tub. Nevertheless, Sundays are busy here at the Marina. Every fat boat-owning industrialist brings his family and business associates to the boat, turns on the expensive sixty-mile radar unit to make sure he doesn't run into any nearby apartment buildings, revs the boat's engines, and then waits for his wife to finish broiling the swordfish they just had delivered from the nearby Gelson's market.

On the Fourth of July, Memorial Day, and Labor Day, the three biggest boating days of the year, some of those floating luxury condos will actually leave the slip for a brief harbor cruise and then return, never actually venturing out past the breakwater into the open Pacific Ocean. They don't need the open ocean for adventure because they have a daring trial of nerve and courage waiting for them when they finish their harbor-cruise - getting the boat back into the slip. It usually starts out with a slow approach, but as the wind and current affect the boat's progress, it starts to slide sideways toward other boats. The inexperienced owner will then usually make a desperate attempt to over-correct the course by goosing the engine, causing more harm than good. The boat will lunge towards the slip, banging into the sides of the dock and bouncing around, while the husband-driver yells obscenities at his family-crew, blaming them for his own mistakes and inability to handle the twin-engine vessel properly in those close quarters. It's a good possibility that in Southern California, poor boat handling causes more divorces than infidelity.

I wanted to avoid making a fool out of myself, so I went online to a well known website called Boatingdvds.com and bought a program on how to properly handle a large twin-engine cabin cruiser. I've never actually driven a boat, but after watching that DVD about fifty times over the past year, I'm sure that I'll do okay if and when I ever get the chance.

Melvin suggested that I have the phone company install two additional telephone lines to my boat for fax and e-mail capabilities. Because he'll be too busy to personally assign work to me, one of his office staff will be either faxing documents or e-mailing me assignments to work on. This arrangement works out quite well. The faxes are mostly papers to be served on non-paying tenants, and the e-mails are research assignments that are easily completed down the street in the law library of Alfred Nieman, a local attorney who I've known in the past and do a little extra assignment for now and then. Melvin's e-mails are signed off by a "Suzi B," obviously the 'staff' member he alluded to.

I follow through on my assignments, leave my Proof of Service Affidavits and research results in the mailbox attached to his houseboat, and always find a paycheck from his office tucked under the doormat in front of my boat's main cabin door shortly thereafter. The other thing that seems to be a constant is the lascivious smile on Laverne's face as she waves to me each time I pass by her boat in the evening. One time she held up a wine glass, beckoning me to join her... I politely nodded and pointed to my wristwatch, trying to signal her that I didn't have the time at that moment. I'm sure she interpreted it as my asking for a rain check.

After a month or two of steady work from his office, one e-mail in particular from Melvin's staff is curiously encouraging: it suggests that I petition the State Bar for a review of my allegedly unfair suspension sentence, and ask for early reinstatement to active status so that my new employer (Marcel.' Bradley & Associates) can utilize my services more efficiently – and supervise my conduct in accordance with the Bar's high standards. The message even offers the free assistance of L. Martin Unger, one of Melvin's staff attorneys, to prepare all the paperwork. I e-mail back that I'll think about it, now that Mr. Unger had generously offered to prepare the briefs, points and authorities and other crap that the Bar requires before allowing you to come in and be humiliated by their refusals.

Thinking about Mel's suggestion more seriously, I take the big fat file of my case over to his office - the address that appears on his letterhead and checks. It's only a few blocks away from the Marina, but when I get there I discover it's one of those private mailbox places. The address is the same as on Melvin's stuff, and it looks like he's using the box number as his 'suite' number – much like Ricky Hansel, the law clerk who got me suspended in the first place. I hope that this isn't going to be a rerun of my last disaster, because the next step down for me will be disbarment and criminal prosecution by my ex-wife.

I think it would be better to visit Melvin personally on his houseboat to get some answers. On the way back to the Marina I stop for a beer or two, finally getting back to the dock at about six thirty in the evening and discover that I'd better stop drinking that much. What convinces me is walking by Laverne's boat, being smiled at, and thinking that she's starting to look better.

Melvin's boat is locked up for the evening. The only sign of life aboard is that small cat glaring at me through the window.

Next morning the little girl and her two partners do their daily parade up to the electric car, and I notice that the dog has something in its mouth. This is too good a chance to miss... I follow them as they drive down the sidewalk in their e-car. When they pull up to a mailbox, the little girl gives a command to the dog in some foreign language. The dog hops out of the vehicle, walks over to the mailbox, stands on his rear legs and with one paw pulls open the mail slot. He then deposits the mail from his mouth down into the mailbox. I haven't seen an animal act like this since reruns of the old Ed Sullivan show, and my curiosity about this trio is really peaking. After the mailbox stunt they drive down the alley to the rear entrance of the private mailbox place where Melvin's 'office' is technically located. I'm able to see through the back door that the little girl is opening up a large post office-type box, mercifully located on a low enough level. She then gets back into the e-cart and drives further down the alley to the rear kitchen entrance of the local Washington Boulevard Chinese restaurant, where all three of them enter the back door. I hope that when they come back out the cat will still be with them. After about twenty minutes of waiting, I give up and go back to work.

Not being the legal-eagle my ex-wife always wanted me to be, I'm not quite sure of the legality of a minor driving that glorified golf cart, or if it's even street legal. But as so often happens in real life, the law doesn't really govern everything. I've eaten in that local Chinese restaurant enough times to realize that the little girl obviously has a connection with the place. All the local cops eat there and treat her like their mascot, so she shouldn't have to worry about ever getting a traffic ticket in this neighborhood. Come to think of it, I never saw any cop in uniform ever getting charged full price there. Maybe that's why like clockwork, they're in there every day at the same times: Noon for the morning watch's lunch and four-thirty in the afternoon for the day-watch's lunch time. There are also second-Tuesday-of-the-month interagency luncheon meetings of all the local police authorities to discuss their new policy of cooperation and sharing of intelligence and computer files. The lunch checks all get paid in full on those days, and from what I've seen, the brass is allowed to drink while on duty.

The restaurant doesn't have too much competition in the neighborhood. There's an Italian place across the street, and a seafood place a couple of doors west, but they don't compete for customers. No-one can eat Chinese food or Italian food every night of the week unless they're Chinese or Italian, and then it's not Chinese food or Italian food: it's just food.

The real competition between them is for parking spaces on the two city-owned empty lots on both sides of the restaurants. The other two eateries are both owned by some rich old guy who lives in a penthouse down the street at the Marina City Club, so the fighting is left to the operators of their two car-parking valet companies.

This evening I'm considering allowing myself to be invited onto Laverne's houseboat for a drink. I'm rationalizing this daring move as an attempt to get some information from her about Melvin's small cadre and that fifty-foot Grand Banks, the new love of my life.

Right on cue, after the gangway gate slams loudly behind me, Laverne appears at her window. As I walk by she smiles and holds up two elegant plastic wine glasses. She gives me a wink, and clicks the glasses together. Once before in my life this phrase passed over my lips and it caused me quite a bit of trouble over the years. My wife and I had been living together in her house for over a year and one night she gave me the dreaded ultimatum that every man will probably hear at least once in his life: "either get married or get out." It was then that I said those romantic words of acceptance: "aw what the hell, I might as well." I hope that this time it'll lead to nothing more than a glass of wine and some information.

Laverne's metallic houseboat is furnished rather interestingly. For lack of a better description I guess you could call the décor 'early whorehouse.' There's a lot of gaudy red velvet wallpaper and a framed picture on one wall of some dogs playing poker. Another wall has a picture hanging there that looks like a sober Laverne. It's one of those phony oil painting type of prints that is really a touched-up enlarged photograph. Some cheap imitation fringed Tiffany lamps are lit. One of them is a hanging 'swag' model. This is probably the first residence she's ever lived in that doesn't have wheels. I guess you would expect Tonya Harding or Paula Jones to have decorating styles not much different. Also not too surprising is what's playing on her television set: one of those crappy reality shows, but with the sound turned off. When I ask her how she can enjoy it without the sound, she tells me not to worry, because she's taping it. What a wonderful videotape library she must have. All that her living room lacks now are some vibrators mounted on the flocked wallpaper. I'll have to remember to leave a couple of twenties on the dresser when I leave.

Aside from the gaudy trappings, Laverne is pleasant enough, and when she sits down, her housecoat momentarily opens to reveal a little more than I was expecting to see. I'd like to believe that housecoat's 'grand opening' was an accident, but I soon learn that no matter how drunk she gets, Laverne doesn't do anything accidentally. After my third drink and her third 'reveal,' our conversation turns toward more personal matters and I discover that she really doesn't drink that much. Her tolerance for alcohol must be very low because after just four or five glasses of wine, she's totally plastered, but not too drunk to remember courtesy towards her guest: she suggests that it would be safer if I stayed over, to avoid any accident trying to make it home at such a late hour. Not wanting to be a rude guest, I accept.

Depending on how you judge success, the meeting at Laverne's is hard to rate, but I do remember that most of the pumping was to get information and I never learned what Laverne does all day. She did tell me that neither she nor anyone else on the dock knows the inside information on that cute little Asian girl, except for the fact that she never speaks to anyone. That may be because she doesn't speak English. I also learned that another dock tenant with a forty-two-foot Californian Motor yacht is a retired eye surgeon with a bad back, who is reputed to espouse that the mere existence of a female's curvaceous rear end is proof that there is a God. Maybe that's why his nickname on the dock is 'Snatch Adams.'

Some lecherous sixty-something lawyer named Unger who works for Melvin owns that fifty-foot Grand Banks I admire so much. He's probably the L. Martin Unger who volunteered to help with my petition for re-instatement. I thought it would be nice to be able to visit with my new attorney on his boat, but Laverne said he was out of town for a couple of months, making a semi-annual trip to his personal Mecca – some smorgasbord hotel in Thailand that offers its clients all the young Thai girls they can eat. A fantasy races through my head: if L. Martin can afford that big boat by working for Melvin, then maybe I'd better get that petition through as soon as possible so maybe I could move up from my old wooden junk to fiberglass luxury.

The evening wasn't a total loss - she made some breakfast for me. I guess it's for me because the table is set and it's on the plate waiting for me. She's already been picked up for the day... to go wherever she goes and do whatever she does. Not wanting to be a rude guest I finish the greasy French toast, do the dish, and then go to my own boat to shower off the evening's experience. She isn't exactly a raving beauty, but you could tell that about twenty years and twenty pounds ago she must have really been something to look at. I don't plan on making a steady thing out of this, but at least I know that as long as I live on the dock, Laverne will see to it that my complexion is kept clear.

Stepping off of her houseboat I notice a Norman Rockwell scene taking place down the dock in front of Melvin's houseboat: the huge Saint Bernard is sitting up next to the dockbox, and standing on a milk crate to reach all the way to the top of its head is the little Asian girl, complete with floppy sun hat and sun dress, using a Flowbee type combination comb & cutting device. She's softly singing some foreign song to the dog, while giving it a haircut. I'm not the only one watching... the small cat is on top of the dockbox, half asleep and half watching the haircut – and me. When she finishes with the dog, there are several dock neighbors waiting to sit on the milk crate for their monthly trims.

My next assignment requires going to the Courthouse to research some civil suits there, and while in the filing room I run into a few attorneys I've known over the years. Several of us went to school together, so they know Melvin. Each one has a different story to tell, but averaging all their information and gossip together, it goes something like this:

Jasmine, a bow-legged waitress at the local Chinese restaurant, was having some trouble getting a green card. Maybe it's because she was an illegal alien, having overstayed her student visa and smuggled her young daughter into the country through Canada. Of course having a steady job didn't help either, because even if your student visa is valid, you're not supposed to be employed. That must be because our INS doesn't want foreigners taking busboy jobs away from all the Americans who go to college just to prepare for that career.

As the story goes, Melvin ate in the restaurant so often that he had his own regular table there. When he learned about Jasmine's problem, he offered to fix it in his own inimitable way, and he did... he married her. Her little daughter Suzi was supposed to be a real cutie, and they certainly got that part of the story right. Unfortunately, a year or so later Jasmine died in a car accident (not having

37

anything to do with the driving ability of Asian females) and since then Suzi has been living with her stepfather on the houseboat that the Marina provides.

It wasn't surprising that Melvin got a wife in that manner, because any other way would probably have been out of the question. He set the bar rather high for his 'perfect' woman, who he said must be a super-model who could read the Torah. When we were law students together he once bragged to several of us how he was dating a nice Catholic girl until he noticed a cross over her bed and refused to sleep with her. As the story goes, he told her that if he was going to get into bed with a woman, he wanted to be the only illegitimate Jewish con man in the room. Needless to say, he lost out that night to the guy on the wall.

Armed with this information it isn't hard to start piecing together the rest of the story. Melvin practices off the boat. He sends out nasty letters and makes threatening phone calls to delinquent debtors and tenants. L. Martin Unger does Melvin's court appearances, with flunkies like me serving the papers and doing the occasional legal research.

Most collection agencies were worried that when the federal Uniform Debt Collections Act was passed that it would crimp their style... but not Melvin. Whenever he made a threatening call outside the bounds of the UCDA (too early in the AM, too late in the PM, harassment at the debtor's place of employment, etc.), he would also ask what the debtor thought of some political issue polarizing the country at that particular time. This was his devious way of setting up a defense for himself, so if anyone ever tried to prosecute him for violation of the Act he could claim he was conducting a political poll, and it was his right to free speech to call and ask those questions. The main secret of his success was an uncanny ability he displayed in finding the debtors that nobody else could find. No one knows how he does it, but it's the main reason he gets a heavy load of collection and skip-tracing work. Someone on his staff certainly knows how to search on the internet. From what I've been told, everyone in the country is in there somewhere. One of these days, I'm going to have to learn how to surf like the kids do. They can find anything online.

Because he didn't have to go out very much, his main traveling was about a mile, to a massage parlor on Washington Blvd., where he keeps his regular appointments every Tuesday and Thursday for 'physical therapy.' Being so overweight, his back is always giving him trouble, so he bamboozled his insurance company into paying for his alleged therapy. What a wonderful state of affairs... the insurance companies refuse to pay for patients' life-saving bone marrow transplants, but they're paying for Melvin's blowjobs.

As clever as Melvin was though, I don't think he ever came across the defense that I used once: four or five years after passing the Bar, some jerk collection agency was going after former students of a Bar Review Course I took, for not turning back in their study materials. Of course the statute of limitations had already run, and no one ever turned back in that study material because it was all marked up and obsolete. New cases came down each year and the materials were always getting annual updates. I decided to take a new tack with the collector. A

Federal anti-pornography law had been passed to fight the mailing of unsolicited obscene materials, and any Classification as 'obscene' depended solely on the opinion of the mail's recipient. I informed the collection agency that *in my opinion* the mail and phone calls I was getting from them were obscene, and if they didn't cease and desist immediately, their agency would be turned in to the Federal authorities and they would be fined five thousand dollars for each violation of my privacy with their calls and letters.

At first the collector thought I was joking, but I never heard from them again. It's a good thing the State Bar didn't know about that little incident, because in their myopic eyes, it might have led to an additional year or two of my suspension.

I decide to take off this warm Tuesday afternoon, relax on the boat, catch up on some reading, and wait for George to walk by. It's around three o'clock, and being so involved in my Nero Wolfe mystery story I don't pay much attention to the sirens down the street in the business district, but I do hear some muffled sounds of crying and sobbing coming next door from Melvin's boat. Worried that something might be wrong, I walk over there to check on Suzi and her pets, when a dock neighbor stops and asks me a question.

"Hey Peter, did you hear the sirens?" I don't know why the sirens should be such a big deal to him. There's always a siren or two heard around here… we're just down the road from the fire station.

"Yes, I heard the sirens. Probably a fire engine going by."

"No, not this time, Peter. Those were police cars. They were responding to a nine-eleven gunshot call... the elderly owner of that Chinese Restaurant was gunned down in his parking lot... in broad daylight!"

Just as our brief dock conversation ends, I turn and see the trio speeding away in their electric cart.

3

I want check this event out myself. By the time I reach my car the kid's electric vehicle is already out of sight, but I know where they're going, and my car can outrun their little cart. The Chinese restaurant is around the corner on Washington Boulevard, only a few blocks away from the Marina so I have no problem beating Saint Bernard & Company there. Approaching the restaurant, the sight is much like one you might see in a science fiction movie, where a spacecraft crashes and all the local police agencies show up. There must be twenty black and white squad cars sitting there with those light bars on top flashing and up to fifty cops milling around the parking lot. This must be one of those Tuesdays when the inter-agency police lunch meeting takes place here. Who said there's never a cop around when you need one?

Try as I can, there's no way to get close to where the action is, especially not being able to wave a current 'active' State Bar I.D. Several rings of uniforms surround the parking lot. All civilians are being told to "go home – the show's over." Off to the side, I notice something remarkable: the police line is parting like the Red Sea, but it isn't Moses coming through... it's the little electric vehicle with the dynamic trio. The cart drives straight though the police lines and pulls up to where the Culver City Police have set up their temporary command post. The police look relieved when she shows up. The little girl and her partners are escorted over to where a group of restaurant employees are seated next to the police van. Accompanied by several uniformed officers, she starts to talk to one employee after another, while the uniforms tape the conversations and feverishly take notes. She must be helping the police get witness statements from the non-English speaking people there.

My main purpose in coming here is because I'm concerned about the little girl. She was crying when I heard about the murder and I want to make sure she's holding up... but with fifty police officers to look after her I guess she'll be okay. This is one of the afternoons when Melvin has his regular appointment at the massage parlor that's almost next door to the restaurant. I'd like to see the look on his face if he walked out and saw all those uniforms. He'd probably think they were there to raid the massage parlor, because of his insurance/therapy claim.

After hanging around for a while I pick up the same gossip that will probably be on the evening news. I think that the local news stations have a universal witness or two tucked away that they bring out for occasions like this – a woman with her hair in curlers, or some old fart who needs a shave, and they all say the same things: "gee, he was a quiet guy, always kept to himself," or "I never thought anything like that would happen in this neighborhood." All the statements of witnesses and neighbors on local news shows are about the same quality of statements made by professional athletes during locker-room interviews. There must be someone somewhere who teaches these people how to talk without saying anything even remotely interesting... and it passes for local news.

By the time I pick up the evening's frozen dinner and newspaper it's almost six P.M. and I'm not surprised to see who's on her front porch waiting as I come down the gangway. No doubt she's already heard about the shooting on the news and wants me to join her for a glass of wine to discuss it. Fortunately my TV dinner is sticking out of the grocery bag, so I have something to point to as I politely give her an apologetic 'not tonight' expression and keep on walking to my boat. It sure is a strange feeling to be the one using a 'not tonight' excuse, because I've been on the receiving end of it so many times.

After a day or two the parking lot murder no longer gets any time on the local news shows, having been pushed out of the way by more important news events like car-chases, car-jackings, car accidents, drive-by shootings, auto thefts and the auto show - now appearing at the downtown convention center. One gets the impression that if there were no cars in Los Angeles, there would be no news at all.

Fortunately another job has come in. I receive an e-mail assignment instructing me to look into a certain matter and that a police report is being faxed to me. I'm supposed to dig up whatever info is available on a Robert Palmer, who supposedly lives nearby in a sixteen stories tall group of crescent shaped towers called the Marina City Club that I can see from my boat. The assignment specifies digging up details on corporations he's involved in. The Culver City police report that comes in by fax is the official crime report on the murdered Chinese restaurant owner. This is strange because those crime reports are supposed to be confidential and I don't

44

see any connection between it and my present assignment.

Not being bi-lingual, I decide to do as much research as possible in the nearby Santa Monica Courthouse, instead of the downtown Los Angeles Civic Center. Most of the case files I need are there, as well as the main office of an attorney service my boss authorizes the use of... they can dig through the files downtown, if necessary. Another part of the assignment is rather good to hear... until my investigation is completed, the attorney service is to be given all the papers that needed to be served on people, including Summons & Complaints and subpoenas for depositions.

When an attorney gets suspended, all of his active clients must be notified so they can seek other counsel to handle their cases. Because most of my clients are now serving time, the only client that the State's computer came up with was Stuart. My name appears as Attorney of Record on that asbestos lawsuit I filed for him. He was notified and given my new phone number so that he could have another attorney call for his file... but Stuart is a loyal friend, so instead of using the Bar's Referral Program, he'd rather have me find another attorney for him. He calls to let me know that he's pleased to hear that Melvin has associated in on the case, and that I'd be doing the trial work after my suspension is over. And while he has me on the phone, he tries to lure me into a new business, which he insists on explaining to me: you can use a 1991 federal law that clamps down on people who send out unsolicited faxes to people. The law gives each fax recipient the right to sue for five hundred dollars, and for triple that amount if the fax sender had previously been notified not to send again to that specific number.

Being at least as clever as Stuart, the Santa Monica-based Foundation for Taxpayer and Consumer Rights filed lawsuits in the Superior Court against two California-based mass fax broadcasting companies, alleging that their transmissions of unsolicited faxes violated that federal law Stuart is so fond of – the powerful Telephone Consumer Protection Act (TCPA).

One of the Foundation's defendants was a firm sending out thousands of unsolicited faxes to the Santa Monica area on behalf of the new owner of Arnold Schwarzenegger's restaurant, 'Shatzi' on Main Street, notifying everyone of the management change. The Foundation won a class action judgment against the new restaurant owner and its fax broadcaster, thereby setting a new precedent in the Superior Court, and more specifically in Santa Monica.

Stuart heard about that case result and saw an open opportunity. He established a business address in one of those private mailbox stores in Santa Monica, placing him inside that judicial district. He then started soliciting people who were receiving unsolicited faxes from Southern California marketers and had the recipients assign the matters to him for collection. He filed Santa Monica Small Claims Court actions on their behalf against the senders. If you've been assigned a matter for collection, the Federal law says you can take it to Small Claims Court without being an attorney. Stuart advanced all of the filing fees and costs to have the Marshall's office serve the papers. If he goes to Court and wins,

Stuart gets his costs back and then splits whatever damages the Court awards with the 'client.'

From what he says, it sounds like business is booming. After talking to a few friends of mine, I learn that everyone is getting those pesky unsolicited faxes, and it's a real pain... it uses up fax paper, depletes ink supply and most annoying, keeps the fax line busy so that customers can't get through. Stuart claims that business is so good he's thinking of expanding. He wants me to join in with him to make the appearances. Reading between the lines, what he's really looking for is someone to also advance money for the filing fees and service costs. Not being in a 'partnering' mood at the time, I politely beg off... and also turn down another invitation to get together with him and his boat-owning uncle Label.

I think my present position occupies a place about as low on the legal food chain that I'd like to be at, and Small Claims Court would be a step down from there. As politely as possible, I tell him my social and business calendars are both on hold for the next couple of weeks so that I can tend to an urgent wiring problem on my boat – which really isn't too far from the truth, but far enough away to keep me from actually tending to it.

A day or so later the attorney service e-mails us that our Robert Palmer is involved with a whole bunch of things, but to really get to the bottom of it requires a trip to the State Capitol in Sacramento where all the original corporate records are kept. They must have quoted Melvin a really high fee for the job, because he turned them down and has instructed me to go up there and do it instead.

I like visiting Northern California, so it's good news. The expenses Mel offer are quite generous and there's no specific time deadline mentioned, so I decide to use the airline allowance and rent a new yellow Hummer from the local Budget Rent-a-Car on Lincoln Avenue, and take a leisurely drive up there. This will give me a chance to stop off in San Francisco to visit Fisherman's Wharf and see that barge they used for filming the old Nash Bridges TV series. The last time I was up there was when I was almost ten years old: it was the seventies, and when my parents took me on the cruise-boat Alcatraz tour, some American Indians who had taken over the abandoned prison for their months-long sit-down demonstrations, were shooting arrows at us... what a day to remember – being seasick and getting shot at.

Before leaving, I see that retired ophthalmologist on our dock. He's supervising the Asian crew do some varnish work on his boat. I'm still sure I've seen him somewhere before, but just can't place where... it'll come to me someday. I sure wish there was some answer as to how that old cocker managed to get a gorgeous girlfriend like the stewardess who visits him each week. I start to perspire every time she walks by and smiles at me.

4

IT'S A HOT, sticky day in Memphis, and the small office is buzzing with activity. Though only the middle of June, the August anniversary of Elvis Presley's 1977 death is rapidly approaching and the office staff wants to do something special in remembrance of that date that so affected their lives. This particular branch of the Elvis A. Presley Fan Club has just received some big time donations from a couple of older broads who really loved the King and want to remember him on that date that will live in infamy. Patty Sue, one of the females (most Elvis Presley fans are middle-aged women with middle names) excitedly jumps up with an announcement: she has found what they were looking for... Elvis' old yacht!

In 1967 Elvis appeared in the film *"Easy Come, Easy Go,"* in which he played the part of a singing, gyrating scuba diver looking for buried treasure. A portion of the movie centered around some people on a forty-foot Chris Craft cabin cruiser. In real life, Elvis' company actually owned the boat during that period of time and rented it to the production company for use in the film, giving him that extra few dollars he really needed so badly in those days. Patty Sue's computer screen shows that the vessel has changed hands quite a few times, but was most recently transferred to the family of Mr. And Mrs. Peter Sharp in Brentwood, California.

Her inquiry to California's Department of Motor Vehicles comes back with Peter and Myra Sharp's address on Waterford Street in Brentwood Glen. In California, if a vessel isn't documented with the Federal Government, it's registered with the State's DMV and gets a pink slip (proof of title), just like all California cars do.

Patty Sue's next step is to locate the new owners and offer whatever it takes to buy that boat so it can be trucked to Memphis for the August ceremonies. A local boat surveyor tells them that if it's running and restored to original condition, it might be worth a quarter of a million dollars... and they believe him, because they want to. People have always believed that those high beehive hairdos had some affect on the female brain, but they never could prove it. If the scientists went to an Elvis Presley fan club office and did some brain scans, they'd probably be able to re-write the medical journals.

Deputy District Attorney Myra Scot Sharp has just returned home from a trying day at the office. On her way past the picket fence, she stops at the mailbox and removes some letters. One in particular catches her attention, because in the return address it has a fancy logo consisting of three the letters TCB, which was a gaudy ring Elvis Presley used to wear and had monogrammed on the white sequined jump suits he wore while performing. The letters stand for 'Taking Care of Business,' a catch phrase he was fond of. Of course Myra has heard of Elvis. Everyone has. Once inside the house, the fancy envelope is the first one she opens. It's short and to the point, and absolutely makes her day. What she is staring down at is a wonderful opportunity to stick another pin in her favorite Peter Sharp effigy doll.

Dear Mr. and Mrs. Sharp:

It has come to our attention that you have become the registered owners of one 1963 forty-one-foot Chris Craft cabin cruiser, hull number CC16506156.

Our organization is desirous of obtaining that boat for a celebration to be held in Memphis in August of this year and we would like to make you an offer to purchase the vessel, if you still own it.

If the vessel floats, is seaworthy, and capable of restoration, we will pay you the sum of One Hundred Seventy-Five Thousand Dollars for it, by certified cashier's check drawn on the Bank of Memphis. Due to the time limitations, we must have your answer in ten days.

Very truly yours,
Elvis Aron Presley Fan Club,
Patty Sue Ehrstrieme, exec. Secy.

Myra puts down the letter, laughs an evil laugh out loud and calls her divorce attorney Gary Koontz. He's out of the office, so she leaves a message on his machine: "Hello Gary, it's Myra, and here's what I need. Do whatever it takes to get my jerk of an ex-husband to sign that crummy boat of his over to me. If you have to, threaten him with breach of our property settlement agreement. He should have known he was going to get suspended when he signed that promise to give me half of his law practice earnings. If he wants to avoid more trouble with the State Bar and a suit for fraud, he'll sign over the boat – and if you want to sweeten the pot a little, tell him that in exchange for the boat, I'll give up my claim to half his future earnings, but the boat must be delivered to me at the Marina boat yard no later than five days from now. And, if you succeed in pulling this off, there's a special bonus in it for you, and I think you know what I mean. It's something you've always wanted from me."

Defense attorneys claim that the only efficient railroad in this country is the Los Angeles County District Attorney's office. A black comedian named Richard Pryor once said "if you want to see justice in the Los Angeles Criminal Courts, go there, and that's what you'll see, *just us!*" Prosecutors have a special outlook on life. Right is on their side, so whatever they do is justified - no matter who gets threatened, bullied, put in jail, or forced to sign over a boat.

The Coast route is a beautiful trip from Los Angeles to Northern California, and the Hummer is a great ride. This big yellow brute is king of the road and gets looks from absolutely everyone. I'm going to make the almost five-hundred mile trip a two-day drive each way, so at the first evening's motel stop I check my voice mail to pick up messages. There's one from beady-eyed Koontz. He has great news for me. I've heard the old warning that after you shake hands with some fast-talking operators, make sure to count your fingers. Well, the same thing applies to this slimeball attorney: when you hang up the phone after talking to him, make sure to count your ears.

By the time I return his phone call it's after office hours, so instead of his answering machine I get his answering service and then get patched through to him at home. His pitch starts. "Listen Peter, I know we've had some differences over the years, but believe me, this could be a great opportunity for you." I don't say anything in response. A book I once read said that when someone is trying to sell you something and you clam up, they go into their 'I'm not okay mode,' and that's where Koontz is now going. He breaks the silence and his speed picks up. "Now this was against my advice, but Myra insisted on it. She wants to give you an opportunity go get your life back together again without the burden of paying her half your net income once you start practicing again, so she'll sell out that right for a paltry sum. And if you haven't got the cash on hand to pay her the forty thousand she'd like to get, she'll take that old boat off your hands."

I may have been born at night, but it wasn't *last* night. Myra wants the boat and is willing to give up future income she values at forty K to get it. Am I missing something? We both know I paid only eight thousand for it, and with the extra ten or twelve thousand put into it over the years, it's still an old piece of crap, probably not worth more than ten thousand, even if it was running. Maybe the best thing to do is try to talk her out of it. That way she might not be able to come back at me with buyer's remorse later on. "Listen Koontz, the boat doesn't even have engines installed yet, and it really needs a lot more work. I don't think she should..." He cuts me off.

"Peter, Peter, don't worry about it. She knows what shape it's in, and she doesn't care."

I'm still a little cautious. "I don't know, Koontz, if she's not happy with whatever she wants it for, I don't want her coming back to me with a lawsuit."

"Not to worry Peter. Tell you what I'm going to do... we'll put it right in the agreement that she's taking the boat on an "as-is, where-is" basis, with no intention of getting any money out of you for repairs that might be needed, no matter how serious they might be."

Hmmmn. This sounds too good to be true, and I know what they say about things like that.

There must be something going on that I don't know about. "Listen, I'm in a motel now on my way to Sacramento, so I'll call you when I get back the day after tomorrow. And don't worry, you'll get my answer within five days."

"I certainly hope so, because she's already got a towing service on stand-by waiting for instructions to tow if from your slip to the yard. I'll fax you the agreement, for you to look over."

"Yeah, okay... fax it over, when I get back in town I'll look at it and let you know whether it's a deal or not." I hang up, count my ears and send a message to Melvin's office to watch out for Koontz's fax to. I had my fax line call-forwarded to his boat's fax line while I'm out of town.

Plenty of things are going on now and it feels good to be back into a little action. L. Martin wants to help with my petition for re-instatement, Myra wants the boat, Laverne wants me, and Robert Palmer, the mystery man from the Marina City Club, may be involved in some domestic intrigue. One item about him was quite interesting: his real name isn't Palmer – it's Pearlstein. I'll never know why most people insist on changing their names.

Maybe it's understandable if you're a professional wrestler: Dwane Johnson became *"The*

Rock" and Terry Eugene Bolea is now *"Hulk Hogan."* Of course there's 'legitimate' show business where Bernie Schwartz is *Tony Curtis*, and singer *Steve Lawrence* was Sidney Leibowitz. It seems that even authors don't want to use their real names: *John LeCarre'* was David Cornwall and Eric Blair became *George Orwell. Ellery Queen* was really two people: cousins Frederic Dannay and Manfred Lee. Hardest for me to understand are the animals: *Eddie,* the dog on that popular TV show *"Frasier,"* was played by a dog named Moose, who even had his own book published. I guess anyone can get a book out nowadays. I still can't figure out why a dog needs a stage name. *Lassie* didn't use her real name – in fact, she was a male dog named Pal, who Rudd Weatherwax the trainer was forced to substitute in at the last minute when the original female Collie picked for the first movie balked at going into some rapidly moving water. Instead of ethnicity being something to avoid, sometimes it's the desired result: Karen Johnson, a good enough name to use in show business changed hers to *Whoopi Goldberg*, and Dana Owens is now *Queen Latifah.*

Robert Palmer's name change isn't the most interesting thing about him. Searching deep enough reveals that in addition to owning the two restaurants that are next door to and across the street from the Chinese one, he also owns controlling interest in the valet car parking service that competes with the Chinese place's valet service for parking spaces. Although the other two restaurants each have more square footage for interior eating space, the people coming for Chinese take-out orders raise their dinner total to more than both of Palmer's restaurants combined, and because the to-go customers are usually in and out in less than ten minutes, the Chinese valet that parks their cars makes several times more than the other two services due to the high turn-around of parking spaces. A conspiracy nut could probably make a good case against this Palmer. He tries to muscle the Chinese place's owner for a bigger portion of the parking lots, and when he can't get his way, he has the Chinaman wacked. It's an interesting theory. Good thing I don't have to prove it.

If my ex-wife hadn't turned into a super-shrew, I might consider cluing her in on my theories, because I'm sure that nailing a local big shot would be a feather in her cap and a definite career booster for her. But she's going to have to be a little nicer to me for a gift like that.

I take my time getting back from Northern California, and after dropping off the rented Hummer and picking up my own car, I stop at the Jr. Market around the corner from the Marina to pick up some things. There are some sirens in the area, but that's to be expected because the local fire station is less than a mile down Admiralty Way, and the trucks have to pass by here to get to this side of the Marina.

Looking around this place I finally figure out what the meaning of a 'Jr. Market' is… it's a liquor store that also sells milk and bread. Never having learned to cook anything but pasta I eat all my meals out, so the Marina's Junior Market is just fine for me. Another good point for it is that they carry Laverne's favorite boxes of wine.

After a six-day trip involving four days of driving, it's good to know that I can now go to my

57

yacht, relax, have a snack, finish another Nero Wolfe mystery and unwind from my road trip. Driving down the access road that leads to the boat docks I see a huge cloud of black smoke in the air and three large red fire engines blocking my way. I park and walk over to the gangway where the action is and look out towards the end-tie to see what's going on. A fireman is bringing up some equipment as I approach the gate. When I ask him what's happening, he sums it up for me. "Some old wood boat burned up."

A watched pot doesn't boil, but an unwatched boat does burn. That wiring I never got around to fixing must have given up and started to short out. Unbeknownst to me, the boat was probably smoldering when I left town. If you love boats nothing looks worse than one that's burned out, especially if you own it. All that's left of mine is the hull from the waterline down. From there up, it's gone. There's absolutely nothing left of it but a flagpole on the rear of the boat and enough of that back end so that the name of the boat is still legible. It's sickening for me to look at. I now have nowhere to live, my Nero Wolfe book is probably nothing but ashes, and seven years of my labor of love have been totally wasted. The Foghorn Hotel is around the corner next to the Market, so I guess I'll just go over there and check in for the evening. Just as I'm about to go into a deep depression, I manage to do the only thing that a sane person can do at a time like this. I pick up my cell phone and dial a number. When it answers, I calmly say: "Hello Koontz, this is Peter Sharp. We've got a deal."

My fax line was call-forwarded to Melvin's boat while I was gone, so Myra's agreement is saved. I quickly sign it and fax it back to Koontz's office. He must have been sitting next to the fax machine, because in about fifteen minutes I see the towboat coming down the channel towards our dock. Boy, she must really want this boat. I don't know why, but it's probably for some sneaky reason.

The towboat guys pull up, and burned out hull or not, they don't miss a beat. After verifying the slip number and seeing the name of the boat on what remains of its stern, they ask me to sign their release form. They then hook up the towlines and slowly pull the still smoldering hull out of its slip and down the channel towards the boat yard. From a distance, it looks like they're dragging a huge black whale through the water.

Before leaving, the tow guys mentioned that Myra and her attorney are waiting for their prize to be brought to them at the boat yard. I wait a couple of hours and then call over to the boat yard to hear about what happened. Art, the boat yard manager, is a serious type of guy, but he and I have gotten along quite well in the past. When the boat was originally trucked over there from my back yard, he was the one who helped me select the proper bottom paint to be put on before lowering the boat into the water. I remember him telling me that the brand of bottom sealer he suggested would outlast the boat. I can't wait to tell him how right he was.

After a few minutes of having him paged over the yard's loudspeaker, he finally gets on the line and proceeds to tell me about the scene at the yard. Myra and her attorney arrived at the yard just as the towboat company radioed ahead that they had the cabin cruiser in tow and would be needing dock space near the yard's crane. They both heard the radio call and then began to smile, laugh and happily high-five each other, like they had just won the World Series. Everything was fine until about five minutes later, when the towboat came into view. Their looks slowly changed from glee to horror. People have told me that they've never seen Art crack a smile over the past ten years, but when he tells me about 'that lady beating the guy in the cheap suit on his head with her briefcase,' he can barely catch his breath from laughing. It was definitely a Kodak moment, and exemplifies that old saying, "to the victor goes the spoils."

After a night at the hotel, I go to see Melvin. He's fumbling with his computer, trying to get it to boot up so that he can check his e-mail. He had read Koontz's fax to me while I was out of town and in his twisted mind he created a scenario that turns me into the Marina's Dr. Evil. He thinks that I engineered the whole chain of events, from talking my ex-wife into taking the boat, to having it burned up just before she had it towed away. He looks at me like I'm his new hero.

Maybe that's why he's so understanding of my present situation, and probably why he goes so far as to make me an offer that must be the nicest thing he ever did for anyone other than his ex-wife Jasmine: L. Martin Unger decided to buy a condo and spend the rest of the year in Thailand, so Melvin got his permission to let me stay on the fifty-foot Grand Banks until I can get another place to live.

This really blows my mind. That fifty-foot fiberglass Grand Banks trawler yacht has always been my dreamboat and now I'll actually be living on one. I can't stop thanking Melvin, who only says "hey, what're friends for?" Somehow I can't help but think that Melvin has another agenda. Kindness isn't in his bag of tricks unless there's something in it for him. But this has to be a good sign. I went from being suspended, divorced, evicted and burned out, to living on my dream yacht. And now when George walks by he'll see me in a different light. The deal apparently also includes the Asian Boys as a maintenance crew and I'm told that they'll clean the boat at least twice every week. The rest of the time that crew will no doubt be working on the other boats on our dock, including George's, Laverne's, Melvin's and the retired ophthal-mologist, 'Snatch Adams.' They're also night busboys at that Chinese restaurant around the corner.

I haven't seen Melvin for the past week or so, but the faxed and e-mailed assignments keep coming in from his office. But where is this 'office?' It isn't at the mailbox place around the corner, because that was only a box in the wall. It can't be on his houseboat, because all that's there is a small laptop computer, a fax machine and the dynamic trio. This is starting to get interesting. There was never a need for me to visit his office, so I think it would be a little out of line for me to question him about it because if I did, he would be justified in answering "what's the difference, your checks keep getting delivered on time, don't they?" And that would be a good answer, because the checks do arrive on time, usually within one day of my leaving an invoice in his boat's mailbox.

Somehow I have a feeling in the back of my mind that the little girl knows all the secrets, but would it be proper to talk to her? Does she even speak English? All questions that I'd love to have the answers to.

Over the next week or so I arrange my schedule so that I can be around the Marina at the same times of the day that the little girl and her 'gang' do their traveling in the electric car. I see that a pattern is being followed. Every day like clockwork, they go to the mailbox place to pick up the incoming mail. At least twice a week, they drive up to the outside ATM at the Wells Fargo Bank around the corner, where she uses the walk-up ATM that's lower than the others, probably installed for use by people in wheelchairs, but the perfect height for her to reach from the e-car, and a good thing too, because making deposits would have been too tough a trick to teach the Saint Bernard. Another stop is the rear alley kitchen entrance to the Chinese restaurant. They always go there before lunch time and I never have the time to sit and wait until they come out again, but they're always back on the houseboat before it gets dark.

So far I have their schedule down pat, with only one morning a week missing from my calendar of their regular stops, but that missing piece gets filled in the following week when I make a visit to the Courthouse. On my way back to the parking lot I see their e-car illegally parked by a back entrance to the building, and there's no parking ticket on it, even though it's less than twenty feet away from the Police station's entrance and uniformed cops constantly pass by it. There's no mistaking it for another e-car just like it, because the odds are astronomical against finding a similar vehicle that contains a Saint Bernard sitting behind the wheel, and a cat sleeping on the back seat.

Their once-a-week visit to the court house bothered me for a while until I poke my head into the Courtroom of the Municipal Court where almost all of Melvin's cases are handled. The Court isn't in session at this moment because the judge is probably in chambers negotiating and trying to settle cases with opposing counsel. Behind the railing is the person who runs the courtroom – the clerk, an extremely attractive Asian woman who looks vaguely familiar, and she should. I've seen her eating dinner at the Chinese restaurant many evenings.

It's a funny thing about remembering people. You can see the same face several times a week in one particular place, but when you see it somewhere else outside of its normal surroundings, all it looks like is a familiar face. For several years I went to the same market three times a week to pick up stuff my wife wanted brought home in the evening. The clerk there wore his usual apron and we exchanged the same small talk each time about the weather, the Lakers, Cubs or Dodgers, yada yada. One time I bumped into him in a department store. I saw his face but for a while couldn't place where I'd seen him before. It wasn't until in the car on the way home that I realized it was the clerk from the market. The same thing happened one time when I was in a criminal arraignment Court, where the criminal defendants all appeared with their attorneys only for the purpose of making a plea. A case was in front of the judge, who looked down at the defendant and said "you look familiar, sir – have you appeared before me on other matters?"

The defendant said "no." The judge wouldn't give up, and over the defense attorney's objections he kept badgering the guy as to why he looked familiar. Finally the judge's patience gave out and he gave an order to the defendant.

"I know I've seen you somewhere before, so either you tell me where or I'll throw you in jail for contempt of Court!" The defendant looked at his lawyer, who grudgingly nodded an assent.

The defendant looked up at the judge and reluctantly spoke. "Judge, I'm your bookie."

The clerk isn't the only familiar face in this courtroom; the uniformed bailiff looks familiar too. He isn't Asian, but I still know that I've seen him around somewhere, but can't put my finger on where. He's probably one of the many uniforms that frequent the Chinese place for lunch every day. I really don't give it much thought because after years of appearing in courtrooms, all the uniformed bailiffs start to look the same.

After the kid leaves through the court's private rear exit, I go up to the clerk's area and see the reason she was there. It was to bring in a check for court costs and to pick up the cards of attorneys who made appearances for Melvin during the week. She probably comes in once a week to pay the accumulated costs and get stamped receipts for the case files.

The Asian clerk must be new here because she mistakes me for an attorney. When I tell her that we have the same restaurant in common, she becomes a little friendlier, explaining that she has a few minutes until Max returns. My look tells her I didn't know who 'Max' is, so she explains that it's Maxine, the judge recently assigned to this Court, who is usually either in chambers approving settlement deals, or down the hall running the Small Claims Court. Cutbacks in the court's budget require her to do double duty.

This courtroom is like a lot of them, where the judge hardly ever takes the bench, preferring to clear up the calendar by doing all the business in chambers. Still under the impression that I'm on active status with the State Bar, she asks if I would like to make an occasional appearance for an attorney who is disabled and can't make it to court. She mentions that his name Marcel' Bradley, and lets me know that any attorney in the courtroom who temporarily fills in for Mister Bradley by making a special appearance (which means not being put on the case as attorney of record) will be sent a generous one-hundred dollar appearance fee by his office.

Not wanting to deceive her, I confess that at the Bar's request, I'm taking a brief leave of absence from the 'appearance' scene. She appreciates my honesty. To show my gratitude for being offered the appearances, I offer to buy her a drink at the restaurant next time I se her there. She blushes and turns back to her duties.

On my way back to the parking lot, I realize that Melvin doesn't have to come to Court. Hell, he doesn't even have to exist, because the clerk helps out by hiring attorneys to make any appearances that attorney Unger can't cover, and the kid sends out the checks. In fact, Melvin probably doesn't even know most of the things that are going on in the practice, but someone has to be running the whole show. Could it be that little Girl? And if it is, does she do it all from Melvin's houseboat?

Life aboard the Grand Banks is a dream come true. Beautiful parquet floors in the main 'saloon,' which is what the real boaters call it, not 'salon.' It has a full gourmet kitchen, called a 'galley,' plus an island bar and raised pilothouse. Now that I'm living on a real yacht I'm starting to learn the proper vocabulary, being helped out by some old fart down the dock that lives on his fifty-foot Columbia sailboat.

Using the semi-circular teak staircase you can step down 'below,' where there are immaculate engine rooms on both sides of the companionway - and in back at the rear of the boat, or 'aft,' there's a guest stateroom and a master stateroom that rivals any sleeping quarters I've ever seen, complete with rear windows that look out onto the water. I don't know how to start the engines on this yacht, and could probably never learn how to drive it, but I'll sure try to use the right words describing it to my friends. At least I can 'sound' nautical.

Having such a great place to stay also means not having to leave as often because L. Martin has a small law library lining the walls of the saloon and both staterooms. Now I can do my legal research here and use the ship's complete computer set-up to print reports, case pleadings, or whatever else might be required. Having a large full-sized side-by-side refrigerator will also require fewer trips to the market. I'm even considering learning how to cook, to utilize the gourmet facility aboard. The idea is quickly forgotten after my first meatloaf comes out looking like something an elephant dropped.

The boat also has a satellite dish, so I can watch all those great classic black-and-white movies. I love seeing those grand old cars, dial telephones, guys who wear fedoras, and hard-boiled cops that all acted like *NYPD Blue's* Andy Sipowitz. Most remarkable are those elaborate murder plots motivated by as little as the husband/victim's five thousand dollar insurance policy, which was big money in those days.

But, just as the T-shirts say, 'stuff happens.' I receive e-mail from Melvin's office requesting my help. Melvin went to Thailand to visit with L. Martin and he hasn't sent any messages back to the kid for a couple of weeks. If he doesn't get in touch with the office soon, I may be required to go to Thailand to find him. The mere fact that Mel's law practice is running quite smoothly in his absence supports my suspicions about the little girl, court clerk, and outside attorneys really doing all of the work.

Never having been to Thailand, it sounds like a different world. All I know about it is that it used to be called *Siam*. One of the guys who works on boats here in the Marina goes there every year, as does my barber, and neither one of them can stop talking about the place. Aside from allegedly being the sex capitol of the world, it's also supposed to be a beautiful place to visit. Just in case, I think I'll stop by the Culver City Auto Club office on Sepulveda tomorrow and have some passport pictures taken.

In 1974 a James Bond movie *"The Man With The Golden Gun,"* was shot there, the Thai beaches and its jungles 'doubled' for Viet Nam in *"The Deer Hunter," "Good Morning Viet Nam," "Air America"* and many other films. I'm going over to the Odyssey video store on Lincoln to rent that James Bond DVD, just to see what Thailand looks like. Maybe If I go there I'll meet a descendant of Anna.

Unable to avoid it any longer, I make my regular monthly appointment to see Burt Cohen, my divorce lawyer. After the burned-out boat caper there's a good possibility my ex-wife will be out for evens, and it would be nice to have some strategy to fight her off. Burt's office is on the twelfth floor of the Cal Fed Building on Ventura Boulevard, just East of Sepulveda in Sherman Oaks, and as I drop off my car with the lot's parking valet, I spot someone I have no difficulty in recognizing. It's my old law clerk and wannabe associate, Ricky Hansel. He's wearing a bright yellow ski jacket, so it's easy to spot him at a distance, and I want see where he's going. If it's to an attorney's office, a courtesy warning to that unsuspecting brother member of the bar would be in order, so that another sucker lawyer may not have to suffer what I went through with those disciplinary hearings.

I stay as far back as possible so as to not be noticed, but not being a trained gumshoe I lose him when he enters the building. This is the same one that my lawyer and about a hundred others have their offices. Luckily, I see which elevator he gets into, and it looks like it was empty when he got in, so I watch the floor display to see where it stops. He gets off on the ninth floor. I have no way of knowing which office he went to on that floor, so I'll just have to go up there and check it out.

Getting off on the ninth floor I step into the lobby of a Fegian suite, one of those huge whole-floor office set-ups named after an attorney named Paul Fegian who created the idea of a bunch of lawyers all sharing a large suite. Each one rents a private office, but there are a bunch of amenities included in the rent that they're all allowed to use like a receptionist, copy machine, law library, coffee room, conference room, and a little display of class.

This is good and bad. Ricky is nowhere in sight but at least I know he's visiting one of the attorneys in this suite, so my search is narrowed to the twenty or thirty names on the business cards in the three-tier rack on the receptionist's desk. The Fegian suites never bother to have the attorneys' names put on the door because of the cost and the frequent tenant turnover.

I'm going to have to play private eye now, so using my best *Rockford Files* personality, I give it a shot. She's filing her nails and I hate to interrupt her. "Excuse me, Miss, but I wonder if you could help me out." That seems to get her attention. She waves me off for a second while speaking into her headset microphone, checking the calendar book on her desk and telling a caller that the attorney is expecting him. I hesitatingly continue, being new to this detective routine. I think I've got her attention again. "I have a new case that I'm supposed to be bringing in to an attorney I was referred to, but I forgot his name." She looks confused. Why am I not surprised?

"Well, sir, I'm sorry but if you don't have the lawyer's name, there's no way I can help you."

Here's where watching television sleuths for years comes in handy.

"Well, I don't know the attorney's name, but the fellow who referred me to him was supposed to meet me here. He usually wears a bright yellow ski jacket and told me that after he met with the attorney he'd see me out there in the hall and fill me in."

It worked! A dim light bulb goes off over her head as she happily gives me the information. "Oh yes, that would be Ricky, the paralegal. He's been working several years now for one of the attorneys here, Mr. Gary Koontz."

5

I don't know how to mentally process this this new information, because if Ricky Hansel's been working for my ex-wife's lawyer Koontz for several years, that means he must have been with him before and during my entire suspension proceedings. Several possible scenarios come to mind.

One of them is that Attorney Koontz could just be some innocent jerk that Hansel will destroy sooner or later. It's true he's a real putz, but he's not the innocent type. If that's the case, my instincts tell me to keep my mouth shut and let nature take its course. Another possibility is too dark to imagine, but more likely: Koontz used Hansel to set me up for the suspension – maybe to get me out of the way so he could go after my wife. Who knows what evil lurks in the hearts of men? The third scenario is the worst of all - my ex-wife may have been involved in it too.

Looking at all three situations side-by-side I think that the second is the most probable. Koontz is a schmuck, but he isn't stupid. There's no way Hansel could have been with him for a couple of years without Koontz knowing he was a crook. They must have both been in on my frame-up together. My ex-wife should be ruled out of the conspiracy, because up until the suspension, we were having some communication problems in our marriage, but nothing bad enough to force her over to the dark side. Besides, getting me suspended would endanger her share of my future earnings. No, it's just Koontz and Hansel, but I have no way to prove it. I'll turn over this new development to Melvin's office so he can let L. Martin figure out what to do with it. He's the attorney handling my State Bar appeal, if he ever comes back from Thailand, so it should be his call.

Having finished up meeting with my attorney a few stories above Koontz's office, I feel better. He looked at the fax that Koontz sent me and is pretty confident that Myra's acceptance of the boat on an "as-is, where-is" basis regardless of any repairs that might be necessary will hold up in any court – even the divorce court, should she want to drag me back in there for a modification. I was out of town when the boat burned and any experienced boat mechanic should be able to testify to the fact that the wiring was bad and could have gone at any time, without warning. True, I may have been negligent in not having the necessary repairs done in a timely matter, but negligence isn't the issue here, so I'm home free on her waiver of half my law income for two years of practicing. And because the boat was insured, I should be getting a check that will cover me for most of my loss. I also think that because the loss took place before she took the boat as-is, she won't even have a claim for any part of the insurance money. Life is good.

Back at the boat, I e-mail my report on the Koontz-Hansel matter to Melvin's office for forwarding to L. Martin in Thailand and decide to catch up on my reading. Several years having passed, it's once again time to re-read *The Complete Sherlock Holmes*, sixty of the best crime stories ever written. I try to read this tome at least once every five years, and when I do, it's like making the same new discoveries over again each time. The only thing that comes close to these gems of crime detection are the seventy-two short mysteries written by Rex Stout that feature *Nero Wolfe*, the original armchair detective.

A good crime story is a lot tougher to solve than a television mystery because most TV shows give away the bad guy in the casting. If the only face you recognize in the television mystery show is the featured guest star, you can make book on the fact that he's probably the one whodunit. Most of the television one-hour crime shows follow the same pattern: you meet the bad guy in the first act; someone will die before the first commercial break, and someone (usually the hero) will be in a situation of peril before the next-to-last commercial. The only TV crime story to break this pattern was Peter Falk's *Columbo,* which wasn't really a whodunit... right from the get-go you knew who 'done it' - instead, it's a 'how's-he-gonna-catch-him.'

In a way, Columbo resembles the police lieutenant in Fyodor Dostoyefsky's all-time classic, *Crime and Punishment.* The reader knows that starving student Raskolnikov killed the usurious pawnbroker Alyona Ivanovna, and so does detective Petrovitch of the Saint Petersburg Police. Just like Columbo, he keeps dogging Raskolnikov until he wears him down and gets the confession.

When I first started night law school, two classmates of mine and I became close friends and formed a study group. Both were L.A.P.D. sergeants, and knowing about my fascination with crime stories, they talked me into applying for the police force.

My written test, physical exam, agility, and oral tests went fine, but the colorblind test stopped me cold. My U.S. army induction exam determined that I had a slight red-green deficiency not severe enough to keep me out of the service, but their test wasn't as tough as L.A.P.D.'s. Maybe it's because people were trying to get *in* the L.A.P.D., while people were trying to get *out* of the army.

As usual, it's a gorgeous day outside. My assignments for the day are completed and my deck chair is all set for some reading. A voice down on the dock calls out "ahoy, Grand Banks!" It's the retired doctor. He comes over and welcomes me to the dock, apologizing for the fact that it took him so long to get around to it. We shake hands and have a cordial conversation. Most of the boat owners in the Marina can tell you the same story about have long conversations with boat neighbors on the dock without ever knowing their names, what they do for a living, or their opinions on anything in the world except boating. Maybe that's the way it should be all over, instead of deciding to like or dislike a person because of what political party they belong to, or what they think about the half-dozen issues that continuously polarize us.

Of course the topic of his girlfriend doesn't come up in our conversation, but he does mention that one of these days he'd like me to join him and "Rita" for dinner on his boat. At least once a week he prepares a gourmet meal. I'm sure he's referring to the times when his gorgeous stewardess girlfriend is between flights and staying with him. Feeling pretty sure that she'll be there for any dinner he invites me to, I graciously tell him I'll be looking forward to an invite, and hope it's soon. He tells me that it won't be until next week, because since his weekly 'guest' is out of the country, he's decided to take his boat over to Catalina Island for a few days of relaxation and will be back by Noon next Wednesday, when Rita is expected to be coming by.

I never could quite understand why people have to go somewhere to relax. People who hear that I live on a boat usually tell me about their dreams of 'sailing away into the sunset.' They really don't want to do that, spend weeks on end without hot water or a shower, constant motion, always heeled over ten to fifteen degrees with constant pitching and rolling, no comfort, no television, no restaurants, no nothing. What they really want to do is sail away from their in-laws, boss, job, bratty kids, mortgage payments, alimony, ex-wives, etc., etc… and no matter how far you go, you never really get away from things like that because they stay with you in your mind. But if the Doc wants to go to Catalina, that's OK with me. I've taken a plane over there several times, and if you don't suffer from seasickness, it seems like it might be a nice boat trip when you're with people you enjoy.

The Island's a really quiet place that's only accessible by boat or plane and if own a boat, you're bound to be bumping into other boaters walking around there that you know. I enjoy going to Avalon, the island's only city.

Up the mountain a little way there's a restaurant called "The Landing," where you can have a serving of cerviche while you drink Patrón Margaritas and look down at the harbor until the sun goes down and the drinks get to you. There's a water taxi service that ferries people from their boats to and from the landing dock, and the last one out in the late evening is the most fun to be on, because it's usually full of half-loaded boaters trying to tell the driver how to find one of the mooring cans that their boat is tied up to.

I tell the doc that I'll watch his slip for him while he's gone, and give him my cell phone number in case he runs into trouble on the way there or back. Watching an empty slip seems like an empty promise, but if you know someone's boat will be returning at an approximate time of the day, you can make sure that people who bring their boats over to visit friends on the dock are not in the slip when the rightful slip tenant returns from a trip.

Sunday morning, he leaves and I start watching.

It's doubtful that the doc is having a good trip over to the island. I've been told that Californian trawler of his only does about nine miles and hour, and it's almost forty-five miles from our dock to Avalon, making it at least a five-hour trip if the wind and current are with you. It's now about three hours after he left, and the skies are getting dark, the wind is coming up, and pretty soon I'm sure the rain will start. The wind is coming out of the North, so it's not likely the doc turned around to return, because then he would have been slowly going against the wind and current. He'll probably ride it out and reach the island late in the afternoon.

Just before dinner I turn on the early evening new broadcast. L. Martin recently installed a new forty-two-inch high-definition flat-panel plasma television set, so watching TV has just become a new experience for me. As I'm potchkying around in the galley, a familiar-sounding voice on the news catches my ear. I turn to the television, and there she is, my ex-wife. She looks like she's lost almost two-hundred non-essential pounds: Me! Super-imposed on the bottom of the screen under her face is "Deputy District Attorney Myra Scot." I guess they just didn't have room on the screen to include the last name we shared. The purpose of her appearance is to confidently state that the authorities expect to make an arrest soon in the murder of that Marina del Rey Chinese restaurant owner.

She explains how their investigation is focusing on members of an Asian gambling syndicate involved in the casinos that are so prevalent in neighboring cities of Inglewood and Gardena. They don't have roulette or Vegas-style blackjack, but they do have lots of card games and other gaming methods that closely resemble what you can do in Las Vegas, which is lose your money quickly. A very high percentage of their customers are Asian. Most of the others come in once a month, cigarette in mouth, both hands on their walkers, and social security money in hand. These local card casinos rarely attract out of town tourists. Instead, they just cannibalize the local economy, all in the cause of paying taxes to support schools, so that the future graduates can wind up spending *their* social security money in the casinos.

One apparently strange thing about her announcement that doesn't quite compute is that it sounds wrong. I've done some investigating into the competing restaurants' owner Robert Palmer, and he looks more like a suspect than some Asian gang. If Myra's office is investigating the gang, it's a good bet they're wasting their time, because they don't have a very good track record for crime solving. It would be a lot better if they left it to the Culver City

Police, who are the primaries on this case, as indicated by that police report faxed to me. I guess this is just another case of the D.A.'s office trying to showboat for headlines. I turned all of my reports over to Mel's office and I'm sure they finally reached the Culver City detective assigned to the case.

For some time now I've owned a DVD entitled *Celestial Navigation for the Complete Idiot.* It was a gift from a friend of mine and notwithstanding the title, it really does a good job of reviewing the techniques of Coastal Piloting and then explaining in plain English the principles of celestial navigation, what a sextant measures, and how to navigate around the world.

Any guy like George Clooney, who is interested in things nautical, and who also owns a boat, should appreciate a DVD like this, so I wrap it up and stick on a post-it note to let him know that it's a gift from a dock neighbor. After rubbing my knuckles almost bare knocking on the battleship-like hull of his mega-yacht, I hand it up to the full-time skipper and ask him to give to his boss next time he's aboard. I'm sure George will like the gift and we can start that friendship I'm so sure was meant to be.

While waiting for a thank-you note from G.C., I receive a most encouraging fax from Melvin's office. In between servings of Thai girl, L. Martin Unger finished my Petition for Reinstatement. Mel's office filed it with the State Bar, and a hearing date has been scheduled. There's no indication that Mr. L. Martin is planning on coming back to the States to attend the hearing, but that isn't a big issue and can be worked out later. I don't even take time to read the Petition, knowing in my heart that the whole process will probably just be an effort in futility. I don't want to get my hopes up. After a while you get tired of disappointments.

It's late Tuesday afternoon, still raining, and now really getting dark. At four in the afternoon I see some outgoing mail on the counter, next to the front window of Melvin's houseboat. I know that the kid's e-car doesn't have side curtains, so I knock on her door and offer to do the mail. She doesn't refuse, but doesn't exactly accept either. Instead of responding to me, she turns and says something to the dog that sounds like Chinese. Hearing what is obviously a familiar command, the dog picks up the outgoing mail in his mouth and walks off the boat, probably to the mailbox. He returns without the mail about fifteen minutes later, soaking wet. She dries him with a towel. From this point on I realize that there's no way I can ever offer any assistance to this kid, because she's got everything under control. Now if we could only teach the dog how to make some court appearances... but I'm sure she's probably already working on that.

It's almost midnight. The wind has blown some loose items off of people's decks and something is floating in the water banging against my hull. If I don't get off the boat to pick it up out of the water it'll probably stay there and bang all night long. As I'm down on my knees, bending over trying to reach a floating kayak oar making that noise, I hear a disappointed female voice behind me. "Oh no... damn! Where is he?"

When I turn around and stand up I see that it's the doc's girlfriend Rita, and I realize what has happened. She's probably returned twelve hours earlier than expected, and while standing there under her little umbrella in the rain discovered her boyfriend and his boat are gone. There's no choice at that point, so I offer an invitation for her to come onto the Grand Banks to dry out.

As usual, when it comes to doing the wrong thing I'm consistent. Not only does she come aboard, she winds up staying aboard. I know that this is a dangerous thing to do, but after she got out of her wet clothes and into one of my robes, had a few glasses of wine and joined me on the couch to watch the late show on that big plasma television screen, the wine had its affect and then one thing led to another – and then another.

As wonderful an experience as this is, a terrible thought just occurred to me: if it's possible for *her* to get here earlier than expected, it's also possible for the doc to come back early and discover us together. In between rounds, we discuss this possibility and come up with a brilliant solution. The plan is for her to wait until early tomorrow morning and then get fully dressed and sit on my boat's covered aft deck, sipping an iced tea as if she just arrived and is waiting for the doc to return.

The rain is over, the sun is now up, and two amazing things are happening. First, Rita is having a conversation with Melvin's kid, in English, which means that she's another person the kid'll talk to other than me. And second, our plan works perfectly.

Right on schedule, at around eleven thirty this morning the doc's boat pulls into the basin. As he makes the turn towards his slip, Rita is all smiles, happily waving at him and welcoming him back. Her glee looks so genuine. I wonder how they do that so well.

I'm sure their reunion went just as we planned it. She told him she got in an hour or two early and that their neighbor Peter was gracious enough to offer some refreshment and a place to sit and wait for his return. He shows his appreciation by coming over later that afternoon and invites me to join them tonight for dinner on his boat. I accept. While we're talking I glance over his shoulder and see Rita standing on the foredeck of his boat, smiling and giving me a 'thumbs-up' sign. As we speak, I can't get his face out of my mind and the feeling that I know I've seen it somewhere before.

Here in Southern California, there's always a possibility that a familiar face you have trouble placing may have been one that you saw in a movie. A lot of people out here have worked as extras. I'll have to ask him about that some day. The doc and I chat for another few minutes about his return trip from Catalina Island during that offshore storm. He doesn't mention what must have been the wild ride he had on his boat and I don't mention the wild ride I had on his girlfriend.

Now I can honestly say my dreams have been answered. I had the greatest all-nighter in the world with the most beautiful girl in the world on my dream yacht. Life will probably be all down hill from here, but it was worth it.

This evening I arrive at the doc's boat promptly at seven, and am invited aboard. His boat isn't as luxurious as the Grand Banks, but he's arranged a very nice table setting. The eating area in his boat's saloon consists of an L-shaped settee around a small rectangular table, which is just perfect for three people. After the usual small talk and a few cocktails, he announces that 'dinner is served,' and that we should sit down. The settee is arranged so that two people can sit close together on one side, with the third person sitting alongside on the 'ell' couch extension. Rita grabs my hand and drags me over to the two-person side. "Come on, Mister Lawyer, I want you to sit close to me." The doc seems amused by this. I feel a blush coming on, but comply with her request. She maintains her grip on my hand after we're seated. I'm hoping that this isn't one of those kinky arrangements where the older boyfriend likes to watch his young girlfriend enjoy herself with another man.

Doc excuses himself for a minute and steps off the boat to get a large bottle of wine out of his under-the-dock-steps wine cooler. Rita comes close to me and whispers in my ear. "You know, he's not the same doctor Gault you think he is."

Bang! It just hit me. This is the famous Doctor Sherman Gault. Now I remember why his face looks so familiar. It was plastered all over of every newspaper front page and television screen during his arrest and trial for the murder of his wife!

Most people think that the Los Angeles District Attorney's office blew the O.J. Simpson case due to lack of experience of the main guy upstairs, the district attorney, who was elected to the office and tried to micro-manage the trial. But the people were wrong – he had plenty of experience – in how to blow a good case. Before completely screwing up the O.J. case by making a series of fatal mistakes, like ordering O.J.'s premature arrest before DNA tests were in, moving the case to downtown Los Angeles, assigning two hot-headed arrogant deputies to try it, having a preliminary hearing instead of going the indictment route, not opting for a more competent judge who wasn't married to a prospective witness, not preparing their witnesses properly, etc., etc. Oh yeah, he had plenty of experience. Unfortunately, most of it was gained from his management of the Doctor Sherman Gault murder case two years earlier. Fortunately, the district attorney lost the next election and we've had better luck with the series of new replacements - up until now.

If I remember correctly, Mrs. Gault's body was never found. Doc supposedly had taken her out with him on a rented fishing boat, and it was a one-way trip for her. The story was that she fell overboard, and because he never learned how to swim, he couldn't save her. There also were suspicions that she never was on the boat with him at all, but that he hired someone to have her wacked so he could be with some new young girlfriend. And if Rita was the reason, I can almost understand him wanting to do it.

When my ex-wife first joined the district attorney's office, all she could talk about was how her newly elected boss was someday going to nail that bastard doctor's ass to the wall for some other crime, to show the public that he's a better D.A. than his predecessor. She seemed to idolize that idiot boss of hers. As far as she was concerned, he was right and the doctor was guilty of that murder, only getting off on 'technicalities.' We defense lawyers call those little technicalities the Constitution, and a fair judicial system.

She still feels the same way. I only gave her one piece of advice, which was a quotation from someone I greatly respected: "It is a capital mistake to theorize before one has data. Insensibly one begins to twist facts to suit theories, instead of theories to suit facts." [Sherlock Holmes – *A Scandal in Bohemia*]

Unfortunately for the entire District Attorney's staff who botched that case, the jury disagreed, and notwithstanding what could have been damaging testimony if brought out properly by the trial deputies, the doc was acquitted amid loud protests from numerous women's organizations and a stinging commentary by the city's most noted crusading female attorney. She puts on a red dress and comes out of the woodwork every once in a while for a press conference, to complain about something that someone has done to a woman – all while getting free publicity for her law practice.

Perpetual losers have a strange view of things that is a lot different from the way that winners see the world. A loser always manages to place blame for the loss on someone or something else. It's never their fault for losing. On the other hand, winners usually credit their victory to the help of others. Our district attorney's office seems to have adopted a prosecutorial culture handed down from one losing boss to another. They never admit to being wrong. It would be refreshing to see someone actually come out and say, "I really goofed this one up. I made the mistakes and I take the blame." Former president

Harry S. Truman had it right with his desk placard that said "the buck stops here."

The assignments are still coming in regularly from Melvin's office, while I bide my time until the State Bar hearing. They're getting more lawyer-like, with requirements that case files be analyzed and trial strategies planned. This is a little more than I expected to be doing, but it's a pleasant change from doing the grunt work of serving eviction notices on people and sitting in the courthouse's basement archive going through the record books.

As my Bar hearing date grows near I decide to put some effort into a prepared statement, and spend a good deal of time at the downtown Los Angeles Law Library researching cases over the past ten years in which similar charges were filed against other attorneys. They all seemed to have resulted in much more lenient disciplinary sentences than mine, so I'm starting to feel a little better about my chances of getting an early reinstatement to practice.

The State Bar has a rule that requires attorneys to take and pass an ethics examination prior to reinstatement, so I've started preparing for it by going over some of the casebooks and outlines used to teach the subject, which wasn't part of the curriculum at Betty Crocker College of Law when Melvin, Koontz, and I attended. I don't think you can teach ethics to anyone in law school because by the time they get that far with their education they've either got some basic sense of what's right, or they don't. However, there are some specific rules concerning the practice of law that have been laid down, so it won't hurt to become familiar with them.

86

Most of the discipline that the Bar doles out is for mismanagement of trust funds, and I don't think you have to be a brain surgeon or take courses in law school to know that stealing your clients' money is not the proper thing to.

If you drive towards downtown Los Angeles on any freeway between seven-thirty and eight in the morning, you'll see people in alone their cars, but they look like they're arguing with someone. They're not talking on cell phones, they're actually arguing, but not just with themselves. What you're actually seeing is a rehearsal of what they intend to argue in court that day. It was practiced in front of the mirror last night and now it's being repeated in the car on their way to the courthouse. You never lose that habit, so until my Bar hearing, people driving near my car will look over and be convinced I am a nut case. To remedy this almost-correct diagnosis I ride with a visible cell phone earplug in my left ear. That way, I appear almost sane while arguing with the non-existent Bar examiner.

Rita's flying schedule is pretty regular, so it isn't too difficult to arrange not to be around the dock the times she arrives or departs. She managed to get my telephone number from the doc's Rolodex, so the occasional phone call comes in. Rita flies over the Pacific, so her calls usually are from Australia. I repeatedly tell her to cool it because I don't want to antagonize the doctor and she repeatedly tells me that he's no problem, she can handle him, and everything will be okay. The thing that really bothers me is her intention during one of her visits, to openly spend her 'layover' on my boat and not on his. Great. This is just what I need. Let a guy who killed his wife to be with a woman see me sleeping with that same woman. As if I don't have enough problems. I might as well get a t-shirt with a big bulls-eye on it. Koontz and Hansel are probably cooking up another thing to frame me with, the Bar wants me out, Laverne just wants me, and I'm sure that after the burned-out boat caper, my ex-wife wants me dead. If the doc finds out about me sleeping with Rita, then my ex-wife'll have to get in line to have me wacked. And if Mister L. Martin Unger returns for my Bar hearing, it's goodbye Grand Banks, hello Foghorn Motel - if I'm still alive.

About the only thing good going for me this week is that Stuart hasn't called. Come to think of it, the last time we spoke he mentioned a new two-bedroom condo he's renting. Maybe I ought to be nicer to him: he and his extra bedroom may come in handy during my next emergency.

My State Bar hearing has been set for two P.M. two days from now, and there's still no word from L. Martin. His being present at the hearing would be nice, but if he doesn't show, then the written papers filed along with my oral argument will have to suffice. The State Bar Judges have probably already read the brief L. Martin had Mel's office submit, so their minds are probably already made up. The hearing will only be a formality for them to let me know what they've already decided they don't want me to practice law for a while.

The night before the hearing, I receive a message from Mel's office that contains two items: first, L. Martin will not be attending the Bar hearing:

second, for some reason, I'm being sent to Thailand. Air travel and hotel arrangements have already been made and I'll be leaving a few days after my hearing ends. I'm supposed to learn my assignment when I arrive there. No other explanation is given.

The day of the hearing I drive towards the State Bar's Los Angeles offices rehearsing my statement and imagining the worse case scenario, like more trumped up charges being filed as a result of new evidence brought in by Gary Koontz's office. Not wanting to blow things by being late, I make sure I get there at least an hour before I'm scheduled to be heard, and given the fact that the worst case scenario is still fresh in my mind, I glance toward the State Bar's office building and what I see sends a cold chill down my spine. It's happening. The scenario is going to come true. My arch enemy Koontz is now walking out of the State Bar's building. No doubt he's been upstairs spilling his guts to the Judges, helping them dream up new charges against me.

You might as well stick a fork in me now. I'm done. No wonder L. Martin didn't fly in for this hearing: he must have been informed that Koontz was coming in with more charges, so there was no sense wasting a plane ticket on a lost cause. At this point I'm contemplating turning around, driving back to the Marina and spending the rest of the afternoon getting smashed while reading another Sherlock Holmes story, but for some strange reason of morbid curiosity I'll go up there and watch my own funeral. I might as well see things through all the way to my bitter end.

The surprises aren't over yet. As I approach the hearing room another witness is coming out. I know he looks familiar, but as usual, can't remember where I've seen him before. As the Sergeant at Arms leads me into the hearing room and tells me to sit down at the table where a "Petitioner" placard is attached, it strikes me: that guy walking out of the room was Jack Bibberman, the clerk from Ricky Hansel's mailbox place on Ventura Boulevard. He walks over to a bench and sits down in the hallway, probably on call to come in and nail me further. They didn't miss a trick. Shoot me now, please.

The hearing judge starts to speak, but I can barely hear him. I guess that's what happens when you're partly in shock. Your hearing ability starts to fade and the only thing that brings you out of it is the sound of someone saying your name. The worst-case scenario I dreaded is now in play. They've probably heard testimony this morning from everyone who wants me ousted, and this afternoon is just a formality to drive the final stake through my Bar license. I hear the judge mention L. Martin Unger's name and that brings my attention almost all the way back to what's going on.

The judge says my name and brings me back to reality. "Mister Sharp, do you have anything you'd like to say to this court?" If I didn't already think that my goose was completely cooked, now would be the time for my opening statement. Maybe I'll do a little prep work for it by calling Bibberman in from the hallway as a witness. The least I could do is to have him describe Hansel as the one who rented the box. When I was there that day with the adjustor,

Bibberman said that he came in once for a UPS package.

"Your Honor, Petitioner would like to call Mister Jack Bibberman to the stand. He's already been before the court and we believe he's seated outside in the hallway." The judge instructs the Sergeant at Arms to fetch him. He gets seated in the witness chair again and the judge reminds him that he's still under oath. I start out by asking him a question. My mouth is dry, so the sound comes out a little raspy.

"Mister Bibberman, do you recall the day that I visited your place of employment to inquire about a certain mailbox there?" He answers immediately, without any hesitation. Somehow I get the feeling that he'd like to help me if he could. "You mentioned that someone came in one time to pick up a UPS package." He nods in agreement. "Do you remember telling me that?" Again, he complies quickly with a 'yes' answer. "If possible, could you please give the Court a description of that person?"

"Sure, he was a slender guy, probably in his forties with a mostly bald head. The thing I remember most about him was that he had these 'beady' eyes. He looked sort of like a guy you wouldn't buy a used car from. I never saw him before that day, but he did have a key to the box, because he used it to identify himself as a person authorized to pick up the package. I saw him out in the hall, when I came in earlier today. Maybe he was in here, too."

Ricky Hansel is in his twenties, a little pudgy and has a full head of hair. The court must have realized this too because he no doubt had been in front of them for over an hour of testimony earlier this week. Koontz had also been in the witness chair today, and even the kid's Saint Bernard would be able to tell that it was him who Bibberman was describing as the guy who had the mailbox key and picked up the package.

I go silent for a minute, trying to figure out the best way to continue my attack, but the judge interrupts my train of thought. "Mister Sharp, we have read and considered the brief filed on your behalf, as well as evidence from both Attorney Gary Koontz and Mister Jack Bibberman, the clerk at Mail Boxes Unlimited in Van Nuys, California. We are now going to take a brief recess to confer in chambers. This hearing will resume in ten minutes, and we suggest that you not go very far from this room Mister Sharp, because when we say ten minutes, we mean ten minutes."

How nice of them. Instead of calling in the carpenters to nail me to the cross here and now, they've decided to toy with me for a while. They're probably going to spend their ten minutes having a beer and laughing about me sitting out here 'dangling in the wind.' I hope that Stuart's offer to make appearances in Small Claims Court is still on the table, because when these old farts get through with me, for sure there'll be no practicing of law in my future.

The Sergeant at Arms sticks his head in the door and informs me that the Judges will be taking an additional fifteen minutes. Why not? They can use the extra time to figure out how to add some criminal charges too. I'm going to sit here with my elbows on the table and my head in my hands. They can come back in whenever they feel like it. At this point, I don't care what they do.

True to their word, their fifteen-minute extension period is up and they're slowly walking back into the room and taking their seats. The head judge is leaning over and conferring with the others. They all nod in agreement. Good, it's a unanimous decision to hang me from the ceiling light fixture and leave me up there for another year or so, as a deterrent to all other lawyers who trust their paralegals.

The head Judge bangs his gavel on the table and starts talking. I hear the voice, but the words are just drifting through my head as he states the case name, case number, a brief description of the facts, yada, yada. I wish he'd get it over with already. When he says my name, I reluctantly regain my consciousness.

"Mister Sharp, we have fully considered the facts and points of law cited by your attorney Mister Unger in the Petition For Reinstatement that he has caused to be filed with this Court. And, in view of the contentions stated therein, and testimony you have elicited from Mister Jack Bibberman, contrasted with the testimony we have heard in this matter from Attorney Gary Koontz, we have come to the conclusion that the facts alleged in your attorney's brief are true. Therefore, this Court finds that it was attorney Gary Koontz who rented the mailbox in Ricky Hansel's name. Further investigation that our outside staff conducted has revealed more about this Ricky Hansel's criminal past and affected his credibility before us. Apparently, his transcripts submitted to enter law school were forged, and his continuing association with Attorney Koontz before, during and after your disciplinary matters has led us to believe that you have been wrongly accused of unethical conduct.

"Accordingly, your previous suspension has been expunged from your record and you are now reinstated to the active practice of law in the State of California, said rein-statement to be considered retroactive, back to the date of your original wrongful suspension. Furthermore, we have decided that new disciplinary proceedings should be instituted against Attorney Koontz.

"You will be notified if your testimony is required at his disciplinary hearing and if so notified, we expect your cooperation in full without the need of a formal subpoena.

"That's all Mister Sharp. This hearing is now concluded."

That's it. He bangs the gavel down and the panel of judges all get up and walk out of the room.

6

My head is reeling. Can this really be happening? The Sergeant at Arms slides a document in front of me and gives me some instructions.

"If you would please sign this standard agreement releasing the California State Bar from any liability for its past handling of this disciplinary matter, your reinstatement as an active member of the California State Bar in good standing to practice law will be effective immediately." I knew there would probably be a string attached, but I don't care. I don't even read the statement. I seem to remember signing it.

Everything that's happening now is just a blur. I must have signed the document, thanked him, and walked out of the room. At least I hope that's what I did. All I know is that I'm now in my rented Hummer, driving back to the Marina with a CD blasting. I'm singing a duet with Frank Sinatra. The song is *That's Life*.

L. Martin sure did get the job done. I can't wait to meet him because an in-person thank-you should definitely be made... and to Melvin too. Evidently the info I turned in about Ricky Hansel working with Koontz panned out. I don't know who did the rest of the investigation, found Jack B. the mailbox clerk, served the subpoenas and made the case airtight, but whoever did it pulled off a bang-up job and I'm forever grateful. When the Bar's through with Koontz, my wife will probably be looking for another jerk to represent her. She should have no problem. There are a lot of them out there.

A celebration is definitely called for now, so on the way back to the Marina I stop off at Mi Ranchito, a gourmet Mexican restaurant on Washington Boulevard just east of Centinela, and order the most expensive burrito on the menu, along with several topless Patrón Margaritas. The first time I heard that description, I thought that it was the waitress being described, but as usual, I was wrong. With respect to Margaritas, all it means is without salt on the rim of the glass, and has absolutely nothing to do with the waitress' attire. And that's a good thing, because today the owner's morbidly obese wife has been bringing my drinks to the booth.

After about 32 ounces of Patrón Margaritas I'm partially anesthetized, so I have them call a cab for me. I can always come back for the rental car tomorrow.

As the dock gate slams behind me and I happily stroll down the ramp to the dock I'm in a weakened state and have no energy to resist the abduction as Laverne grabs my arm.

I must have had a good time last night. All I can remember is that I made a wonderful discovery concerning the reverse correlation between alcohol and aging.

In my eyes, every Margarita I drank erased ten years from Laverne's appearance, so I was able to journey backward in time and sleep with a very, very young Laverne. Unfortunately the magic spell only lasts as long as the Margaritas, so the sobering-up process reversed the fountain of youth and she aged back to the present while I was sleeping.

Melvin's office already knew about my reinstatement before I could tell them and I've just received my next assignments, which are five court appearances in Santa Monica. Now that I'm a full-fledged attorney again, I'll be paid the full one hundred dollars for each one of those appearances. This money, along with the five hundred owed to me for the past two weeks' assignments gives me over a thousand extra dollars to waste, so I'm now making a request to Mel's office. Because I'm not due in Thailand for another four days, I suggest a slight change in my travel arrangements: I'd like to leave the next morning and stop over in Maui for a few days before continuing on to my appointment in Thailand.

Surprisingly there is no objection, and as a congratulory gesture, the office will be picking up the extra charges incurred by the flight changes, as well as my two-night stay at Lahaina's Pioneer Inn on Front Street, across from the huge Banyan Tree.

When we discuss my travel plans, Laverne apologizes for not being able to make the trip with me because I'm going during the week, and she just can't get away from work I try to look disappointed and say to myself "as if!"

Several years ago my wife and I spent a week's vacation in Hawaii and visited Maui, a 729-square-mile island seventy miles southeast of Oahu. Maui has a population of less than one hundred thousand people and it's a charming place to visit. After landing at Kahului Airport, we took a thrilling 27-mile ride on winding roads to the island's main tourist area, the small oceanfront village of Lahaina. While we were there, our conversation with some people we bumped into at one of the Island's many art galleries turned to the boat I was restoring in our back yard. John Williams and his wife, the people we were talking to, happened to be members of the local Lahaina Yacht Club, and upon learning we were interested in boating they graciously invited us to be their guests for dinner at the club.

We spent several more days in Lahaina, and always seemed to gravitate back to the friendly atmosphere of the Yacht Club, where we were allowed to purchase a fifteen-day guest membership privilege card, courtesy of arrangements made by our new friends.

Before leaving the island, John offered to sponsor me for membership in the club. At first it seemed like a strange idea, but upon hearing that as a member I'd be entitled to reciprocal privileges at thousands of other yacht clubs around the world, the idea sounded like a good one so I accepted. Six months later I received my membership card in the mail and have kept it current to this date. It's only for an Associate non-voting membership. In order to be a Regular Member with charging and voting rights you must have a residence on the Island. The club's logo of a large whale looked very impressive on the triangular burgee that I had fastened to my boat's flagpole, and it was the last thing I saw as the burnt-out remains of my Chris Craft were being towed away. I'll have to buy another one when I get back there this time.

The flight is a little over five hours and I'm spending most of it reading some Sherlock Holmes stories. I can't help but think of a strange coincidence: Arthur Conan Doyle, the Holmes' creator, was an ophthalmologist, just like Doctor Sherman Gault. But unlike Gault, Doyle was never accused of killing anyone.

Doyle was born in 1859 and got his medical degree from the University of Edinburgh, where he studied under Dr. Joseph Bell, who used to tell his students that no matter how good the eye can *see*, many times it doesn't *observe*. To prove his point, Bell would have a student go outside on the street and bring in any passer-by at random. Bell would then amaze his students by doing a Sherlock Holmes-type of 'rant,' telling all about the stranger by just observing him. According to Doyle, every one of Bell's observational presumptions would invariably wind up being correct.

Having a slow medical practice, Doyle began creating stories featuring the fictitious Sherlock Holmes, influenced to a great degree by Doctor Bell. There have been some new versions of the Holmes stories, written with the permission of the Doyle estate, but a pure Sherlockian won't read them. All that we would consider poring over is referred to as *'The Canon,'* the set of sixty original stories (fifty-six short stories and four novellas) by A. Conan Doyle. Any book written by another, while still being a Holmes story, is considered outside the Canon and not to be read.

I sometimes wish I could have been around in 1887 to read Sherlock Holmes' first appearance in *A Study In Scarlet,* which was an addition to the Beeton's Annual Christmas publication. Someday I plan to visit London to see Mrs. Hudson's rooms at 221b Baker Street, where Holmes and Watson allegedly resided from 1881 to 1904. The tourist guides say that Holmes' study overlooking Baker Street is still faithfully maintained. Only the non-believers doubt its existence.

My timing is perfect. At the last page of The *Adventure of the Speckled Band,* the announcement of our approaching landing is being made, so we straighten up our seats, put up our food trays, fasten our seat belts and with white knuckles, wait to touch down. You can always tell when a flight is about to end when you hear those flaps on the wings being lowered to slow the plane down. I think they're called ailerons.

The twenty-seven mile taxi ride to Lahaina is as exhilarating as ever. As I look out the left-side rear window, I see a sight that always fascinates me: waves are coming in toward the shore, but the wind is blowing very hard against the waves. This conflict of waves versus wind causes a spray off the top of each breaking wave to be blown back offshore, toward where the wave was coming from. Next on my list of interesting sights is a certain empty bar stool at the Lahaina Yacht Club which, after showing my membership card and signing in, is filled by my rear end while the bartender serves my first topless blended margarita of the day... ordered in advance via cell phone when we're about five minutes from the club's Front Street location.

Lahaina Yacht Club is only the width of a slightly larger-than-normal storefront, as are most of the places on Front Street, whose back-ends are balconies hanging out over the Pacific Ocean.

It's very relaxing sitting on the balcony, sipping Margaritas and having pleasant conversations with other members of the club. They all notice my small suitcase and are aware of the fact that I just flew in. I get some respect for placing a higher priority on visiting the club than trying to get a hotel room down the street at the Pioneer Inn. Being surrounded by people who you can immediately bond with, people who all share a common interest and would like to get to know you better is a wonderful experience. It makes you feel like a celebrity. Probably a lot like being a black Republican.

The time flies by and in no time at all I'm looking at the club's dinner menu. This is great: no fax, no phone, no Stuart, no Laverne, no ex-wife, no distractions. My before-dinner cocktail is brought over to the table and the waitress tells me that someone at the door wants to see me.

"I'm sorry honey, but there must be some mistake. Tell whomever it is that I've recently deceased and am therefore not accepting visitors. I only know one person on the island, and that's my club sponsor John Williams. He's also a member, so he wouldn't be waiting at the door."

I was hoping that would do the trick, but I notice that she's still standing here.

"Mister Sharp, I can assure you that it's not John Williams who wants to see you."

"My dear, I don't intend to get off of my chair until it's either time to pee or go to bed, hopefully in that order, so you might as well usher whoever it is over here to my table."

It's a good thing I'm partially embalmed, because it helps to absorb the shock of discovering who my visitor is. I feel a gentle tap on my shoulder.

Without turning around, I once again instruct the waitress.

"Honey, I told you that I don't know any non-members on the Island, so please tell whoever it is that I'm not..."

I don't get a chance to finish my sentence because I feel some warm, wet lips on the back of my neck. If the waitress thinks that a stunt like this will increase the amount of her tip, she is absolutely correct. I turn my head around to give her an opportunity to earn the biggest tip of the year and am stunned to see who's kissing me. It's not the waitress. It's the doc's girlfriend, Rita.

7

By reflex action I stumble to my feet and graciously pull out a chair so Rita can sit down. She has another type of greeting in mind and after the longest, wettest kiss of my life, my red face and eyes and I sit down next to her. I hear some applause from the bartender and the waitress.

Her presence makes my head start to clear up enough to try a conversation. "Well, well, it's a small world, isn't it? What's a nice girl like you doing in a place like this?" Hearing that lame remark come out of my mouth tells me that my head really isn't cleared up enough to try being clever. She knows that her showing up here must have shocked the hell out of me.

"Hello sailor, wanna have a good time?" I look around the room to make sure she came by herself.

"Not if you're with Doctor Death." I can tell immediately that was the wrong thing to say to her, so I back off on insulting her boyfriend. Like a real trooper, she lets the remark slide right past her.

"Peter, honey, where are we sleeping tonight?"

"Frankly, my dear, I don't give a damn. But to answer your question more seriously, I'm afraid it will be right here at this table if I don't get down the street pretty soon and register at the Pioneer."

Standing in the lobby of the Pioneer while leaning against the counter for support, I am informed that the Inn is completely filled, and has been since yesterday.

As expected, Rita comes through perfectly. There's some sort of underground network of stewardesses [who from this instant on I'm informed, are to be referred to as 'flight attendants,' any violation of said rule to result in a loss of consortium] who have an international chain of apartments available to them. On Maui they have one a few miles north of Lahaina at the Hale Kai Apartment Home Complex on Lower 'H' Road, which is where we taxi to after completing one of the most enjoyable dinners I can ever remember having. That was the first meal during which I rushed to get through the first dessert, looking forward to the upcoming second one.

The evening is another memorable one, but carries with it the biting feeling that this is too good to be true, and will end sooner or later in some conflict with a person who has probably taken the life of one human being already. Rita is unflappable and constantly assures me that everything is going to work out just fine between me and the doc. Denial is not a river in Egypt.

My flight to Thailand isn't scheduled to take off until nine this evening. Rita has already left to catch her connecting flight to Los Angeles, so I decide to spend my remaining daylight hours on Maui sitting under the Banyan tree, reading some more Sherlock Holmes. If you've never been to Maui or India, you might not be familiar with the Banyan tree [real name *ficus benghalensis*]. The shady branches of this tree from India cover almost an acre, and its roots extend nearly fifty yards. This one was planted in 1873 to mark the 50th anniversary of Protestant missionary work in Lahaina and is now the largest tree in the United States. You can sit under it until four in the afternoon, at which time about a thousand squawking birds come flying in from somewhere and descend into the branches of the tree. From that moment until the sun goes down it's too noisy to sit there, so once again, it's Patrón margarita time.

This evening I bid farewell to the gang at the club and try to answer all the questions about where my good-looking girlfriend is. The taxi picks me up at seven sharp and I'm on my way to the airport, and then to Thailand. This leg of the journey will be more than twice as long as the one getting to Hawaii, so I prepare to finish the Adventures of *The Five Orange Pips, The Musgrave Ritual, The Red-headed League,* and *The Six Napoleons,* all of them classics in true Sherlockian fashion.

I seem to remember getting through the first three before the club's last Margaritas kick in, and then sweet sleep comes. The stewardess, er, flight attendant wakes me and I discover that I've been out for several hours, and it's now time for the usual stuff – seat up, tray up, and belt fastened. We're going into the landing pattern.

This is my first trip to Thailand, and the farthest away I've ever been from the States. Being a strong believer in our wonderful American judicial system, notwithstanding many of the ignoramuses that inhabit it, I always feel better in an environment where I know what my rights are and how to handle myself in any kind of situation. That good feeling doesn't exist outside of the U.S. of A., so left to my own choice I'd rather not be a world traveler.

Come to think of it, ignoramuses probably belong in the judicial system, because the very first ignoramus was a lawyer. George Ruggle wrote a play

106

in 1615 entitled *Ignoramus*, named after its lead character - a lawyer.

Years ago, before I got married, some friends and I sailed about twelve hundred miles South one winter, from California to Puerto Vallarta, on the Mexican mainland. I remember feeling uneasy every time we went ashore. It's probably due to bad memories from all those dramatic noir movies, in which completely innocent Americans always seem to get unjustly prosecuted by people like my ex-wife and her gang. Somehow I usually feel like Rick, the Humphrey Bogart character in *Casablanca*, fearful that there's always a Claude Raines-type policeman ready to take me away on a politically motivated charge. Fortunately, it isn't like that at all in Thailand.

I was told that a government official would be meeting me at the airport. He had been sent a picture of me, so I wasn't to worry about being found. And I was. A short, well-dressed, pomaded government-type individual introduces himself to me. He must have seen me looking around at the surroundings like I'm some hick tourist. "Mister Sharp, why don't you sit down for a minute until I return; we'll be riding to my office soon. I'll go and get my elephant."

It isn't until we're sitting in the back seat of his air-conditioned government vehicle that he gives me one of those "gotcha" smiles, but I do actually see some elephants. They have them in several rural areas for people to ride and have their pictures taken with, but the Bangkok officials are getting tired of the mess they make with their droppings, so eleven new city bylaws are being strictly enforced to keep them out of the urban areas. In the past I've been irritated by seeing some dog droppings around where I live, but learning that an elephant can drop up to a hundred pounds a day now makes me realize how lucky I am that there aren't any of these huge critters in Marina del Rey, California.

When the official sees me looking at the elephants he tells me the tragicomical story about what happened several years ago when a twenty-one year old elephant named Phlai Rungruang got mad at a tourist, after having been teased by a withdrawn offer of some sugar cane. The young elephant ran amok downtown for three hours until subdued by tranquilizer darts. Evidently his trainer never taught him to obey the command "Stay." I'd hate to have been the tourists sitting in that little seat aboard Phlai during his temper tantrum. It was probably like John Travolta's riding that mechanical bull in the motion picture *Urban Cowboy*. Fortunately, some very good lessons are learned at an early age: I remember a traumatic incident about thirty-six years ago when my father tried to have me sit still on a pony for a photo-op. After that I was forever convinced that guys raised in big urban cities like Chicago are not meant to be on top of animals.

During our trip to the official's office I'm fascinated by the areas we're passing by, and barely hear him as he keeps repeating how wonderful it is for me to come all this way on Mister Bradley's account; how good a friend I must be to sacrifice my time and how grateful his government is that I could come to finalize this segment of their procedure. I keep thinking to myself "what the hell is this guy talking about?" I have only one question to ask him: "will I be seeing my associate soon?" He assures me that within the hour my anxiety will be completely removed.

Following the instructions given to me before leaving Los Angeles, I call the office to check in. Amazingly my cell phone works fine. All I have to do is use (310), my local California area code. The international code must be automatically programmed in. Our office answering machine picks up, so I leave a message. "Hi, this is Peter. I'm in Thailand now, and that government official who found me at the airport is taking me to see Melvin. I'll check in again later. If there's anything you want me to tell him or L. Martin, leave word for me at Bangkok's Peninsula hotel. I should be checking in within the next hour."

At the official's office I'm led into a waiting room with a large picture window on one wall. I have no idea what purpose it serves, because all you can see through it is a hallway on the other side of the office, and another office door. The official pokes his head into the room and says that Mister Bradley is on the way. I'm sitting down looking at a magazine when I hear a knock on the glass of the picture window. On the other side is the official, beckoning me over to the window. When I get to the window, someone in the hallway rolls up a gurney with a sheet-covered cadaver on it, and pulls back the top part of the sheet. Lying on the gurney is a corpse. It's Melvin!

8

When the official comes back into the room, I grab him by his lapels.

"Jesus W. Christ! Couldn't you have told me what to expect?"

He's caught completely off guard. "But Mister Sharp, I thought you knew I was the coroner. Oh, my Goodness."

"No, I didn't know that. All they told me was that you were a government official who'd be taking me to see Melvin. No one said he'd be dead! What the hell happened? Was he murdered, or what?" The coroner is not taking this well, so I release my grip on his jacket. It's difficult for him to believe that someone would travel so far not knowing that the real purpose of the trip is only to make positive identification of a body.

"Mister Sharp, you really must calm down. There are others here who would be disturbed if you continue making a scene."

"Scene? Scene? You want to see a scene? Wait'll I get my hands on the person who sandbagged me into this trip. That'll be a scene! What're you worried about? Are you afraid I might wake up some of your other customers? They should only be so lucky."

I sit down with my head in my hands. I can't remember ever having been this upset. Not even my separation from Myra or the State Bar suspension affected me like this. Maybe it's because they weren't unexpected surprises and I had some time to prepare. But this one is different, and I hope I don't have to ever experience anything like it again. A quick appraisal of the situation doesn't look too good: I'm in Thailand, Melvin is dead, my boat is gone, my job is probably gone, a killer's girlfriend lusts after me and I have no idea what's going to happen next in my life. This makes the divorce and suspension look like a walk in the park. Oh, I've got my license back all right, now all I have to do is get my life back together, find a job, find a place to live and make sure that Doctor Death doesn't find me.

No matter what part of the world I'm in I seem to wind up with a Doctor Death, but at least this one in Thailand only gets involved after the fact. With his help, an hour's time, and three or four Thai beers, I start to regain my composure. He tells me what he believed happened. "Mister L. Martin Unger owned and flew his own private plane here in Thailand. He filed a flight plan at the Chiang Mai International Airport, up in the hills North of Bangkok, giving his destination as James Bond Island. Mister Unger's only passenger we later believed to be an American tourist named Marcel' Bradley - a friend of his who he wanted to show the country to.

They must have had some mechanical problem, because the plane crashed during take-off. The local authorities were able to identify Mister Unger because they knew him, but we still needed someone to make a positive identification of his passenger. And because there was a good probability he was an American citizen, we wanted to avoid any problems with your local embassy. The body's clothing contained a hotel key, so we checked his room and found a passport and business card for Mister Marcel' Bradley. When his United States office was contacted they assured us that one of his close associates would fly here to make the identification.

At that time, there was still a remote chance that it was not Mister Bradley, so maybe your office was correct in not telling you he was dead. Your picture was e-mailed to us and you were met at the airport. You know the rest. We're sorry for your loss and that you weren't told in advance. Perhaps it was a terrible oversight on your office's part to not let you know of the exact nature of your trip."

I can't be mad at the guy. He's the ultimate professional, courteous and patient with me. I thank him and he offers to drive me to my hotel. As I'm getting out of his car, he hands me an envelope: "Mister Sharp, this is for you. We found it among Mister Bradley's things. It is addressed to you."

Once in my room, I sit down with some ice cubes wrapped in a towel around the top of my head and open the envelope. It's a handwritten letter from Melvin:

Dear Peter:

If you're reading this letter, it's because something terrible has happened to me. I'm going up in a small plane with L. Martin today, so I thought that leaving this behind might be a good idea.

As you must know by now, my stepdaughter Suzi really runs the practice, so there's really nothing for me to do there. If L. Martin's brief worked, and I'm sure it did, you've probably been reinstated by now and can take my place in the practice, doing more than I did, because you can actually make appearances; the judges probably like you better than they did me.

My main concern is Suzi. My will, which a Century City attorney will probate, appoints you as her legal guardian. I know it's a lot to ask, but please take care of her. She's a good kid, and with me gone, you're all she's got in the world. And please tell her that even though I never said it, I really loved her.
Thanks,
your law school bookstore partner, Melvin

Melvin and I were never close friends. Like most other people, I didn't give him a lot of respect, but I have to admit that he went out with some class. The friendly local coroner tried to be as cooperative as he could, but he had his own problems getting the bodies ready for transport back to the States. Now that both bodies have been positively identified, he must deal with their final disposal. There's no 'Potter's Field' in Bangkok where unclaimed bodies are buried. They use them as 'donors,' for the country's rapidly growing medical system, and then dispose of them some other way that I really don't want to know about.

After several e-mails are exchanged between my hotel room and the office, I get authorization to bring the remains of both Melvin and L. Martin home with me for proper burial. The office must have wired some money to the coroner, because when I give him the request, he's already done the paperwork, and the bodies have been packed in dry ice, crated, and ready to be loaded onto the plane.

It must be the lawyer in me. How does a thoroughly inspected plane suddenly develop a mechanical problem and crash during take-off? Not ever having flown a plane or been very interested in flying, I sent my thoughts about this question back to the office the first day I arrived here, and now two days later, some action has obviously been taken. The office knew about the incident before I did - they usually do. A package has been delivered to me at the hotel containing the personal affects of Melvin and L. Martin, and along with that package is another small box containing two pieces of what look like a broken airplane part, and several officially-stamped documents that establish the part's purchase from a reputable aircraft supply company in the United States. There's also an affidavit from the local aircraft inspector, identifying it as a counterfeit part, and officially states that there were several other parts all purchased from the same company that were all delivered in the same recent shipment.

Even though I have no knowledge of the law as it pertains to aircraft crashes and counterfeit parts, it looks to me like this case is a slam-dunk. My work is completed here, so it's time to return to the States and make an attempt to locate the remaining family of both plane crash victims. I don't know where I'll be working from now, because with L. Martin gone, I'll probably have to vacate the Grand Banks, but with my license to practice having been restored I should be able to make a decent living off of Melvin's practice – if the little girl doesn't fire me.

Before leaving Thailand I make one extra stop. I want to have my picture taken on top of an elephant. This will be a trophy photo to be sent to the remaining members of my family who may still remember that long-ago unfortunate incident at the pony ride park. This picture should prove once and for all that it was the pony's fault, not mine. I am perfectly comfortable on top of an animal…. for very short periods of time.

Both wooden body crates are now loaded onto the plane and I bid farewell to both the coroner and Thailand. He promises me that on my next visit he will introduce me to 'alive people' only - young, attractive, female alive people. I can't help but think that I'd like to take him up on that invitation, as soon as they discover a vaccination for every sexually transmitted disease ever known to medical science.

There'll be no reading of any Sherlock Holmes on the flight back. I have too many other things on my mind to concentrate on a detective who knew what he was doing. I'm too busy concentrating on my own tasks, and I certainly don't know what the hell I'm doing.

There are just too many unanswered questions. Did Melvin have any family other than the little girl? Is she supposed to live with me now? What am I supposed to do with a little kid and a big dog? Where am I (or we) supposed to live? With Melvin gone, will he keep his main Marina client, or is the law practice gone too? And of course the never-ending concern that now I'm practicing law again, my ex-wife will be coming after me for her share of the profits. She's probably been staying up nights trying to figure how to get even with me for the burned-out boat thing that happened. I'm sure she thinks that I had it burned just to spite her. And all that may be nothing, compared to what can happen to me if the doc finds out I've been sleeping with Rita. And, I'm sure I've made another enemy out of Koontz, who definitely is not too happy with me for getting his license lifted because he conspired with Hansel to frame me. I'm sure he'll be out for evens, so I'll always be looking over my shoulder.

Thinking about all the junk I have to deal with is too much for me. Fortunately, out of guilt for not giving me a heads-up on the real reason for my trip, the office upgraded my return trip to first class, so I'm now relaxing in a comfortable seat and have my own private LCD television screen with a satellite hook-up to watch. I give CNN a try, figuring that no matter what's going on in the rest of the world, it can't be worse than what's happening in mine. After Wolf Blitzer, Larry King and my nap, their *"People In The News"* segment covers some high-profile court cases taking place around the country. To my surprise, I see a familiar face. My ex-wife is on camera, doing an interview about how she's spearheading the investigation into an Asian casino gang suspected of murdering a Chinese restaurant owner over some unpaid gambling debts. The newscaster expresses her doubts that a gambling gang would do such a thing in broad daylight while so many police were inside the restaurant, but Myra is adamant in her office's belief that the gang is guilty. She promises that an arrest is imminent and stakes her reputation on a successful prosecution and conviction.

If she's right, all the stuff I dug up on Robert Palmer has no meaning in the case. For her sake, I hope I'm wrong. The television drones on while I sleep the rest of the way to Los Angeles. First Class is the only way to fly.

Coffins don't get any priority treatment at the airport. They're offloaded last. The office made arrangements for a funeral home to pick them up but I still have to hang around until they're loaded, to sign the release forms. Dead bodies are picked up in what the funeral industry refers to as 'first call' vehicles. They're not limos or hearses, but instead are black station wagons with dark tinted glass all around. Once the coffins are loaded into the vehicle, the driver offers to give me a ride to the Marina. I politely refuse and take a cab instead.

On the way back to the Marina my cell phone rings. It's Rita. As glad as I am to hear from her, I don't want to end up like the freight I just brought back from Thailand, so I tell her that with all that's going on now, it might be better if we 'cooled it' for a while. I can tell by the frost I feel coming through the phone that she's not a happy camper.

It's nice returning home. I always look forward to that part of the ride when you head north on Lincoln Avenue and after passing 85th Street, there's a hill you start to go down, from which you can see the Marina in the distance. When the taxi drops me off at our dock entrance I'm greeted at the top of the gangway by Carolyn, the marina's assistant dockmaster. "Mister Sharp, I understand that you're now the managing partner of Mister Bradley's law firm." I nod, waiting to hear what this jerk with a clipboard has on her alleged mind. "We still intend to retain your law firm, but the arrangement to give him the houseboat to live on was a personal one and not connected to the retainer agreement. Therefore, since Mister Bradley is no longer living on the boat, we've rented it out to another tenant who will be moving aboard tomorrow morning." With that said, she turns and marches off. Walking down the dock, I'm greeted by a motley crew consisting of the little girl, the big dog, the cat and four Asian guys, all of them standing in front of L. Martin's Grand Banks.

The conversation that takes place may be the most amount of thought conveyed in the least amount of words ever spoken. One of the Asian boat maintenance guys acts as spokesman: he comes over to me, points at the trio and then at the Grand Banks, and proclaims "they live with you now on big boat." After this stunning oration has been completed, the parade boards the Grand Banks, with the Asian guys carrying her computer, printer, monitor, fax machine, dog food, cat food, litter box and suitcases. At the same time, one of the Asian boys picks up my suitcase. The phone company is also there moving phone lines from the houseboat over to the Grand Banks.

Once everyone is aboard, the boys set up the dynamic trio in the forward crew quarters and then start cleaning the boat. They find things to clean that I never knew needed cleaning. I haven't seen a cleaning operation like this since I was living with my wife. Whenever she got mad at me she started cleaning. I could usually tell how mad she was by how long she cleaned. About a half hour was average. A full hour meant I was really in trouble, and if the vacuum cleaner went on, it meant celibacy for at least three days.

I have no idea how long this arrangement on the boat will last, but as long as I still have the master stateroom to sleep in, I decide to keep my mouth shut. The Marina obviously doesn't know about L. Martin's death, so if the office keeps paying his slip rent, I guess we're okay.

My most recent copy of the California State Bar Journal says that the current membership total is almost 200,000. That's a lot of lawyers. The state's population is about 35.4 million, which means there's a lawyer available for every nineteen people. Or even worse, every 20th person in the state is a lawyer. Most gangs know that there's strength in numbers. Lawyers don't have *gangs* - they have *firms*. The same principles are involved. If you attend a performance of Shakespeare's *King Henry VI*, there's one line that when spoken never fails to get a roar of approval from the audience as well as the cast: in Part two of Scene two, Dick the Butcher says to Jack Cade "the first thing we do, let's kill all the lawyers!" I wonder what would happen if someone started telling lawyer jokes about black female lawyers. Maybe then, Gloria Allred and Jesse Jackson would probably get together and we'd finally be replaced with Doctor jokes on all the late night television shows.

9

Law firms that do collection work and landlord-tenant evictions are saved from being the most despised of all lawyers, because beneath them on the food chain are the firms that do insurance company defense work. Their job is trying to defeat the claims of people who have been injured by large multi-billion dollar republican businesses like the tobacco industry, toxic polluters, faulty product manufacturers and other holier than thou types with big political clout. One of those delightful groups of lawyers is now meeting in their luxurious conference room, with a large important client. He is the CEO of a respected supplier of aircraft parts to civilian and government aeronautical groups.

The obese, white CEO addresses his lawyers. "Gentlemen, we have a problem. An attorney has placed us in an embarrassing position. Some non-genuine aircraft parts were inadvertently shipped to one of our accounts, an aeronautical supply house in Bangkok, Thailand. These parts were then mistakenly installed on an aircraft, and they are now being alleged to have caused that plane to crash, resulting in the death of both passengers.

Now I'm sure that you boys can out-paper any law firm in the country, and stall this thing off forever, but due to other pressing business matters we'd like to get this situation cleared up as soon as possible." One of the lawyers in the room is a little too curious.

"Excuse me sir, but how did those 'non-genuine' parts happen to be in your company's inventory?" Big mistake. His partnership just got sidetracked for another couple of years. The CEO is not happy about being questioned.

"How it got into our inventory is none of your damned business. Your only responsibility now is not to cross-examine me, but to make this thing go away. And I mean quickly. We're about one month away from getting what will be a two-billion-dollar contract to provide aircraft parts to the United States Government over the next five years, and if any word of this unfortunate incident gets out, we're in danger of losing that contract. The letter we got was from a small-time firm out somewhere near the Marina, and from what our contacts tell me, all they usually do is some collection work and tenant evictions. Can you imagine that? Some small-time penny-ante shysters trying to bring us down? They probably see this as their one chance at a big pay-day, so let's not let this thing go more than one round." There's a murmur around the table. Mental wheels are spinning. One of the senior law partners speaks up.

"What kind of offer would you like to authorize? Any particular ceiling on this one?" The CEO thinks about it for a minute, before answering.

"If we go to trial and lose, there might be a multi-million dollar judgment, and after being dragged through the mud we wouldn't stand a chance in hell of getting that huge government contract. And with all the political correctness crap going around, your firm's stock options with us would also be in the toilet. And before we even get to trial, your legal fees over the next couple of years will come to about four million, so I'll tell you what we're prepared to do: if you can make this case go away in the next month and before the press gets wind of it, your fee will be one-half of what you save us from the four million we'd pay you and the five million we'd lose in a jury verdict."

After the client leaves their office, the lawyers use a scale of justice to balance their own greed against the better interests of the client and the injured parties. Guess who wins. Their mental calculators indicate that if this matter goes through to verdict, the client will be out nine million. If they can settle this thing for a quick five million, that will save their client four million, and their fee will be two million. The down side is that it's only half of what they could bill if they take the case to trial. The up side is that they don't have to actually work on the case for five years to get the two million. It's decided. They'll try to settle for less than five million.

I hear the pitter-patter of large soft paws entering my stateroom. It's the Saint Bernard, and there's an envelope in his mouth. This must be the kid's new method of delivering messages to me: Dogmail. I retrieve the envelope and then tip the messenger with a pat on the head. He turns and returns to his office. The damp envelope contains a letter from the defense firm representing that aircraft parts manufacturer.

I have to hand it to them. They sure work fast. Their letter contains an offer of settlement, and the amount is the largest one I've ever been involved with: three million dollars total. Smart. They must have figured that if they could get the client out for only three million, their fee would be in the neighborhood of the same amount, due to the combined savings to the client of legal fees and the exposure to a jury verdict. I know that if that's their first offer, if we get to the discovery stage and take some depositions, we can probably get the amount up a little higher, but then we run the risk of their paper mill creating too many Motions for us to handle.

The sad fact is that we're just not set up to handle a case this big, so I think that instead of trying to get a bigger settlement, I'll just take a much lower fee and the clients will wind up fine. What they came up with was an offer that was low enough to keep their client happy, while still having enough zeroes in it to make it attractive to me and the plaintiffs. And it is all of those things.

They offered one million dollars for L. Martin's estate and two million for Melvin's. If not accepted, the letter lets us know that their client demands that the case go all the way through trial. I call the lawyer who signed the letter. His response is typical. "Mister Sharp, you and I both know that our client's settlement offer is fair, but to tell you the truth, we don't care if you take it or not. It's the absolute top dollar the client will authorize and if you don't accept it, our firm will be looking at several million in legal fees, so please don't feel you're disappointing us by turning it down." I answer with the usual lawyer's response

"I'll let my clients know and get back to you." I wish my answer was true, but unfortunately, at this point in time, I'm not even sure who my clients are. I know there's Suzi, but that's about it. I have no idea if there are any other surviving relatives of either Melvin or L. Martin who might have some claim to their estates.

But as far as the negotiations go, this is a done deal. I'll let him wait for a while before formally accepting. No sense letting him know how easy it is, and I need more time to find some heirs. This is a game that we're all familiar with; he knows that when I accept, I'll be sure to let him know that it was at the demand of my clients, and against my advice to proceed to trial. Typical saber rattling that all lawyers do.

After checking through the State Bar's records and his application for admission to our old law school, the only living heir of Melvin's that we can establish is little Suzi. California law requires that the Court approve any settlement for a minor, and now that Suzi has agreed to the amount, the office gets a Request for Court Approval started. Until I meet our dock neighbor/actor George C., this kid will be the richest person I know.

We're still searching for L. Martin's living relatives. Among the things requested by the defense firm prior to sending any settlements are court approval for the minor, all original documentation provided by the Thailand authorities, copies of the death certificates of both victims, and the execution of a privacy agreement which prevents anyone involved with the case from disclosing any details of the incident or settlement amounts. The defense firm also informs me that the offer will only be on the table for a certain amount of days. I think that an offer coming in this quick is odd. There's no doubt something is going on that I don't know about, but as long as I take care to see that my clients are properly served, that's all that counts to me.

Life aboard the boat now isn't as bad as I thought it would be. I've never been this close to a kid for any length of time before, but there's no conflict between her and me. That's probably due to two main things. First, she's my boss, and second, it's because we haven't had a conversation yet. I still don't know if she understands English. We manage to keep out of each other's way, but somehow I get the feeling that she's the one who's really in charge of this boat. Most of my time is spent in court making appearances for the firm. With my license back, the office now has in-house counsel and no longer needs the services of all the other lawyers who filled in from time to time. Suzi is gone most of the day, to wherever she goes. By the time I get back to the boat it's usually seven or eight in the evening and there's always some delicious Chinese dinner waiting for me on the stove. The dog is quite friendly, and always not more than two feet away from the girl. The cat glares at me and stays close to the dog.

Due to the fact that I probably owe my law license reinstatement to the cooperation of Jack Bibberman, the mailbox clerk who testified against Ricky Hansel and Koontz, I go back to his place of employment and offer him some extra part-time employment: he now takes my old position and serves papers on people for the firm. Stuart has also been using him to help solicit junk fax recipients in the Valley. Come to think of it, I haven't talked to Stuart in quite some time. I'll have to call him and say hello one of these days soon. He'll be pleased to know that I'm now on a big yacht, and probably take

125

the opportunity to once again try to introduce me to his dear uncle Label.

Just as I suspected, something is going on with the defense firm's client, because they're sending me urgent messages requesting that I get back to them about settlement offers. They obviously want the matter wrapped up as quickly as possible. Sensing some weakness on their side, I tell them that there should be no problem settling, and that while we're still searching for Unger's relatives, all we want to do is take the defendant's deposition to find out how many other potential disasters are going to take place because of their shipments to other aircraft supply houses.

As you might imagine, this doesn't sit too well with them. The phone rings. "Peter, Peter, what's the problem here? We've made a generous settlement offer, and you can take my word for it that our client has definitely asserted that there were no other shipments. The one that allegedly went to Thailand was an anomaly caused by a greedy, now-fired warehouse manager who made the switch and sold the genuine parts to a local distributor. It can never happen again."

Whenever your adversary starts out by using your first name, you've already got the upper hand. I also know that without spending thousands of dollars in discovery and investigation, I'd never be able to find out what the real truth is. And if I try, I might jeopardize the settlement offer that's already on the table. I might as well close this case out. One way or another, we'll find L. Martin's heirs. I decide to put him out of his misery.

"Okay, I think we can wrap this thing up. All that's holding us up is my clients' being unhappy with our expenses for the trip to Thailand. They don't think it's right for them to have to reimburse our firm for those costs, plus the expenses to ship the bodies back, funeral costs, time lost, etc., etc."

"How much are we talking about, Peter?"

"Well, as a matter of practice, we always use first class on any trip over five hundred miles, so taking the air fare, hotel and miscellaneous expenses into consideration, including shipping the bodies back and funeral arrangements, I'd say that an extra ninety thousand should handle it." He gives me the typical lawyer answer: he'll check with his client and get back to me. We both know it was all baloney, but those are the dues his client will have to pay for a quick settlement, so that their hidden agenda, whatever it is, can stay hidden.

In addition to the possibility of getting some more money out of them, I hope that this delaying tactic will give me more time to locate any relatives of L. Martin. As it turns out, I may not need the time.

While preparing the documentation that the defense firm wants, I take a closer look at the death certificates. If what I'm looking at is correct, this will be the one of the most amazing coincidences I've ever encountered. L. Martin Unger's full name appears on his passport and on both his birth and death certificates: his first name is 'Label.'

10

LABEL isn't exactly a common name, so the question has to be asked: can this really be Stuart's boat-owning uncle Label? Does this mean that Stuart will now inherit the boat of my dreams, the yacht that my 'family' is now living on? How can this be happening? I call Stuart. His answering machine picks up, but he must be monitoring the calls because as soon as he hears my voice he cuts in: "Peter, what a pleasant surprise. I'm glad you called. I wanted to tell you about a new weight-loss product I'll be marketing. This one really works. All you..."

Rude as it is, I cut him off mid-sentence with only one question: "Stuart, please tell me your uncle Label's last name."

It's true. L. Martin Unger is Stuart's uncle, and Stuart has no idea what happened in Thailand, or that he might have a million dollars coming his way. This is the kind of information that's better served in person. We make arrangements to meet at Lido Pizza on Victory Boulevard in Van Nuys. It's right off the San Diego Freeway and not far from Stuart's Valley apartment. They serve a delicious whole-wheat egg-free rigatoni there.

Taking one look at him waddling through the restaurant's door makes me happy to hear that he's now involved in a weight loss program. I insist that he have a couple of glasses of wine first, because I've got some unpleasant news to give him. I think I need the wine more than he does, because breaking news like this to people is not my specialty. We talk about his uncle and I finally get the nerve up to let him know about the fatal plane crash. He takes the news about it much better than I expected, and tells me that he was Label's only living relative. After another few minutes of conversation he pops the question: "Pete, do you think anyone responsible should be made to pay for my uncle's death? I mean, I'm not looking to get rich offa this or anything, but if it was someone's fault, shouldn't there be some penalty?"

Stuart doesn't miss very much. I finish another mouthful of rigatoni and signal Nick the waiter for a side order of anchovies.

"Stuart, I looked into the matter. We conducted an investigation in Thailand and found a defective airplane part that was traced to an American corporation. There's a good possibility that a settlement can be made with them." As a matter of practice, a good lawyer never blurts out any amount to a client, because invariably, the client will never be happy with it. No matter how much you tell them is on the table, they'll always want more. Instead, you have to subtly and professionally lead them toward the right conclusion, so that they're mentally prepared to accept a fair amount when it's offered.

"In wrongful death cases, people's lives are often measured in terms of how old they are and how much they could have been expected to earn if their life was allowed to continue to a natural end. People called actuaries calculate morbid statistics like this, and every insurance company has them on staff. In your uncle Label's case, he was already over seventy, and other than his monthly social security check and some minor legal work he performed for a mutual friend of ours, he was almost completely retired."

"So how much do you think they'll offer? A hundred thousand?" I was pleased to hear that he didn't have 'billions' in mind and think that now is the time to bring the conversation to the point where he'll be amenable to what I can actually get for him.

"Stuart, I think in addition to the condo in Thailand and the boat in the Marina, you should wind up with a settlement much more than that." He bit eagerly.

"Yeah, how much do you think? A half a mil?" "Well my friend, my goal is not to stop working on them until we can get them to part with at least three quarters of a million dollars."

Stuart turns white. "Seven hundred fifty K? Are you serious? You think we can even get close to that?"

"It couldn't hurt to ask. They're a wealthy corporation and if they did something wrong, they should pay for it." I can tell from the wheels I hear spinning in his head that he's already spending it.

"What would your fee be?"

"Well Stu, normally, a wrongful death contingency is in the neighborhood of forty percent, but in your case, I'd like to be a little more creative." His face is a blank slate waiting for me to create a work of art. "If I can get them to make a check out to you for seven hundred fifty thousand dollars, I won't take one cent of a fee out of it. I'll hand it over to you as a favor from one friend to the other, in exchange for one dollar from you. But then, I'd like you to do me a favor: when your uncle's estate is settled, I'd like to buy that boat of his for the sum of one dollar."

Stuart's no dummy. He's seen that boat on several occasions and knows that it's easily worth several hundred thousand dollars, but he also realizes that if not for me, he wouldn't be getting any money at all, and that a legitimate fee could be close to four hundred thousand. It only takes him another few seconds before he sticks out his hand. We shake on it and order some spumoni to seal the deal.

Less than two months have passed by and a series of completely predictable events has taken place: we got Court approval for Suzi's two million dollar settlement, and her check was sent. It will be deposited into an certificate of deposit, arranged by my Farmers Insurance Agent, Murray Uniman. I was named executor of her funds and she'll be able to withdraw a reasonable amount of the interest each year for living expenses. The CD will roll over until she reaches the age of twenty-four. The court asked me to file a written fee request and I complied. The fee I asked for was one dollar. The court happily approved it, as well as my one-dollar annual fee request for handling her trust.

Stuart just arrived at the boat because I called and told him that the settlement check came in, but I never disclosed the final amount. "Pete, did they go for it? Did we get the whole seven hundred fifty K?" This is one of those rare times when practicing law is enjoyable.

"Sit down, Stu, let's talk about it." His face drops. As much fun as it is to surprise him with a big amount, I don't want to force him into a depression along the way. "Stu, we didn't get that exact amount, but I'm sure you'll be happy with what I was able to drag out of them." I hand him the envelope. He looks down at it with the same feeling of trepidation that every high school graduate gets when receiving responses to college applications. I know the feeling too. Every law school graduate gets it when that State Bar letter arrives telling you whether or not you passed the Bar exam. Now it's Stuart's turn. He looks at me as he slowly opens the envelope and takes out the check. His eyes are closed as he holds it up to his face. Fortunately, I have an amyl nitrate 'snapper' handy from the boat's first aid kit, so that if he faints we can wave it under his nose. He slowly opens his eyes and looks at the one-million-dollar amount on the check. Silence. Tears. A big hug for the lawyer.

After the celebration winds down, true to his word, Stuart pays me my one-dollar fee by cashier's check and further follows through on our deal by signing an option that gives me the right to purchase the boat for one dollar any time during the next five years. I think it best not to hold title to it, just in case my wife liked the first boat so much that she decides to get another one. Even worse, word of the transfer might reach the Marina office and they look down upon ownership transfers that might affect slip occupancy. It'll only be a matter of time before Myra hears through the court grapevine about me settling several million dollars worth of cases, and her new lawyer will no doubt be sending me a letter. I want the Grand Banks safe from the battle. The foreward stateroom door is ajar and Suzi has been watching the whole show. She doesn't look too happy. I realize what her problem is: she's probably thinking that the boat isn't my fee, because the case belonged to the firm. And she's the firm. I'm just a managing partner. To make her happy, I assign the option to purchase the Grand Banks over to the firm. She glares at me. A typical female: two million with no fee paid isn't enough – she wants the boat too. The glare persists. I look right at her. "What?"

She walks over, takes Stuart's one-dollar fee out of my hand, and then turns around and exits towards her stateroom. Before she turns completely, I catch a glimpse of a smile on that little cupie doll face.

I've already learned not to question things I see going on that I don't understand, because they're usually being orchestrated by the small person who is running the business, the boat, and most of my life – all without talking to me. This time it's the installation of a small antenna on the radar arch over the boat's flybridge. The techie doing the work is Don Paige, one of our dock neighbors, and tells me the thing being installed is a new device for picking up broadband wireless Internet signals. He goes on to explain that a nearby boat owner set up a wireless local network, and that people within a thousand feet of his set-up who are line-of- sight with him can be part of his network by using a password that is assigned to us.

Some people are born with certain talents. If you're having a problem installing your stereo set, VCR, DVD player, computer, modem, or any other electrical device, not to worry, help is at hand. All you have to do is go outside and look for any teen-aged male wearing a baseball cap on backwards. Offer him a Snickers bar and he'll fix all your electrical hook-up problems. There's no need to ask him in advance if he can handle your type of problem, because all male children born after 1990 have that knowledge. It's a special technical gene embedded in their DNA genome. I have a feeling the little princess also has it.

Don is a nice guy who I've had some conversations with in the past. I bump into him on the dock and he lets me know how lucky I am "Hey Pete, that's one heck of a little girl you've got there. She knows as much about my wireless network as I do. She talked me into letting your boat in on it. The doc's got it too." I can't figure out how they were able to communicate. She certainly doesn't speak to me. Maybe these techie people have some new language that I don't speak. Technalese?

11

Beverly Hills' Wilshire Boulevard has more banks and law offices per mile than any other street in the world, and Los Angeles County's premier deputy district attorney, my ex-wife, is now in the office of one of them. She's huddling with her new attorney Daniel Vincent, a lawyer well known for his aggressive legal tactics. "Let me get this straight Mizz Scot, you claim that your ex-husband sold you a burnt-out hull for forty-thousand dollars?" He tries to keep a straight face. "And after promising you half of his law practice income for the next two years, he gets suspended and stops practicing law?" Acting the victim, she admits to the truth of both statements. "And in exchange for that burnt-out hull, you waived your right to any share of his future law practice earnings?" Silence. "Well, you seem to have arranged things in a nice order. Exactly what do you want me to do for you?" Now it's her turn, and she comes to life.

"First of all, he's gotten his license back, due to the incompetence of my first attorney. Second, I hear that he got involved in some big wrongful death cases. I want you to take this agreement he's holding me to, in which I waived my rights to a share of his income in exchange for that burnt out piece of crap boat of his, and I want you to shove it so far up his rear end that it hits his tonsils. I want to nail his ass to the wall for that burning boat stunt he pulled on me, that cost me the loss of a sweet deal. Any questions?"

He's taken aback by her aggressive attitude. "Well, it seems that you're quite serious about this matter. I'll see what I can do."

Vincent gets the point. He doesn't like her very much, but that's never been a requirement in the legal profession.

I remember something that happened many years ago when I was a law student clerking in a law firm. One of the attorneys I worked for gave me the transcript of a deposition to read. When I was finished, he asked me what I thought of the person being deposed. I candidly remarked: "he's an asshole."

To which my boss replied "yes, but he's *our* asshole." The moral of the story is that you can't pick your relatives or your clients; you take 'em as you find 'em. This means that the games will now begin. Much like combat between wild animals, there's a certain amount of circling and snarling that takes place before the fight actually begins. With lawyers, it's more like a chess game. Each player makes his move with a carefully worded letter that contains the minimum amount of facts and the maximum amount of threats. I'll get my first letter from him soon enough.

Back on the dock, things are getting interesting. Rita is stopping by every week, and now that the kid is living in the forward stateroom, I tell Rita that it wouldn't be proper for her to stay over when the doc isn't around. It hurts me to do that, but at least now I have a credible excuse to avoid getting caught and killed.

During the day there are a series of visits to the boat by a team of plain-clothes detectives. They never show me a badge, but they must be police, because no one in the Marina still wears polyester.

I'm never told anything. After getting permission to come aboard, they go straight to the forward stateroom, pet the giant guard-dog and enter the little princess' domain. In a little while they usually leave with a printout of some sort. To my surprise, Jack the mail clerk came to the boat a couple of times to pick up investigation assignments. He never told me what they were about. I get the feeling that I'm becoming irrelevant around here.

The newspapers and local television can't seem to get enough of my ex-wife. She's good to look at, sounds good, and an obvious love affair immediately springs up between her and any news camera within fifty feet. The district attorney's office has two Asian gang suspects in custody for the parking lot murder, and there are sound bites galore in the prosecutor's usual campaign to poison the prospective jury pool. By the time this case goes to trial, the district attorney wants everyone in the county to already believe these guys are guilty.

Television isn't all that she has working for her. As expected, the exchange of letters starts.

Dear Mr. Sharp:

This office has been retained to represent your former spouse, Ms. Myra Scot. She claims you have knowingly and intentionally perpetrated a fraud by inducing her to waive certain spousal rights in exchange for worthless consideration, namely a fire-destroyed, vessel.

It is the intention of this office to pursue these charges against you in the State Bar Court and with the criminal authorities, if you insist on perpetuating this fraud by your failure to voluntarily rescind her agreement and re-instate your original marital settlement terms, by allowing her to share in some portion of your income.

We understand that you have recently been involved in several lucrative matters and should have no difficulty in doing the right thing.

Very truly yours, Daniel Vincent, Esq.

Not a bad opening. His syntax could use a little work, but I get the message. They obviously know about the wrongful death cases and assume that I took a normal fee. Good. Responding too quickly is like calling back the girl you took out last night, the very first thing the next morning. You shouldn't want to seem too eager. The proper etiquette is to make them wait at least a week for your response. That gives the client some time to call her lawyer and pester the hell out of him twice a day with the same question "well, did you hear anything? No? Well what are you going to do about it? Just let him get away with it?" This will bug the lawyer to no end, and possibly lower his aggression level towards the adversary - who he will then look to for a response, if for no reason other than to get his own client off of his back. I think I'll do him a favor by sending a response in four days instead of five.

Stuart has been coming around recently and. he looks paler and slimmer each time I see him, so I finally get up the nerve to ask him about his health. Our office has already gotten his asbestosis case rolling, and as a friend, I want him to be around at least as long as it takes to conclude it. To my relief, he claims to be feeling great and credits his weight loss to a product that he's distributing.

Stuart loves multi-level marketing. That's where each person you sell is encouraged to find other people he can sell to, and then each one of them is supposed to sell to several people, establishing an ever-expanding base of customers who are also distributors. The only problem with this 'pyramid' type of organization is that it grows geometrically so that in a short period of time there are no more available customers. A good example of that type of progression is the old story of a man who does a tremendous favor for a rich person. When asked what reward he would like, the poor man replies "nothing much, just give me a penny the first day and double it every day for a month." This doesn't sound like much to the rich man, so he agrees. If you do the arithmetic, you'll see that by the end of the month, the rich man is probably no longer rich, because the amount due on the 30th day of that month would be $5,368,708.80, and the total amount paid during the month, over ten and a half million dollars.

In a pyramid scheme the numbers multiply in much the same way, but only the first few involved ever wind up reaping the rewards. All that those 'downline' of them ever wind up holding is 'the bag,' and a lot of unsold inventory. Stuart claims that this time it's different, because the product really works, and he's living proof of it. He gives me a bottle to try. The instructions are simple enough: all you do is take one spoonful each night after dinner and then not have anything more to eat or drink for at least three hours before going to sleep. I try it, but taking one teaspoonful of that god-awful stuff the first night makes me gag, so I give it up. I do like the idea that you're to take the teaspoon each evening after dinner, and then not have anything else to eat or drink before going to bed.

Aside from the gag-inducing aspect of the product, the plan looks like a decent one, so I try it, but without taking the teaspoon of snake oil Stuart is selling. The most interesting part of the program is that it denies you the late nite snacking that so many of us do. After a month of having my dinner by seven P.M. and not having any snack between then and bedtime is starting to have some results. I lost almost four pounds the first month, and another four the next month.

Stuart notices my success, but doesn't believe that I haven't been using the product until I give him the unused bottle back. We both agree: what's the difference? If the customers need the incentive of spending money and following a program that works, their weight loss is all that counts. And if they can incorporate the no-snacking routine into their permanent life-style, then they can probably keep the weight off forever, so there's no harm done. Even though the product might make you gag, people are losing weight and Stuart is making money – and those are both good things.

Everything is finally going Stuart's way, and it couldn't happen to a nicer guy.

12

The defense firm that was hired to represent the government and its asbestos suppliers are now considering offering just one mass settlement, so they start to make demands for illness documentation from all claimants. Part of any big defense firm's strategy is to make you jump through a series of hoops that they hold up. This also gives them a chance to pretend to go over the documentation you provide so they can increase their billable hours. When I ask Stuart what doctor diagnosed him, he hems and haws for a while. After pinning him down, he confesses that he went to some holistic medical provider with a storefront office in the Valley. We can't find this person listed in the phone book, so I send Jack Bibberman out there to check it out. His result confirms my thoughts about Stuart's practices. The guy who diagnosed his death-threatening disease isn't exactly a medical doctor. He isn't even exactly a chiropractor. He isn't a doctor of any kind. He's a faith healer.

I've never made an attempt at stand-up comedy, unless you count my first few court appearances, but I'm pretty sure that if I try to settle Stuart's case with a hand-scribbled report from a faith healer, I'll get more laughs than Robin Williams' two-hour HBO special. But what the hell, I've got nothing to lose, so I might as well give it a try. "Stuart, does your witch Doctor have a typewriter? It's going be tough enough to sell his report as it is, so please try to get him to at least type it." Stuart promises me he'll make sure that one way or the other the report will be in a presentable form, even if he has to re-do it himself. I don't really want to hear that, but at this point it probably won't make much difference.

With all the things going on in my life recently I don't have much time to think about it, but I realize that I really miss Rita, and that's not a good thing. She's with the doc and the doc's a killer. This is a similar situation to the classic one Jack Benny found himself in when a robber said "your money or your life." After a pause that seemed to last for an eternity, Jack, the ultimate stingy persona, came back with "I'm thinking it over." In my case, it's like the doc is saying to me: "your girlfriend or your life."

Rita isn't the only female on my mind. I waited the standard four or five days and sent a letter to Myra's lawyer, but haven't heard back from him yet. I can only assume that the long delay in getting back to me is caused by her being so busy trying to build a case against the wrong people in that Chinese parking lot murder.

To refresh my memory and see if I said anything that can back to bite me in the rear, I get out a copy of the letter sent to Myra's lawyer and check it over.

Dear Mr. Vincent:

The vessel your client received was damaged due to matters entirely beyond my knowledge and control and I regret her disappointment, but she specifically acknowledged that she was accepting that consideration on an as-is, where-is" basis, so I feel that she should stick with her bargain.

A copy of her previous attorney's agreement is enclosed, confirming that basis of the transfer.

The lucrative matters you refer to are therefore beyond the scope of any previous agreement, and I will vigorously defend my right to retain any and all fees received from their successful conclusions.

Due to the fact that your client was gainfully employed during my period of suspension, there is a possible liability on her part for retroactive spousal support during my temporary loss of income. We can discuss that at the appropriate time.

Very truly yours,

Peter Sharp, Esq.

My veiled threat to seek alimony is total bunk and specifically intended to put her in a defensive mode and take her mind off of attacking me. It acts much like a person complaining about a headache and getting hit in the shin. The shin pain takes their mind off of the headache. Also, dangling my legal fees on the two wrongful death actions out of her reach is like teasing a dog by holding a bit of its favorite food up in the air and making it jump up and down trying to get at it. The hook has been baited, so now I'll just wait to see what their next move is.

Under the category of 'doing your homework,' I send Jack Bibberman to the courthouse to get some conformed copies of the settlement agreements showing my fees. I always wanted to live out one of my favorite cartoons. And now I'm the *RoadRunner,* and she's *Wylie Coyote.*

Things on the dock are going on as usual, with nothing much new happening. I still haven't seen George C., but I do happen to bump into the doc, and we chat for a while. He also had Don Paige install one of those wireless Internet antennas on his boat, and now he's boasting about how good the deal was. He also mentions that he'll be flying out of town for a few days to attend a funeral. Being the good neighbor that I am, I promise to watch his boat while he's gone.

It was inevitable. Doc leaves town and Rita shows up. I'm glad to see her, but at the same time I'm afraid of what I know will probably happen with the doc out of town and Rita staying on his boat all alone. And it does happen. Doc's forty-two foot Californian trawler has a nice feature: the aft stateroom opens to a small fishing deck at the stern, so that by leaving the back door open you can look out and see the stars from the queen-sized bed, if you aren't otherwise too busy.

It's a lovely evening, and in between serious bouts of intimacy we lie there gazing out at the stars.

The doc's Lexus SUV is a beautiful vehicle, but not the easiest to park in the cramped outdoor spaces reserved for the boat tenants, especially after you've had a few 'for the road.' Doc decided to come back a day early, and at this particular instant in time, both he and I are wrestling to get into better positions, and each one of us is also making several attempts at trying to fit something into its proper place. It will only be another couple of minutes before he finishes backing his vehicle into place and walking down to the boat. After a long drive, he's probably worn out and surely will head directly for his bed, which unbeknownst to him, is presently occupied.

Neither Rita nor I have any idea that doc returned earlier than planned and was up there on the small access road trying to park his car. Suddenly there's a strange sound on the boat and we both freeze as we hear what sounds like footsteps on the deck, and a slight rocking movement. Someone heavy has just come aboard. This is definitely not good. A large form appears on the aft fishing deck, looks in at us from the open back door and growls menacingly. My life flashes before my eyes. All I can see is a large silhouette, but can't make it out. After a second of stark fear, I realize that it's not doc, it's Suzi's huge Saint Bernard!

Seeing the big dog sends shivers down my spine. I'm not of afraid of it, I just don't know what the hell it's doing here. Rita immediately gets the idea that something might be wrong with Suzi, so at her request, I put my boat shorts on, jump off the boat's stern and follow the dog back to the Grand Banks. While entering the wheelhouse of my boat I see a figure walking down the gangplank toward the boats. Because of the darkness I can't make out the face, but as it gets closer, I see that it's the doc walking towards his boat. From that day on, I'll be looking at the dog in a different way. I have a sneaking suspicion how and why he got to me on doc's boat, but I'll probably never really know for sure.

Having narrowly escaped certain death the night before, I'm still in a state of shock. I look up to see the dog walking into my aft stateroom with a letter in its mouth. This must be another dog-mail delivery. The kid obviously hasn't yet taught it to knock first. I remove the letter, give him the customary pat on the head as a tip, and he goes back to the forward stateroom. I hope he never goes 'postal' on me. Too bad everyone doesn't use Tyvek envelopes like Suzi does. I guess the rest of the postal world isn't into dog-mail delivery yet. The moist envelope tells me that we are once again involved in Stuart's asbestos lawsuit.

Dear Mr. Sharp:

We have reviewed with great interest the documentation you forwarded to us concerning your client's alleged mesothelium inflammation.

Are we correct in assuming that your client's diagnosis was not from a licensed physician, but a holistic care provider? Could this person actually be a faith healer?

This is the first time we have encountered documentation in such a fashion and we must caution you that any serious settlement of this matter may now be in jeopardy.

Very truly yours,
Charles Indovine, Esq.

I knew it wouldn't work, but had to try anyway. Now that Stuart's big non-case is entirely blown, I might as well take one last parting shot. Stuart was told that it's a lost cause and agrees that anything I want to do now is okay with him. Knowing the chances of recovery, Stuart insisted that if anything comes in on this case I should take a normal fee, so I agreed, and take one last parting shot with my next letter:

Dear Mr. Indovine:

Surely you must be aware that the world is changing. There are millions of people who do not subscribe to what you consider to be the normal types of treatment.

To question their methods is to question their faith, and in this changing world, it might not be advisable to question one's faith, especially if one questioned is a Muslim, because to do so would be against the policy of the United States Government, and against accepted international behavior, attracting enemies in all quarters.

If you disagree, then we would be willing to let a jury decide the validity of my client's faith in a public trial, which would no doubt garner worldwide attention to the fact that your client has a problem with a certain faith.

Very truly yours,

Peter Sharp,

Esq.

A copy of the letter is sent to Stuart, who lets me know that he doesn't mind at all having undergone a temporary conversion to Islam if it helps settle the case.

Getting back into the legal swing of things really feels good. It's much more interesting than the court appearances, which could have been done by the dog. Almost all of them are in the same Santa Monica courtroom. The judge is never on the bench, preferring to get more work done settling cases and clearing the court's busy calendar by conducting conferences in chambers. Her clerk, the attractive Asian woman, takes care of all other matters. If the Judge's attention is required, the case file is brought into chambers and she deals with it there, sending her answer back with the clerk.

Myra's lawyer won't give in, and neither will I. They're now so swept up in their greedy desire to get a piece of my legal fees that they don't do the basic homework of trying to find out what the fees actually were. This is a common mistake made by emotional litigants. Keeping a cool head and planning strategy can often be much more important than knowing the law.

Years ago when I started to practice law, a case came in where a dog grooming parlor had accidentally killed my client's poodle, which should have been an indication early on where my practice was 'going.' Prior to going to trial, the courts allow what is called 'Civil Discovery,' by which each side can send written questions ('Interrogatories') to the other party and also demand to take oral testimony ('Depose') prospective witnesses, to get information about the case. Defense firms usually bill on an hourly basis, so it's quite common for them to send out at least one set of Interrogatories. It helps build up their billable hours on the case.

The grooming parlor's defense firm must have specialized in automobile accident cases, because the boiler-plate set of Interrogs they sent to us were mostly comprised of many questions about the plaintiff's vehicle, driving record, driver's license number, etc. etc. These questions weren't all relevant to the matter at hand, but we answered most of them anyway except for the one that requested her driver's license number. We refused to answer that one, making a relevancy objection. The defense firm went ballistic, threatening to haul us into court, demanding that we pay punitive sanctions for failure to answer, and did their best to scare us in a way that also increased their billable hours to the insurance company.

An ongoing battle ensued between us, with menacing letters going back and forth. We kept refusing to answer that question and disclose her driver's license number unless a settlement offer was on the table. The battle wound up being a macho matter for the defense firm. They wanted to show their client that they actually could get the number, so they made a settlement offer based on our providing the driver's license info. We accepted the settlement amount, but informed them that we were still going to resist providing the information.

They couldn't take it any more. This was becoming a battle of honor for them and as far as they were concerned, my last refusal was the last straw. A decision was made to go for my throat, so they requested a court hearing date, hoping that the judge could be persuaded to make us answer the question and provide them with her driver's license number. We went to the hearing and I strenuously argued about the relevancy of the question.

Once the case was called the judge, being a nice old guy, let me know his feelings about the matter. "Mister Sharp, I tend to agree with you. Your client's driver's license number doesn't seem very relevant to the death of her dog, but quite often a defense firm likes to have that information for other reasons, like seeing if there are any suspensions for drunk driving or vehicular manslaughter, or some other reason that might reflect on one's credibility as a witness. So in this particular case, seeing as we're all brother officers of the court, I'd like you to do me a personal favor: would you please, here in open court, state for the record what your client's drivers license number is?" I hesitated for a while. The defense firm was gloating. They looked at each other with smiles of success.

"Your Honor, we'll be glad to comply, but for the record, we'd like the court to know that there has been a settlement offer made and accepted. The offer is contingent only upon our providing the information you just asked us for. What we'd appreciate now is you asking the defense firm to let the court hold their settlement check and act as an independent escrow officer. My client would feel much better if you did, because she seems worried that once we give them this information they'll come up with some other reason to not pay her. I tried to explain to her that there won't be any other problems, but she still wants me to ask you to hold the settlement draft."

The judge looked out over the top of his glasses towards my client, who was sitting next to me, wearing her overcoat and babushka. She looked like she just got off the bus from Moscow. "Well all right, Mister Sharp. Bailiff, please pick up that settlement draft and bring it up here." Once he had it in his hand, he waved it in the air, looking towards my client for approval. She nodded at him with an appreciate smile on her face. "Your turn Mister

Sharp." I took a deep breath and then gave him my answer.

"Your honor, my client does not now and has never possessed a driver's license in the State of California or any other jurisdiction. She's never learned how to drive a car."

The lead defense lawyer jumped up "your honor, our offer of settlement was contingent upon us getting her driver's license number, and we didn't get it, so she shouldn't be allowed to get the settlement."

The judge knew what I'd done to the defense firm and appreciated my tactic of whipping them into a frenzy that ultimately embarrassed them. They were so intent on getting the irrelevant information, that the amount of the settlement was relegated to no longer being the main issue.

The moral of that story is simple: when something asked for is denied, quite often the battle centers on getting that which is denied, and the underlying reason for the request is put on the back burner, if not ignored completely. And I am about to teach that lesson to the rapidly becoming famous female deputy district attorney who was formerly my wife. A court hearing has been set for next week, and with Jack Bibberman's help I have all the documentation I need. Let the games begin.

The hearing will be held in the downtown Los Angeles Courthouse, so that Myra doesn't have to travel too far from her office. When I walk into the courtroom Myra and her attorney Daniel Vincent are already seated at the counsel table. As is customary before the judge comes out, the bailiff makes his usual announcement. "Remain seated and come to order. The Superior Court of California, Department 86 is now in session, the Honorable Ronald B. Axelrod presiding.

That having been done, the judge enters the courtroom through the door behind the clerk's desk, steps up and assumes his throne-like position on that raised area referred to as 'the bench.'

When the case is called, each one of us stands up and states our name and representation for the record. Her attorney makes his opening statement.

"Your Honor, as our papers filed with the court indicate, this matter concerns a re-modification of an agreement. We contend that Petitioner was fraudulently induced to enter into this agreement, whereby she waived certain rights, and that there was no sufficient consideration for her waiver. We intend to offer evidence showing that the Respondent intentionally defrauded Petitioner by inducing her to accept as consideration an item that he knew had actually decreased substantially in value. The fact of this depreciation was neither known by Petitioner nor told to her by Respondent. In addition to that fraudulent act, Respondent knew or should have known that his ability to earn income would be substantially reduced, so that promises made to Petitioner about future earnings could not possibly be fulfilled.

"Based on this evidence, Petitioner will ask the court to invalidate Petitioner's agreement to accept said worthless consideration, and reinstate her original waived right to a share of respondent's income, which has greatly increased in value to date."

Very nice. I couldn't have done better myself. I wonder, should I fold now, or make them work a little harder? I think I'll push them a little further towards the edge. Having just had my goin'-to-church suit cleaned and pressed, now might be a good time to give it a workout. I walk over to the lectern that stands between the counsel tables. The court reporter looks up at me, no doubt admiring the suit and my yellow 'power' necktie.

"Your Honor, if it may please the court, Respondent would ask the court to take judicial notice of the fact that Petitioner's former attorney has been arrested on a charge of conspiracy to practice law without a license by assisting a non-licensed person to impersonate Respondent, thereby causing this Respondent to wrongfully be suspended from the practice of law. The State Bar Disciplinary Court case number and criminal court case numbers have been included with our response, filed with the court.

"The Court is also being asked to take notice of the fact that said conspiracy having been exposed, Respondent's license to practice law has been reinstated to active status with the State Bar. Respondent therefore contends that the Petitioner knew or should have known about the possibility of Respondent's suspension in advance of Respondent becoming aware, due to the possibility of Petitioner having been involved in the frame-up as an un-named co-conspirator"

That does it. Vincent and Myra both jump up out of their chairs. Vincent is shouting. "We strenuously object, Your Honor. Respondent hasn't the slightest basis of fact upon which to base that accusation and we demand, er, we request that the court have that portion of his statement stricken from the record. Furthermore..."

It worked out just right. The buttons were pushed, the expected reaction occurred, and the judge is getting sick of it. He taps his gavel a couple of times to shut Vincent up and interrupts him mid-sentence with a pronouncement that will ultimately help me get what I'm going after.

"All right, counsel, this is a court of law, and I don't want to see it become a pissing contest between separated spouses who obviously are not enamored of each other. All I've heard so far is this 'he-said, she-said' argument about evidence that'll surely be mostly hearsay and innuendo.

"I've read the complete file on this case including all of the documents, exhibits, pictures of burning boats, affidavits, etcetera, ad nauseum, and at this point, I'd like to give you both an indication of my leaning in this matter. The Petitioner may have gotten screwed royally, but the Respondent also got a raw deal. I don't think that a deputy district attorney would have gotten involved in that mess with former attorney Koontz. He's appeared in this Court many times and I have the greatest confidence in his ability to have done the entire frame-up of this Respondent without the help of Petitioner.

"Here's the bottom line. Mister Sharp, I'd suggest very strongly that you and Mister Vincent take the opportunity of the recess I'm about to take to sit down and work this problem out, because if this hearing goes to its conclusion, you may wind up with the short end of a very big stick.

"I'll see you both in chambers in thirty minutes. And Mister Sharp, I hope you've brought your checkbook with you today."

With that, the learned judge rises and exits the bench, lighting a cigarette as he opens a door leading to the chambers hallway. Looking over to the other table I see my dearly departed wife grinning like a Cheshire cat. It is now time for my Academy Award performance. I intend to take a dive so spectacular, that if in the ring, it would make boxing history. Vincent gets up from the table and nods toward the jury room, and we all step into that unused area to settle this matter.

Once in the room I decide to keep my mouth shut and let Vincent and Myra do the talking. When this settlement is locked down, I want it to be more of their doing than mine. Vincent sums it up. "Sharp, the party's over. You've been nailed and you know it. Forget about the burning boat bit, that deal's dead. Your original agreement is back in place and you now owe Mizz Scot a substantial amount of money."

My turn. "Okay, okay, but there's no way I intend to reimburse her for the money spent towing that boat to the yard or having it demolished and removed."

This tactic is called 'closing on a collateral issue.' A perfect example of this is when I once sold an old restored Mercedes Benz to a guy who offered me several thousand dollars more for it than I thought it was worth. I didn't want to accept too eagerly, but I also didn't want to give him time to re-consider the fact that he was voluntarily overpaying for the car. So, referring to the new set of custom wheels on the old car, I said: "okay, but that price doesn't include the wheels."

At that point he started arguing about the wheels. For the next fifteen minutes all he could do was concentrate on how badly he wanted them to be included in the price, so that when I finally gave in, he was happy to write out the check. I took his mind off of the main item, the total price, by distracting him with a non-important 'collateral' issue. And it works in law too. To some extent, it even applied to the dead dog case. It usually works every time.

Myra jumps right up and grabs the piece of candy that I'm holding up and dangling. She temporarily loses it. "There's no way in hell I'm going to be out that seven hundred dollars. I had to have the damned..." Her lawyer stops her.

"Mister Sharp, we're talking about some serious money here, so what exactly is your intention?"

"Mr. Vincent, if we can settle this matter up, I'm willing to come up with her fair share of my fees on the wrongful death cases with only two conditions: first, I'm not paying for towing that boat away. I had no idea it burned. I was out of town at the time, and having been exposed to a new saltwater environment the old wiring gave away. Those old wires..."

"All right Sharp, enough with the wires. What's your second condition?"

"I want your office to prepare the settlement agreement and I want it made clear that this is her last trip to the well. No mas, and that we each pay our own legal fees."

Vincent is almost as sharp as I gave him credit for. A settlement agreement was already prepared for us to sign. He opens the door and signals to his paralegal sitting out in the courtroom. The assistant comes in to the jury room with a laptop computer and a small portable printer. They briefly discuss the new terms and the paralegal makes some changes and prints out three copies of the new one-page agreement. After looking it over, we all sign the copies and tell the court clerk that counsel would like a chambers conference to have a settlement agreement approved.

The announcement that a settlement has been reached is the best news that any judge can hear. They *love* to see cases settled without the necessity of a trial. Thirty years ago there was a judge in Burbank who was so anxious to help lawyers settle, that if they said they were close and would like to finish up in chambers, he'd meet them in the courthouse parking lot at seven A.M. Using his own key, he'd bring the parties in through the back entrance and up to his chambers, where he'd serve them coffee and Danish. If they actually settled then and there, he would give them Green Stamps, a marketing device item that merchants gave out in those days for people to earn discounts on purchases, much like air miles are used as premiums nowadays.

The clerk ushers us all into the judge's chambers. "Well, I'm glad to see that you guys finally came to your senses. Now, what have you got for me?" The clerk hands him the settlement agreement. The judge nods at the court reporter, letting her know that the record is about to begin. "Okay boys and girls, in the matter of Sharp versus

Sharp, California Superior Court case number 8222985, the parties have agreed to a settlement whereby…" He reads the entire settlement agreement into the record. And then looks up at me. "Mister Sharp, it's now time for the commercial. Did you bring your checkbook?"

"Yes, your honor. I have my checkbook right here, and also brought along confirmed copies of the court documents showing settlement amounts and legal fees."

My favorite movie of all time is Jose Ferrer in Edmond Rostand's 'Cyrano de Bergerac.' I love to watch the opening act, where an insult is made about Cyrano' s nose and he starts a prolonged swordfight with the insulter, all the while composing a lyric poem. At the end of the fight (and end of the poem), Cyrano thrusts his rapier into the chest of his opponent with a majestic "thrust ho!"

I never got around to taking up fencing, but I've always dreamed of some day being able to end a battle victoriously with a "thrust ho…" and now, 'some day' just arrived.

I remove all of the documents that Jack Bibberman had prepared for me from my briefcase, along with a check made payable to 'Daniel Vincent and Myra Scot,' in the sum of *one dollar* and, wielding them like an epee, (with a 'thrust ho' being said to myself mentally), lay everything down on the judge's desk. I then thank the judge very much, pick up my copy of the agreement and exit the now-silent chambers. I think it best to get out of the room quickly before Myra's head starts to explode.

Once back at the boat, I call the court and asked to speak to the court reporter for a blow-by-blow description of what happened after I left the judge's chambers. Myra must have been on good behavior that afternoon, because she didn't give Vincent the 'briefcase-on-the-head beating' that Koontz got. Instead, I'm told that her mouth dropped open when she saw the check. She started sucking air like a fish out of water, then grabbed at the documentation and read it in disbelief. The judge sat there with a contained smirk on his face and thanked them for their cooperation, letting them both know that the conference was over and it was time for them to get out of his chambers. Myra and Vincent walked out and went in separate directions. The last words the reporter heard said were Vincent' telling Myra "My invoice will be mailed to you."

After hanging up the phone I notice that another call had come in. The caller ID shows a telephone number I recognize. It's the defense firm on Stuart's asbestosis case. They don't know it, but at this point I'd recommend that Stuart take their settlement offer for anything more than fifty dollars, so if they're calling with an offer of *any* amount, this case is closed. I'm just about to return their call when I hear a knocking on my hull; it's doc, my wife-killing neighbor.

He asks if we can talk in private. It's a beautiful Southern California day, so we climb up to the Grand Bank's flybridge. It's completely covered with a custom canvas awning and enclosed with clear side-curtains, like a mansion's sunroom. He starts with a semi-confession. "I suppose, being involved with the criminal justice system, you've heard of my past problems with the law." I nod, wondering if he's finally going to admit that he really had her put down, or if he'll continue with that old 'I didn't do it' routine. He does a combination of both, which really surprises me. "She's dead, you know, and there's an insurance policy on her life that I'd like you to help me submit."

That's it. This guy's really got stones. I've heard a lot in almost twenty years of practice, but this takes the cake. Here's a guy who kills his wife and wants me to help him collect on her life insurance policy. He obviously needs some professional help, but not legal. It should be psychiatric. I know there's absolutely no way I'm going to get involved in this mess, so I try to get out of it as politely as possible, because there are some people you just don't want to antagonize. "Doctor Gault, there are so many reasons why I can't help you that it's hard to list them all. First, I've read that your wife disappeared and has never been found. For you to now claim that she's dead implies that you know where the body is and therefore were responsible in some way for causing her death, and there's no statute of limitations on murder. Second, there's no way I can help you perpetrate a fraud on an insurance company..." He stops me mid-sentence.

"Peter, I didn't kill her eight years ago. She just died last week."

13

This guy is certifiable and should be institutionalized immediately so he can get some sort of drug therapy. That's supposed to do wonders. Like professional athletes, who are capable of putting on their 'game face,' cops, lawyers and judges learn how to have a 'non-reaction' face, no matter what's being said to them. I've been using that face successfully for many years now, but it never got tested in a situation like the doc is creating now.

"That's right, Peter, she's been alive all this time. She just died last week, and in anticipation of your next question, no, she hasn't been locked up in my basement. She was in a private convalescent home up above Avalon, on Catalina Island."

Out of the corner of my eye I spot a uniformed Rita walking down the dock, wheeling her small carry-on luggage case behind her. She doesn't see us up on my flybridge as she enters the doc's boat. "Does Rita know about this?" It's probably no business of mine, but I want to know to satisfy my own curiosity.

"Yes and no. She knows about the long confinement, but I haven't told her about the death yet. He turns and sees Rita stepping into his boat.

"I'm going to do that now."

The only sure way to positively avoid sticking your foot in your mouth is by keeping your mouth shut. I've heard that saying before, but never seemed to get the knack of it, so I go right ahead and start to wedge a size eleven boat shoe between my pearly whites. "Well, now that you're finally single, I guess that paves the way for you and your girlfriend." He looks surprised.

"My girlfriend?"

I can't figure out why he should be surprised. If she's not his girlfriend, what's she doing sleeping with him? Oops. Maybe I did it again. What if he's a bigamist and he married Rita while his wife was alive? I make a concentrated effort to painfully extract my foot from my mouth.

"Yes, you know, Rita."

For the first time since I've met this serious man, I see him crack a smile. He gets up, and as he starts to climb down the ladder from the flybridge, he tosses a closing line at me.

"She's not *my* girlfriend, Peter, she's *your* girlfriend. She's my *daughter*! Please, join us for dinner tonight." The look on his face lets me know that he realizes I was caught off-guard, and that he's always been aware of my awkwardness being with her in his presence. This old doc is one sharp cookie. I just hope he's not a killer too.

Every non-fatal illness usually has a recovery time; a number of minutes, hours, days or months that it takes before the afflicted fully gain their senses and can perform as good as before the illness. In my case, a chronic illness seems to be making a complete fool of myself, and the recovery time varies from minutes to years, depending on the severity of the attack and the number of witnesses.

My mind flashes back to a past foot-in-mouth incident, when I was given my first court appearance to make. In most courtrooms, as you face the judge's bench, there are usually two counsel tables. The trick to knowing which one is designated as yours is to notice on which side of the bench the jury box is located. The bench nearest the jury box is for the moving party, the one who has asked for this matter to be heard by the court. This is usually the plaintiff, prosecutor or petitioner. The other table, the one that's farthest from the jury, witness box and court reporter's station, is reserved for the defending party, which is the defendant, or respondent. Not wanting to be discourteous to the court, I arrived about thirty early minutes for my first appearance. This gave me time to spread out my papers on the counsel table so that I might possibly look like I knew what I was doing. Opposing counsel was an old pro who timed his entrance into the courtroom exactly as the judge was taking the bench. The court clerk announced the case we were appearing on, just as opposing counsel came through the swinging gate (the 'bar') that separates litigants from spectators. Seeing me standing up behind the counsel table, he uttered the first three words that appear on the court's official record. Three words he said to me that I ordered a transcript of and had perma-plaqued to forever hang prominently on my office wall: "other table, dummy!"

That first incident of foot-in-mouth disease happened twenty years ago, but every time I look at the wall hanging I'm reminded of it, and a minor relapse occurs. This time it had more serious ramifications. I not only embarrassed myself in front of a potential client, I also found out that I was involved in a serious relationship! This looks like it is going to be one helluva dinner tonight.

Before trying the usual cure of standing in the shower for about thirty minutes, I decide to request that a little homework be done. I send an e-mail to our office manager requesting all the information that could be dug up on Doctor Sherman Gault, his wife, daughter, everything. By the time I get out of the shower, there's an answer on my flat-panel screen. How this happened so fast is almost as amazing as the facts uncovered.

Apparently, the gang in the forward cabin has inadvertently been receiving copies of e-mails that were being sent to doctor Gault's boat. This was probably due to a glitch in the wireless network our boat neighbor Don Paige had set up that all of us on the dock shared. I don't know if our messages were being sent to anyone else, but that's not the issue now, nor do I care. What's important now is what those accidentally intercepted messages to doc's boat reveal. They include several royalty statements for the doc's wife, Robin Gault, who was a successful writer of self-help books. It also reveals invoices and payment receipts from a convalescent home on Catalina Island where she had been a resident for these past years.

Armed with this information, I feel a little better about the dinner I'm going to. It will probably still have its awkward moments, but there's a good possibility that with enough concentrated effort, I may be able to avoid making a complete fool out of myself again, at least tonight.

I decide not to waste time returning the defense lawyer's call on Stuart's case until tomorrow and instead get ready for the evening on doc's boat.

The dinner looks delicious, and it is. Ditto for the daughter. She sits as close to me as possible, never letting go of my hand. It's a good thing it isn't the hand I eat with. She looks like she's been crying, but lets me know that she's okay now. Her mother's death was something that had been expected, but dreaded for several years. Doc goes on to explain that when she was first diagnosed with Alzheimer's, they couldn't believe it. She was so bright, so creative, so successful in writing, public speaking and counseling people with their problems. They were certain that the diagnosis was wrong. But as the months and then years went on, it became apparent that the diagnosis was correct. Due to her pride and love for her family, while still lucid, she requested that she be placed in the convalescent home on Catalina Island. They had made many trips over there over the years, and she thought it would be an ideal place to live out the rest of her life, at least the part she could still appreciate.

Doc and Rita both argued against the idea and wanted her to stay at home. Money was no object, and they offered to hire professional caregivers around the clock when the situation called for it. But no, she wouldn't have it. One of her concerns was the loss of her public image as a brilliant writer. She feared that having that disease would cause her reputation to diminish and cause a loss of royalties that were supposed to go into a trust fund for her daughter and future grandchildren. No, she just wanted to have the public know that she was retired and wanted to live the remainder of her life in privacy. To make sure that her remaining years went uninterrupted, doc purchased the land that the convalescent home was situated on. That way, he could be certain that she'd be allowed to stay there in privacy for the rest of her life.

At first the public tended to accept her announced desire for privacy, but as time went on, curious investigative reporters, always looking for that sensational celebrity item for a 'where are they now' type of story, continually failed to find her. That absence of a satisfactory explanation created a vacuum that the press filled in with rumors about possible foul play. The newly elected district attorney was looking for a new cause to bolster his future political career, and the prosecution of prominent Doctor Sherman Gault for the murder and disappearance of his wife seemed to be just the right opportunity.

This must have placed doc in an untenable situation. In order to easily clear his name he would be forced to violate his beloved wife's trust and secrecy.

If memory serves me correctly, he hired the first real 'dream team' to defend him, and it worked. The jury was hung (meaning they couldn't reach a unanimous decision) and the district attorney, then embarrassed but too involved with newer cases to re-file, decided not to try the case again and the doctor got off.

It's a stunning testament to this man's love for his wife that he allowed himself to be put through the criminal justice system and then constant district attorney harassment until his license was suspended, all to protect her desire for privacy and to live out her life in peace. That's why he bought the boat - so he and Rita could go over to the Island to visit with her. I look at both of them in a different light now and promise that I'll do everything I can to help them process the insurance claim.

I instruct our office to send out the usual letters putting the insurance company on notice that we will be presenting the claim, and that in the event they were planning on contesting it, that we were prepared to disclose a burial site and provide DNA samples that their lab can analyze for positive identification purposes. I don't mention the Alzheimer's or Catalina Island at this point, thinking it not wise to tip too much of our hand at this early stage. If the insurance company puts up a stink, we can always bring out more ammunition. I always like to feel that I know something that the other side doesn't.

Being the consummate professional, doc tells me he informed the insurance company that if and when they ever pay his claim, they have been instructed automatically send me a check for five percent of the total payout. I tell him that isn't necessary, but he insists, in view of the work I'll no doubt be doing on this claim.

For a lawyer who specializes in criminal defense, I'm spending a lot of time dealing with insurance companies. Proof of this is the fact that my own carrier sent me a letter about their looking into my old boat's fire. I decide that I'll send whatever settlement comes in for that to Myra. I've had enough fun tormenting her over the past months and she deserves someone doing something nice for her.

The dinner last night was nice, but now it's time to get back to work on my favorite client's matter, so I dial the asbestos defense firm's number and get put right through to Charles Indovine, Sr.. When dealing with opposing counsel, it's always a good idea to address them formally. If it's going to turn into any less than a formal conversation, it should be their decision and not mine. My opening line is intended to sound formal, not too anxious, and with an irritated tone, indicating that this matter isn't important to me and that I have other more important things to do.

Negotiations are all a game. The most important thing to remember is not to play checkers if the other guy is playing chess. My call finally is put through to the head man. "Indovine here." The game is afoot.

"Hello Mr. Indovine, this is Peter Sharp returning your phone call. What's on your mind?"

"Oh yes, Peter, I'm glad you called back." Good sign, a first name response. That signals he wants something from me; let's see what it is. I'll try to avoid warming up, no matter how hard he tries. "You know, we were talking about your case, and I thought it would be a nice gesture towards your client if we could dispose of this matter without going through all the usual pre-trial procedures." This is good. They must be afraid that Stuart will come walking into court looking like Osama bin Laden. I now feel that a settlement offer may be coming. "Peter, why don't you tell us what it would take for us to make this matter go away?" Very smart approach. They want me to start the bidding for them. I might as well soften them up a little.

"Well, to tell you the truth, I've been so busy with a capital case I'm working on, I haven't had the time to give it much thought. Let's see now, if my memory serves me correctly, the statute of limitations has already run for any other people to make claims like this against your client, so there's no danger of your setting any precedent by settling a case based on a faith healer's report, so I'd say we can probably dump this case for anything in the neighborhood of a million or two." I've really never said that sentence to anyone before, and it feels very good. As expected, there's nothing but silence on the other end of the phone. He recovers nicely.

"Well, Peter, that's a little more than we had in mind. Can we be a little more flexible on this one?" Fantastic! The mere fact that he didn't go ballistic at the mention of several million-dollars may mean that Stuart might actually get more than fifty dollars out of this turkey of a case. Now the end game begins.

"Mr. Indovine, you're a senior partner in one of the most successful defense firms in the country. I'm not privy to your billing rates, but I would think it's safe to say that after the first round of interrogatories and a deposition or two, your meter would probably be reading at least six figures, and if this case went to even a minimum one-week trial, your client would be looking at close to a million dollars in experts and legal fees even if he won the case, so I really don't think that a million is out of the question. And, if your firm really insists, we can get the client out to some specialists for a consult, and with an expert's medical report, you'll be looking at exposure of several times that amount. I'll tell you what: you've been a real professional with me and I appreciate your courteous conduct and honesty so far, so I'll be willing to recommend that my client accept eight hundred thousand, but that's about as far down as I would advise him to go.

My head is now racing. If he comes back with anything more than five hundred dollars, I might consider it, but my last response approached the genius level, so let's see where he goes from there.

"Peter, I appreciate your working with us. If you'll recommend three quarters of a million to him, we can messenger the check and release form over this afternoon." I'm struck speechless. This case was a loser from the get-go. After learning about the faith healer's involvement in the diagnosis process I thought we'd never have a chance to recover the couple of hundred advanced for the filing fees and service of process. If this works, I may be making history. Seven hundred and fifty big ones with only a faith healer's report to prove up the specials? I lose track of the time and don't realize that Indovine is holding a silent phone waiting for my response. He finally brings me be back to reality. "Peter, are you there? Are you all right?" I wait another beat and then play out my final scene.

"Yes, Indovine, I'm here, and I'm all right, sorry about that, I was just handed an important memo on some other case. As for the seven fifty you're offering, we weren't planning on going that low, but okay, send it over. I'll recommend that he accept it. He gave me the final authority to settle, so it's a deal."

For some strange reason, the only thing I'm feeling at this moment is sympathy for my ex-wife. If she would've only been reasonable and hung in there for a while, we both could've shared all this. The sentimentality comes to an abrupt end when the phone rings again and the caller ID display shows my dear departed's private office phone number.

"Hello sweetheart, to what do I owe the pleasure of this call? Her response brings me be back down to earth. She's not in a good mood today. Why am I not surprised?

"Don't sweetheart me, you rotten crook. I just want to let you know that we've finally nailed you. The insurance company had a red flag on Mrs. Gault's file and guess who's name appeared with the filing of a claim? Yours, you ambulance-chasing sleazeball. I'm going to be on you like a cheap suit, and we're going to put you and that murdering rat Gault behind bars, where you both belong!"

I've got nothing to lose now, so I might as well inquire. "So I guess dinner is out?"

My response doesn't serve any purpose, because all I'm talking to now is a dial tone.

This is really unfortunate. It seems that there's just no way to save her from herself. She's under the spell of that nitwit boss of hers, and doesn't even realize she's been brainwashed. It must be like some sort of cult when you work in that district attorney's office. Not only do I think she's prosecuting the wrong guys in the parking lot murder, but she's going to make another fool out of herself with the doc's case too. I'm sorry, but I just can't waste any more time worrying about her. Stuart's settlement is on the way over here, and between dealing with him and processing the doc's insurance claim, my plate is completely full for a while.

Traffic to the boat has been getting heavier in the past week. Detectives are going in and out almost every other day, and now they're bringing uniforms with them, and staying more than a few minutes in the forward stateroom. They're also having conferences in the main saloon. It's so crowded when Stuart shows up that we have to go topside to the enclosed flybridge. "What's going on here? What're the police doing on your boat?" I don't blame him for his curiosity. With all the cops hanging around, it looks like the boat is being raided for something.

"Good question, Stu, I wish I had the answer. I think it's some charity matter that Suzi's organizing." At this point he doesn't know about the settlement of his case. When I called him, all he was told was that there might be some good news and that we should meet to talk about it.

"What's up with the case, Pete? Do you think we're going to ever get something out of it, or should I just forget about it and write a check out to my faith healer?"

"Relax, Stu, in a little while a messenger will be here with a settlement offer and I want to talk to you about how much the case is worth. First of all, how are you feeling? Have you been to the doctor? I mean, a regular one?"

"Yeah, I finally went to the VA and had a chest X-Ray. I hope I'm not screwing up the case, but the doc there told me that I was in the process of recovering from the worst case of bronchitis he's ever seen, so I guess I was wrong about that asbestos stuff. Sorry, Pete, I'll get a check off to you for your time and expenses in filing the suit."

I used to think that Stuart was the biggest loser in the world, but my feelings about him have changed drastically over the past months. He's worked hard. It may have been with some lame-brained schemes, but he finally made something out of himself. He's got a nice income now, and aside from still having some strange personality traits, he's even developed a little class.

His admitting he was wrong about the asbestosis is the first time I've ever heard him confess to a mistake. This is definitely a good sign. "Stuart, I really appreciate your wanting to be fair with me on the filing fees, but it won't be necessary. I think we've got the case sewn up and there'll be some money in it for you."

"Pete, no matter how much it is, I want you to have half of it. No, don't argue with me. You've been great with me, and I want you to take a full fee; even if it's only on a small settlement."

I'm living on my dream boat, which will only cost the firm one dollar to exercise that option to buy; my ex-wife is off my back for a piece of my future earnings, my girlfriend and prospective future spouse is going to come into a few million bucks from her mother's life insurance policy and future royalties, and Laverne is leaving me alone. What else can I ask for? I've been treating Stuart pretty badly for the past twenty years, so maybe now's the time to do something nice for him. "Stu, I'm going to accept your offer to take a fee on this case, but not the fifty percent you offered: I only want the minimum retainer amount that any lawyer would take for settling a case before the discovery process commences; twenty five percent, partly payable in merchandise of my choice."

Stuart sticks out his hand and we shake on it. There's no need for a written retainer agreement between us, because one good thing about Stuart is that like me, his word is his bond.

The police have finished their meeting down below and start leaving the boat, just as Indovine's messenger arrives with the settlement draft and release. Stuart looks at the sealed envelope like he's one of the nominees for an Academy Award and the winner is about to be announced. He sees the smile on my face. "C'mon, Pete, please don't make me go through this again. The last time was unbelievable. I don't think I can take the suspense again this time."

"Stuart, this case was not like the last one, so don't expect to see a telephone number on that check, because it's definitely less than seven figures. All I'll tell you is that it's more than the fifty bucks I thought the case would settle for. And don't worry about the costs for filing; my fee will cover that."

He opens the envelope and stares at the check with disbelief. More tears, another thank you, and another hug for the lawyer that lasts longer than I want it to.

We celebrate for several hours. Next morning, true to his promise and per my instructions, Stuart delivers two items to me at the boat: an envelope containing most of my retainer fee, and something big and yellow. The envelope never really got as far as my hands, because the little one appeared out of nowhere and intercepted it. I had originally brought that case in as a referral to Melvin, so the fee belongs to the firm. All I'm entitled to is the normal one-third referral fee, which in this case is quite sufficient. I take the pink slip to the yellow Hummer, and she takes the money.

14

The problem with driving a Hummer is that it's tough getting it into designated parking spaces. The people who designed our Marina must have imagined that people with million-dollar yachts all drive compact cars. If your vehicle hangs over the painted white lane markers, everyone complains. Fortunately my income has reached a level that affords the additional expense of special underground parking, so I rented two spaces where the adjacent apartment building's residents park, and now have plenty of room for my yellow tank. Extra space isn't the only advantage, because by paying to park under the building, my designated space is just a few feet away from where George C.'s limo driver parks when his boss is on the boat. This will no doubt give me a much better chance of bumping into my celebrity neighbor. I hope he enjoyed that DVD I gave his to skipper for him.

Now that I'm done wiping the Hummer's windows, I'm going up to the boat because it's time to completely read through the Hummer owner's manual. This is a ritual that every new car owner usually does so they can look really smart when showing the car off to some friend whose envy is being solicited. I only get up to the part about how to regulate the air conditioning when more cop-types of people approach the boat and come aboard without even asking permission. Leading the parade is my ex-wife. Once inside the saloon, she points a finger at me and declares in her best official voice: "Peter Sharp, we have a warrant here for your arrest on the charge of attempted insurance fraud. You will be taken to the Culver Boulevard Pacific Division of the Los Angeles Police Department, where you will be processed. Your bail has been set at one hundred thousand dollars." That having been said, she instructs the armed district attorney investigators who were with her to put me in handcuffs and take me away.

On the way out of the boat I notice that Suzi has been peeking through her slightly open stateroom door and taking the whole scene in. It's embarrassing. Even though we've never really spoken to each other, I feel ashamed to be taken away like this with her watching. This isn't a very good example for her legal guardian to be setting.

By the time Myra and her gang drive the five miles or so to the Police Station, I realize that the word must have gotten out about my arrest, because the media is out in front of the station waiting for us. When I see my dear ex-wife parading in front of the news cameras, the mystery of how word must have leaked out is solved. She's in her usual rare form.

Every time you open your refrigerator door, you can be confident that the little light inside will go on. The same type of reliability can be said for my ex-wife. Every time you stick a microphone in front of her face, she starts making a public statement. This time it's no different, except for the fact that today's sounds a little more rehearsed.

"Our office is pleased to announce that we've solved an almost ten-year-old murder case. This afternoon we have arrested a prominent Marina del Rey attorney, who will be charged with conspiring to perpetrate a fraud upon the victim's insurance company. His co-conspirator, also arrested earlier

177

today, is none other than the actual murderer, Doctor Sherman Gault, who had formerly been acquitted of the crime. We can't try him again for the murder, so this time he'll be sent away for the insurance fraud conspiracy. Our office will be issuing a formal statement tomorrow morning. Thank you."

Once I get handed over to the jailer, Myra and her investigators leave, and I'm pleasantly surprised to be treated quite well here. I've known the jailer from past dealings in this police division, but this is my first time as a prisoner. His courtesy surprises me.

"Well, Mister Sharp, it's nice to see you finally decided to give my little domain some business. Why don't you sit down over there and relax. Once we've finished with the booking process, you can go out into the lobby and wait. Your bail has already been arranged and your sponsor will be picking you up in a few minutes. Sorry to see you go so soon. Maybe the next time you'll stay with us a little longer." I remember seeing this jailer recently. He's part of the lunch crowd at the Chinese restaurant, and also no doubt a big fan of Suzi's. No wonder I never see the inside of a cell today. That little kid's got more juice on this side of town than the governor.

The most surprising event of the afternoon isn't the arrest, because I knew that sooner or later my ex-wife would set me up for something or other; it's the fact that the jailer was expecting me and that I've already been bailed out. After the friendly jailer finishes up his paperwork I'm allowed to sit on the 'visitor's' bench near the station's front door. When my sponsor arrives she doesn't come into the building. Instead, she just stands there holding the door open. I know this is a request for me to get up off my rear end and follow her and the Saint Bernard outside and to alleged freedom.

I've never ridden in a little electric car with a twelve-year-old driving, but for some strange reason I feel safe. The dog doesn't give up his usual front seat, so I'm now riding in the back, which is another invasion of the cat's private space and earns me a constant glare from those green little eyes.

As usual, there is no conversation on the way back to the Marina. When we board the boat I think it's time to break the silence between us. I now feel certain that she speaks English, and hasn't said anything to me in the past months because she just didn't have anything she wanted to tell me. I take a chance: "Suzi, I don't know how you did it, but thank you. I hope you realize that this is all a big mistake. Honest, I didn't do what they're accusing me of." To my great surprise, as she's about to enter her stateroom, she finally decides to honor me with a statement:

"I know you didn't do it. The firm's funds were used to bail out both you and the doctor. His daughter was sent to pick him up because he was arrested in town and taken to Parker Center's jail, downtown. We're now preparing documentation for your false arrest suit." But that isn't all. Her final declaration is "dinner will be ready a half hour late tonight. I was busy with other things this afternoon."

Will wonders ever cease? She finally talked to me. I feel honored and at the same time scolded for taking her away from her busy afternoon schedule to bail me out of jail.

Less than an hour has passed and Rita is here with her father. He's apologetic. "Peter, I'm sorry you had to go through all this: it's all part of being involved with an acquitted murderer." His daughter slaps him on the arm for describing himself that way

"Stop it, dad, you're not an acquitted murderer, you're an innocent man who was railroaded." I don't like to see them bicker like that, so I break into the conversation and try to change the subject away from his past accusations of guilt.

"Oh, don't worry about it… I look forward to every meeting with my ex-wife. Let me bring you up to date and then we can plan some strategy." I tell them about the letter that was sent to the insurance company and the fact that all we offered to do was identify a burial site and provide DNA samples for positive identification. Rita questions my letter.

"Don't you think it would have been better to tell them the whole story? That mother has been alive all these years and just died last week? If you would have done that, they probably wouldn't have arrested you and daddy." I disagree with her.

"There's been no crime committed. This is nothing more than the filing of a normal claim to collect on a deceased spouse's life insurance policy. If there had been no past accusation of murder, no trial and no acquittal, and this was just a case of a husband putting in a claim after his insured wife's death, no more than I offered would be asked for or expected. There's no reason for us to jump through imagined hoops.

"Furthermore, the actions of the insurance company probably led to our arrests today. My office staff seems to feel that their pre-mature suspicions were conveyed to the district attorney's office, and they also acted before they had their facts lined up. All of this will lead to a bigger damage award when we rub their noses in the truth about your mother's life and death. I'm sorry to make it look like anything here is being done for profit or to exploit the loss of your mother, but these people have put your family through hell over the years, and now it's time for some payback."

Rita has a question that is shared by many of the news commentators.

"Isn't this a case of double jeopardy? I mean, they're not supposed to try a person for the same crime twice are they?" That's a good question she has there and some clarification is called for.

"They're not, because this is a completely different crime with a different set of facts. In the first trial he was charged with murder, and at that point in time he hadn't made any attempt to collect on her life insurance policy because, as we now know, she was still alive. The District attorney's office probably made sure the insurance company red tagged that policy for all these years, just waiting for someone to put a claim in, and someone finally did. Unfortunately, it was yours truly."

Doc has obviously been doing some reading on the matter. "Aren't they trying to make some changes to that double jeopardy law?"

"Yes, but not here. The Law Commission of England and Wales recommended that the law of double jeopardy be relaxed in circumstances where there's compelling new evidence, but it'll never get passed there and I don't think it will here, either."

"Why not, Peter? The public is against criminals getting away with anything."

"You're right, doc, but who would you have making the decision of whether or not the new evidence is 'compelling?' You can't bring a person back in for another trial and expect it to be fair when a jury already knows that the only reason the defendant's being tried over again is because the judge has seen the new evidence and now knows the defendant is guilty. That completely blows the whole presumption of innocence, which is fragile enough already. The concept of single jeopardy has been on the books since the 12th century, and it's withstood all challenges since then, so I think it'll hold up for a while longer.

"I still say we just go ahead with our plans as if the arrest never happened. I'll take care of the criminal part, and this present incident should be treated as nothing more than a normal claim to collect on a life insurance policy."

No matter how much you try to put a client at ease it rarely works. I can tell by doc's questions that he constantly lives in fear of another arrest and trial..

"Do you think they'll go after me for anything else?"

"I'm afraid so. You took the stand in your murder trial and denied committing that crime. This time around, even though it's only a conspiracy case and they can't get you for the murder, they'll probably try to nail you for perjury, because of your prior in-court statements under oath. They'll want you to have the distinction of being the only person convicted of that crime in this state since Mark Furhman, one of the detectives on the O.J. Simpson case, back in the 1990's. That, coupled you're your alleged partition in a conspiracy to defraud the insurance company, could lead to some serious penitentiary time if they can convince a judge to make the sentences run consecutively."

The State of California has two ways to bring an accused felon to trial. One is by preliminary hearing in a division of the Municipal Court, at which time the prosecution doesn't have to prove the defendant's guilt, it only has to show that a crime has been committed and that there is probable cause to connect the accused to the crime. If the prosecution is successful at the 'prelim,' which they are ninety-nine percent of the time, the defendant then is bound over for arraignment and trial in the Superior Court.

The other way that the authorities can go is usually reserved for high-profile cases and investigations into alleged misdoings of public officials, is indictment by a Grand Jury. That's where the district attorney calls witnesses and presents their basic case to a select group of about twenty-three citizens nominated by Superior Court judges. This blue-ribbon panel hears the evidence in secret and then usually rubber-stamps whatever the district attorney requests by returning an indictment. Once an indictment is filed, the prosecutor can skip the preliminary hearing process completely. After indictment, the defendant goes directly to arraignment and trial in the Superior Court.

This is a complete reversal of the reason why grand juries were created. Hundreds of years ago, they were designed to be a protection for the public, by having disinterested people decide whether a person should be brought to trial on baseless, politically motivated serious criminal charges. But now, all a grand jury does is save the district attorney the trouble of putting on a preliminary hearing and giving the defense a chance to see how weak their case is. This way, with a Superior Court felony trial hanging over his or her head, there's a better chance of coercing the accused into pleading guilty to a lesser crime.

Not having heard anything from the district attorney's office, I'm pretty sure they're going for a grand jury indictment. Myra probably would never forgive herself for giving up a chance to prance in front of those bluenoses. My suspicions are confirmed while watching the local evening news. A good-looking airhead reading from the teleprompter drones on.

"Deputy District attorney Myra Scot announced today that the Los Angeles County Grand Jury has returned indictments against prominent attorney Peter Sharp and doctor Sherman Gault for their alleged conspiracy to commit fraud against the Uniman Insurance Company. They filed a life insurance claim for the death of doctor Gault's wife... the same wife that doctor Gault was accused of murdering almost ten years ago. This reporter has also learned that the case was brought to the prosecution's attention again when attorney Sharp offered to show where the deceased was buried. Not too bright a move on his part. We also want you to know the interesting fact that that attorney Sharp and district attorney Scot were married at one time."

This isn't too bad. I'm described as being 'prominent,' but 'not too bright.' I've been described worse than that many times. Myra got the worst of it though, because her bad taste in men has now been exposed. I'm sure the public will feel sorry for her. The poor girl is an honest, hard-working public servant and deserves more than to have been married to a crooked lawyer. Hell, I'm even starting to feel a little sorry for her, but she's bringing it all on herself.

Preparing for this trial should be easy because all we have to do is bring in one person to testify on our behalf: the convalescent home's attending nurse, who will also establish a chain of custody for the DNA sample. The district attorney will no doubt have done most of our work for us by the time of trial by paying the thousands of dollars required for DNA tests to prove that the person buried was in fact the doctor's wife.

After the criminal part is done we'll go on to the civil part. The district attorney's office will have already been humiliated, so it should be a slam dunk to get a settlement out of the insurance company on two bases: first, they caused our arrests. And if that isn't enough, they should be liable for acting in bad faith against their own insured's beneficiaries. This all seems so easy that it bothers me. Nothing this easy has ever dropped into my lap before. Although being arrested was slightly on the inconvenient side, my guardian angel had me bailed out before I saw the inside of a cell, so all in all, the whole experience may prove to have been worth it.

Both the doc and I agree that until this mess is cleared up, Rita and I should cool it. Once a potentially high-profile situation like this develops with elements including a rich doctor, a 'prominent' lawyer, a beautiful daughter, millions of dollars in the alleged victim's insurance, yachts, alleged fraud conspiracy and murder, there's always someone with a telephoto lens not too far away just waiting for the shot that a tabloid will pay big bucks for and the district attorney will blow up into another legal issue or motive for conspiracy.

Doc has some good news. Judy Marino, his wife's attending nurse, will be taking the tourist boat over from Catalina Island and bringing the death certificate and DNA sample with her. Doc will be putting her up in the Foghorn Motel around the corner. This is fine; now I'll have a chance to interview her and prepare her for what will happen in the courtroom when the district attorney puts her an extensive and through cross examination.

Nurse Judy should make an excellent witness. With the doc and Rita, we've all spent several pleasant evenings eating dinner together, courtesy of Suzi. I don't know where the food comes from, but it's always delicious. And then that old nagging feeling hits me. There's something about this nurse: the way she looks, the way she walks, the way she eats. There's something, but I just can't put my finger on it. This time the stakes are pretty high. If I can't figure out my strange feelings about her before the trial, I might wind up in deep doo-doo, so I've got to ask some questions. "Miss Marino, have we ever met before?"

"I don't think so Mr. Sharp, and I don't think I'd forget meeting a handsome man like you." Great. She's got a good line of bull, too.

Going to trial is always a crapshoot. No matter how slam-dunk you think your case is, there's always something the other side will come up with to knock

186

your socks off, and if there's anything I hate, it's a surprise during trial. As good as this case looks for us to get acquitted, I'd much rather have it dismissed before we get to the Superior Court arraignment.

Forget about avoiding double jeopardy. I don't even want single jeopardy to attach. There's only one way to do this, so I pick up the phone and call Myra's office. When I'm put through to her and she hears my voice, she's reluctant to talk.

"Peter, I'm the Deputy assigned to this case and you're one of the defendants, so I can't talk to you about anything... not without your lawyer being present."

"Yes, I know who you are, and who I am, but this isn't going to be a conversation about the case."

"Then why are you calling? I hope it's not for any misguided social reason."

"Don't flatter yourself. The purpose of this call is for you to set up a meeting tomorrow with your boss. I'm going to come in and help you all avoid making fools out of yourselves."

"You mean you're coming in to make a full confession?"

"Yeah, right. I'm coming in to make a statement to show you all what a wrong track you're on. Maybe I can show you how to avoid a disaster. And while you're at it, you might as well have a court reporter there too… and don't worry, I'll waive my right to have counsel present."

15

District Attorney Bill Miller is a few minutes late to the meeting. We all wait for him in their conference room on the nineteenth floor of the Criminal Courts Building in downtown Los Angeles. Aside from me, there's Myra, her assistant, the court reporter I requested, Miller's assistant, and two investigators - the ones who arrested me. They also have a video camera set up to get my statement on tape, so that no one (meaning me, probably) can get away with distorting the facts in any subsequent press conference or court hearing.

Miller comes in and everyone around the table exchanges polite, but insincere greetings. All I get is a nod of recognition. He signals the camera operator and stenographer that the show is about to begin and then he gives me the floor. I'm surprised he doesn't put a beret on his head and use a megaphone to shout "Action!" Instead, he tries to maintain some small amount of professionalism.

"Mister Sharp, before you make any statement we want to state for the record that you are presently under indictment for the felony of conspiracy to commit fraud against an insurance company, and that anything you say here can and will be used against you in further proceedings." I interrupt him.

"Mister Miller, I'm a licensed attorney in this state and I know my Miranda rights to remain silent and that an attorney can be appointed for me, and for the record, I waive them all here and now." He looks around the room. The general consensus is that a proper waiver has been given, so he nods for me to continue. I look at the camera and begin. "My name is Peter Sharp, attorney at law, and on this date, having willingly waived my Miranda rights to have legal counsel, I make this statement voluntarily. Concerning the indictments brought against doctor Sherman Gault and myself, I would like to explain why the indictment should be immediately quashed.

"First of all, doctor Gault never murdered his wife. She's been alive all these years, suffering from Alzheimer's in a private convalescent home on Catalina Island. Out of respect for her desire to live out the few remaining years of her life quietly, he never revealed this fact and suffered through an unjust criminal prosecution to protect her privacy. She died last week and was buried there, on the island." I pause for a second to see the reactions in the room. They range from surprise to disbelief, but everyone there keeps their cool, trying to look like whatever I'm saying doesn't mean much to them. I go on.

"We are prepared to document this fact with testimony from the attending nurse, who has brought DNA samples from the deceased. The sample can be compared with previous samples of the doctor's wife, as well as one from her daughter. The nurse is now in town and has the DNA sample with her. We will make her available to you and your lab techs.

"Here is a document containing her affidavit and present location. Once you've had an opportunity to question our witness and do your own DNA tests, you will see that I'm telling the truth.

"Now, you have a decision to make. Do you want to take this to trial, and in front of a packed courtroom and media circus have me prove up what I've just said, making complete idiots out of all of you, or would you like to do what you should have done already... complete your investigation, verify the truth of everything I've just told you today, and quietly dismiss the charges. I have no doubt you'll be able to concoct some phony reason that still makes you look good, and don't worry about us. Unlike you, all we care about is truth and justice. We're not running for office or trying to give our miserable careers a boost, so we'll keep our mouths shut and let you save face any way you want to." You can hear a pin if it drops in this room. The silence is deafening.

Miller signals the camera operator and stenographer to stop. Myra doesn't look at me. No one will look at Miller. He finally gets some words to come out of his mouth.

"Sharp, I don't believe a word you've told us here today, but we'll waste the taxpayers' money by checking it out anyway." What a stupid, stubborn ass this guy is. I can't help but believe that everyone at this table including my brainwashed ex-wife must see that I'm right and Miller is wrong. He finally finishes up.

"We'll look into this matter. One of our lab people will be contacting Miss Marino to make arrangements to pick up the DNA sample and death certificate. If you don't hear from us in the next two weeks, then we suggest you prepare for trial. Is there anything else?"

I hold up my parking stub "do you validate?" They are not amused. This is a not a good audience for humor. I know what the two weeks he mentions are for, because that's how long it will take for a complete analysis of the DNA sample to be compared to the sample that was voluntarily given by

Rita. The meeting is over. I look around the room but don't see any eyeballs facing my way.

Driving my Hummer back to the Marina, I feel a lot better. Not just because I think that our criminal indictments might be quashed, but because I probably stopped Myra from destroying herself any further with another losing case. Somehow I think she appreciates my stepping in like that, even if she couldn't look at me during the meeting.

Now back at the Marina, I report what happened at the D.A. meeting to my co-conspirator. The report is also repeated to my boss and her assistant, who sits there panting and drooling. Like so many others, it's a one-way conversation. Later that day, doc tells me that the DNA sample and death certificate have been picked up by a cop.

Tomorrow morning, Nurse Judy is scheduled to return to Catalina Island, so we all decide to have a farewell dinner together on our boat. When I tell Suzi about it, I'm surprised to hear that for the first time, she has decided to join us.

The meal is catered by the Chinese restaurant, brought over and served by the Asian Boys, who disappear into the foreward cabin during dinner. That's where they wait until everyone leaves so that they can clean up. They've probably got a crap game going on in there, but that's okay with me. We all have a very quiet pleasant evening and exchange conversation about everything but the case. Suzi just sits there and listens.

After dessert is served, Nurse Judy stands up, without noticing that the Saint Bernard has taken up residence under her chair during dinner. Just then a quick series of events takes place that goes by so fast that it's hard to tell exactly what happens first. As the nurse stands, she accidentally steps on the dog's tail. The dog yelps and jumps up, knocking Judy off her balance, but not off of the dog's tail. Her chair then falls over on top of the dog's head. Purely out of reflex action, the dog nips at her leg. Everyone is moving. Suzi runs to the dog, doc runs to the nurse, the dog runs to the foreward stateroom, the Asian Boys run over to pick everything up, and the cat sits and glares at everyone. I just sit here motionless with my mouth open.

I haven't witnessed a scene like this since watching a Three Stooges movie on cable.

Suzi quickly returns from her stateroom with a cloth and some bandages. The Asian boys are cleaning up some food that spilled onto the floor. It looks like the dog's bite broke the skin on Nurse Judy's leg and some blood is oozing out. This does not look good to me... that's why I chose law school over medical school. Doc is assuring everyone that it's all right... just a slight flesh wound. Suzi can't stop apologizing while wiping Judy's leg. I guess it takes someone either arrested or bleeding to make her talk. When it looks like the bleeding has finally stopped, Suzi goes to her foreward stateroom and the embarrassed animal follows her, tail between his legs. Naturally, I offer to pay whatever medical expenses Judy might incur in fixing the damage. She politely refuses. Doc assures me that everything is under control and not to worry about it.

Notwithstanding the dog incident, the evening went well. Several after-dinner drinks seem to calm everyone down and doc leaves to drive Judy over to the Foghorn Hotel so she can get some rest before leaving the next morning. While the doc gone I can't help but notice how shook up Rita is… even more so than Judy or Suzi. I try to calm her down. In a while, she looks a little more relaxed and my curiosity takes over.

"Rita, honey, I've got to ask you a question." Big mistake. The expression on her face tells me I should know better than to say that to a female I'm allegedly 'involved' with. "No, it's not a proposal of marriage, you're not rich enough for that yet." Good, the ice has been broken. She manages a slight smile. "Please tell me. What would your dad have done if he were convicted of murdering you mom years ago? Would he have tried to get the conviction set aside by revealing her secret life on the island, or would he have served his time until she passed away, waiting until then to finally reveal the truth?" She looks down for a minute or so.

"We talked about that a lot. He kept telling me not to worry, that he'd be acquitted, but I was still afraid for him. I thought that if he did get convicted for killing her, he might so want to protect her secret and privacy that he'd actually go to prison for the remaining years of her life, only revealing the truth after she passed away. Now we know it would have been almost ten years before he'd get his conviction reversed and be let out of jail."

Wow. That's real love, to do hard time in order to let your loved one live out her few remaining years in peace. I don't know if I could do it, or would want anyone to do it for me. It's the tough type of situation I hope I'm never in.

During the next two weeks everything is pretty much back to normal, with the exception of an occasional reporter or photographer following me around trying to get a 'scoop.' I also start filling out my own insurance company's claim form, hoping that maybe there can be some recovery for my burnt-out boat. The Culver City Police visits to our boat are becoming more frequent now, so it looks like something might be coming to a head pretty soon. From snippets of the conversations I can't help but overhear, it sounds like they're going to make an arrest on some case that Suzi has been helping them with. Her specialty of computer snooping has probably provided them with some evidence they needed of a smoking gun somewhere. From what I've been told, she's really good at finding people and things on the Internet; stuff that average police detectives aren't trained to do and not budgeted to hire specialists for.

Two envelopes have just arrived. They are delivered to me in the master stateroom by dog-mail. One is from the office of the district attorney. I open it up. There is no attached letter, no apology, no excuses, just a folded legal-sized document that I recognize as an original Grand Jury indictment form. Across the front is a big purple official-looking stamp that says two of the nicest words in the dictionary: "**INDICTMENT CANCELLED**." I only hope that Myra appreciates the fact that I saved her and her boss from more humiliation.

The second envelope has information that is less encouraging. It's from my former boat insurance company.

Dear Mr. Sharp:

Concerning your claim to recover for fire damage to your former vessel please be advised that we have been contacted by the new owner, who has informed us that a lien has been placed on any recovery.

In the event that you should wish to continue the claim process and execute the attached documentation, any sum towards recovery will be made payable and sent to the new owner, Ms. Myra Scot.

Please sign and return the enclosed Documents if you wish a check to be issued.

Why am I not surprised? Should I have thought that she would actually allow me to get away with anything? Aw, what the hell. I might as well just sign the damn papers and let her have her pound of flesh.

As promised, I continue pressing the life insurance claim for doc. The insurance company finally agrees to process it, so things are back to normal and now it will just be a matter of time before their check arrives and everyone on the dock will be a millionaire except me. I'm still bothered by my feeling that I've seen nurse Judy somewhere, but just can't remember where.

After two weeks goes by I receive a letter from the D. Riddle Laboratory Institute, a high-tech place out in Van Nuys that does DNA testing for paternity tests and law enforcement agencies. They say that the second sample matches the first one exactly, and that in error we must have sent in duplicate samples, but their accounting department requires that we pay for the second one too. An invoice for two thousand dollars is enclosed. As usual, I don't know what's going on. We didn't send them any DNA to be analyzed... or did we?

It's one thing getting a bill for something you've actually ordered, but I don't know what this is about. I leave the invoice on Suzi's table next to her cart key, with a post-it note to please let me know what this invoice is for. Having no other pressing chores today, I go up to the flybridge to finish another Nero Wolfe adventure, *The Doorbell Rang*. In this one, Wolfe does to the F.B.I. what I just did to the District Attorney. I just love these 'thrust-ho' stories.

I'm going to have to re-think reading on the boat, because every time I try, something catastrophic usually happens. This time it's Suzi. She's too small to confidently climb up the ladder to the flybridge, so she calls my cell phone and requests my presence down below in the main saloon for a meeting. This must be important, because it looks like she's actually going to talk to me again.

The subject of this meeting is that invoice we received for DNA testing. She starts her explanation.

"Peter, I took the liberty of ordering that sample to be tested, and I'm afraid I misled the laboratory." I'm sitting here with a blank face, not knowing what she's talking about, but happy that she's talking to me. She can tell by my expression that I don't understand, so she tries again. "I told the lab that we were doing a follow-up on the sample previously sent to them by the district attorney's office, because the first sample may have been contaminated and we wanted a back-up test done to see what the result would be." I'm sorry, but I have to ask.

"Suzi, what are you talking about? The district attorney's office had two samples they sent to the lab. One was from Rita and the other was from her dead mother. There were only two samples and neither one was corrupted. The lab picked up the sample themselves from Rita, and the other one was taken under strict lab conditions by the convalescent home doctor and then brought here by the nurse."

She could see that she wasn't getting through to me and her eye-roll was a clear indication that I just don't get it. Her mind works much faster than mine and she realizes she's going to have to try harder to make me understand. "Look, I'll try to make it as simple as possible: when Nurse Judy got bitten by Bernie, she bled onto a cloth that I wiped her leg with. That cloth was what I sent to the lab." I understand the words she was saying but... all of a sudden it hits me.

"You mean to say that nurse Judy's blood was a perfect match for one of the samples that the district attorney sent in?" She sees the light bulb go off over my head.

"By George, he's got it."

"Wait a minute. It couldn't have been Rita's sample that it matched, because I saw where that blood came from, and it was from Judy, so how could it have been a perfect match for one of the samples? Oh, oh, we've got a problem." Seeing that I finally 'get it,' she leaves the room.

The fact that Judy's DNA is a match for the sample that wasn't Rita's definitely proves one thing. Nurse Judy is doc's wife, Robin Gault. This is an amazing development, but it then begs the questions of whose body is buried on Catalina, and how did that death certificate get issued, and by whom? Now, my being aware of the fact that doc's wife isn't dead means that if I continue processing the claim for her life insurance I'm back in trouble again, and doc may be guilty of a real murder this time... whoever is buried on Catalina.

Not only may I be arrested for actually doing something wrong now, but I'm sitting here telling my problems to a dog.

The kid saw the same things as I did, but she was able to put it all together. I thought the nurse looked familiar. The same walk, the same gestures, the same laugh, all the things the mother shares with the daughter that I couldn't see but Suzi did. And her hunch paid off. I don't know how she would've ever gotten a DNA sample if the dog didn't help out with that bite, but I'm sure she would have found a way.

This isn't a unique situation. Many times a lawyer discovers things about a client, things that completely alter the way a case is handled. People don't understand why a lawyer doesn't want to ask his own client whether or not he actually did what he's charged with. That's because if the lawyer knows the client really did commit the crime, then he can't put the client on the stand and allow him to deny it under oath, because that would be subornation of perjury, and no lawyer in his right mind would do it. That's a double-edged sword, because most juries are also aware of it, which leads them to place more suspicion on a criminal defendant who doesn't want to waive his constitutional right against self incrimination by taking the witness stand in his own defense.

In this case, I now know that the insured is alive, and as far as I'm concerned, that finishes me on this case. There's no way I can continue with the insurance claim having this knowledge, because if I did, Myra and her gang would probably find so many crimes to charge me with that my indictment could be used as a textbook example for law students to prepare for a Bar examination with. She'd no doubt go for accessory after the fact to murder of some body on Catalina, conspiracy, fraud, theft, perjury, and too many felonies more to count. It would be like a D.A. feeding frenzy, and I wouldn't be surprised if National Geographic or the Animal Channel sent a camera crew to capture the bloody scene for posterity.

Now I understand why doc bought that boat and traveled to Catalina so often. When first hearing about who his wife was, I went to the bookstore and bought a couple of her books, but the author's picture on the dust jacket didn't look that much like nurse Judy. The picture was probably twenty years old, and women always try to get by with their old pictures. If they can't make themselves look younger in person, they might as well at least do it with an old picture. I don't blame her. Unless you're a world famous author making appearances with Oprah or on the Tonight Show, the readers never get a chance to see you in person, so what's the harm?

There was a very slight resemblance, but that's all. It looks like their plan was to have her appearance changed, wait until the time was right, then collect the insurance money and live happily ever after. And it was all going right on schedule until the dog screwed things up for them. What a confidence builder this is; my case was destroyed by a dog that's supposed to be on my team. All I have to do now is figure out how to get out of this mess. The Bar's rules of ethics prevent me from disclosing information that the client tells me, but doc never told me she is still alive to this day, so I'm not betraying any confidence by disclosing it.

Maybe there's another way out. Nurse Judy was never a client of mine, so if I turn this DNA info over to the authorities, they'll arrest her. No, that won't work, because it would put my own client in further jeopardy, and I can't do that either. The district attorney would reinstate the indictment and replace my name on it with Judy's.

I've got to think this thing out. Let's see: another possible solution is for me to just confront doc and tell him about the second DNA test, that we know Judy is really his wife, advise him in writing to drop the insurance claim, resign as his attorney and inform the insurance company that we're withdrawing from the matter. Then, if he really killed whoever is buried on Catalina Island, all he has to do is knock off Suzi and me, and there'll be no loose ends, no witnesses, and no problems. Hmmmn, that's another terrible idea. Maybe I should just leave everything for the kid to solve and hide in my stateroom under the covers until the dog comes in with a note that it's all over. Just as I'm making the decision that this last idea to hide under the covers is the best one yet, I'm brought back to reality by the phone ringing. My caller ID display shows Myra's private number. "Hello Myra, and before you even ask, the answer is yes. Whatever you want to arrest me for is okay. I'll even drive down to your office and turn myself in. I haven't got the energy to fight you any more." To my pleasant surprise, she informs me that I'm not going to be arrested today.

"I got a check from the insurance company for the fire damage to the boat, and I just called to thank you for executing the forms and sending them in, knowing that the money would go to me. You weren't legally bound to do it and I'd like to buy you dinner for that... and for other things." Wow. She really shocks me this time. Is she actually becoming a human being again? I thought that was against the rules of the District Attorney's office.

"I don't know what to say Myra, this is really a pleasant surprise, and the answer is yes. When and where?"

"If you're available, I'll meet you at the Mexican place we used to like. How's next Thursday at seven."

"You got it, kid, I'll see you there." This should be good. During dinner I'll have to remember to speak directly into the flowerpot. I wouldn't want to screw anything up for her or the four guys in a van parked down the street turning me into a recording star.

16

I once heard a popular black comedian named Chris Rock's say: "when a boss tells his secretary to go to bed with him or she's fired, that's sexual harassment. Anything else, is just trying to get laid." Several important people disagree with Chris, and fortunately nine of them are on the Supreme Court.

Another one is my new boat landlord, Stuart. Before living on his late uncle's Grand Banks and having the luxury of a built-in law library, I was doing my research at the offices of Alfred Nieman, a local attorney who's built quite a name for himself by specializing in workplace Sexual and Age Harassment, Discrimination, and Wrongful Termination law. Spending so many hours over there and overhearing his conversations with some of the hundreds of callers his office hears from each month, I've absorbed a lot of that law by osmosis.

I now have the luxury of being acquainted with two notable experts in those fields: Al and my friend Stuart, a non-lawyer who has discovered another way to exploit the law for his own profit. Being licensed to practice law in the State of California and the United States Supreme Court is only one of the two differences between Al and Stuart – the other being the fact that Al is a Harvard graduate and has spent more than twenty years honing his knowledge and experience, so that now he only accepts about one case a month out of the hundred or more calls he gets. Stuart, on the other hand, has been learning about his new 'specialty' for almost a month now – and he also accepts one case a month – the same amount of calls he gets.

Not being a licensed attorney, Stuart can't actually represent these 'clients,' but he can help them prove up their case so that a competent lawyer will at least have some ammunition to walk into court with.

Most of the calls Al gets are people complaining that their boss sexually harassed them. When Al starts to ask them specific questions, he almost always discovers that their alleged case is too weak to prosecute for several of the common reasons: the actions complained of really are not technically sexual harassment, or, the complainant has some private agenda or motive against the boss, or there's just no evidence to support the claim. And that's where Stuart comes in. When he meets a female (and most of the sexual harassment complainants are), he helps them get the 'goods' on the alleged perpetrator by using a 'wire' on the victim, to record and often photograph the accused in action. As consideration for his efforts, Stuart will get a hefty 'private investigator's' fee from any lawyer who successfully obtains a monetary reward for the client.

The State of California prohibits any unlicensed person from acting as an investigator for the general public, but if the assignment is done for an attorney, then it's okay. Stuart gets around this hurdle by having the lady call the attorney first and have him then authorize Stuart to 'look into the matter.' If the alleged facts actually turn into a case, Stuart gets paid an investigation fee. If there's no case, then his efforts go unrewarded. This means that he has a financial motive to succeed.

Actually, he's walking the fine line of falling into the category of being what's called a 'capper,' which is someone who collects money for referring people to an attorney. This type of practice can also get the attorney in trouble, because they're not allowed to share their fees with any unlicensed people. Most cappers avoid problems by having more than one attorney to work for, and I have a feeling that Stuart would like to recruit me as one of his 'specialists.' It's probably due to his knowing about my time spent at Al Nieman's office and picking up some of the finer points of law involved in those types of cases.

Logic tells me to pass on this lucrative offer of his; my ex-wife and her associates are busy enough as it is, and I'd rather not hand myself to them on a silver platter, as another case to prosecute. This is the right decision to make, but I still realize that a lot of what I have today is owed to Stuart. Settling his uncle's wrongful death got me this Grand Banks, and settling his asbestos non-injury got me the Hummer and a savings account, but I still feel that his new business is too much like 'bottom feeding,' until he tells me that Maggie, his latest 'client' is an employee at a local restaurant - one of the several owned by none other than the mysterious Robert Palmer.

Maggie works two afternoons each week as a bookkeeper, and weekend evenings as a waitress in the Mexican place Palmer owns directly across the street from the Chinese restaurant where the parking lot murder took place. Her sexual harassment case sounds weak, but my 'office manager' says it's okay for us to take Maggie on as a client as long as Stuart's investigative services are paid for on an hourly basis and with absolutely no connection to our ultimate success or failure in handling the case.

I look forward to interviewing Maggie, especially after my 'office' boss authorizes an open expense account to handle her alleged case. If everything works out as planned, her sexual harassment suit will be probably be replaced by one for wrongful termination, but it doesn't make any difference what the exact grounds are, as long as they open the door for us to do some civil discovery and depose the mysterious Mister Palmer.

At first I thought it was strange that approval was given for us to spend money on this case, but I figure that the kid must have some reason for wanting us to take this case, so I might as well do my best on it.

The big advantage that civil discovery has over criminal discovery is that in a civil case you can force the defendant to testify. He can 'take the fifth' in either a civil or criminal proceeding, but at least in the civil case you're allowed to call him to the witness stand and are guaranteed a crack at questioning him. If a defendant refuses to answer questions claiming a right against self-incrimination during a civil trial, that fact alone can usually sway a jury against him. It doesn't take a unanimous vote on a civil jury, so things like refusing to testify carry a lot of weight with them.

The basis of Maggie's sexual harassment complaint is a series of uninvited and unwelcome advances and sexual suggestions made by a guy named Vito Renzi, who is a manager of the car-parking valet service that services both of the restaurants near the Chinese place. This car-parking business is one of the companies that my Sacramento research shows as being owned by Mister Palmer. Maggie was also curious why the boss was authorizing her to make out several large checks to the valet company harasser; checks that were much more than the usual bimonthly checks she had been issuing to him over the past three years that she was employed there.

My plan is to have her complain to Palmer and question the wisdom of paying so much money to Renzi. These questions can be justified from any bookkeeper, in view of the fact that Renzi was getting paid far more than the entire car parking business was bringing in. If everything goes according to plan, she'll probably get fired and then I'll have my big chance to depose Palmer and subpoena his books; there might be some interesting things to be found there. More interesting however, are the visits that all those Culver City Police detectives are making almost on a daily basis now to the little princess' forward stateroom by.

It's finally my Thursday big-date night, and promptly at seven I'm sitting here at our reserved table in Pollo Meshuga, our favorite Mexican restaurant, while Myra and I were still together. The place is well known for its food, and the fact that they've got at least four large screen television sets hanging from the ceiling, strategically placed so that no matter where you're sitting or standing, you will have your dinner conversation distracted by one of the screens. Most of the time all the sets are playing a soccer game that's being broadcast in Spanish, but during the early dinner hours they usually tune to an

English speaking CNN channel for us few gringo customers.

Another reason we both like the place is because notwithstanding its not-quite-classy family type of décor, it uses what we consider the best margarita ingredients in the world, including Patron Añejo Tequila.

Myra arrives right on time, but it still seems like I was sitting and waiting for a while. That's probably because I've been here since six thirty, making sure not to be late for my free dinner. Since she's offered to pick up this check, I've already had two Margaritas. I need a little extra support. She looks as beautiful as ever, but in a sort of reserved way. Her formerly bright red hair is now a reserved dark brown, no doubt to not distract jurors; her formerly open blouse is now covered with a reserved business suit, no doubt to not distract me. I made sure to have her Patrón margarita waiting on the table. If she doesn't drink it, then I'll know for sure she's here on business and I'll make every effort to help her out by speaking directly into the flowerpot.

I might as well start with a compliment. "Hi, you look nice tonight. I like what you've done with your hair." That's a safe opening. You can't go wrong with a compliment unless you fail to make it sound sincere enough. God, she looked so much better with that wild red head of hair. It really used to drive me crazy and she knew it. She is a *true* redhead. I'm waiting to hear the tone of her voice when she talks to me. You can tell a lot by the tone of a woman's voice. The lower it is, the more trouble you're in. This time, it's in the medium range.

"Nice to see you Petey... and thanks for having my drink waiting." Good... she's drinking it, and there's no tape-recorder-in-a-briefcase on the table for me to worry about. Maybe this really is a social event. We were always pretty compatible, so maybe she'd like a little more of Petey's Petey. Now that Rita is probably history, I'd sure hate to just have Laverne as my only backup. It can't hurt to talk about something I know she's interested in.

"How's your Asian gang murder case going?"

"Not too bad, there've been some court delays during the jury selection process and the judge was out having some surgery for a while, but it's going along nicely now." Damn. They're still going ahead with that case. What's wrong with them?

"Still convinced you've got the right guys?"

"Well to be honest, at several times during the investigation I had some doubts, but Bill assured me that he'd come through with the final evidence for me, so I'm not worried." That clinches it. Her boss is setting her up to shoulder the full responsibility when this case of theirs goes down the tubes. I want to warn her to be careful, but I know I'm walking on eggshells here.

"You know, if this case goes into the toilet, it'll be you taking the fall, not Mister Bill Miller. He can write it off as the failing of an incompetent deputy trial attorney." That must have been a bad button for me to press. If she wasn't on her second drink, I'm sure the response would be much stronger.

"Can't you get off of it? Bill Miller is not that kind of person. He cares about my career and would never put me in a position like that." I think it best to drop the matter lest she have a change of heart when the check arrives, so I quickly switch the conversation to catching up on what some past mutual friends of ours are doing.

The strange thing about this dinner chat is that it's probably the longest conversation I've had with her since our third year of marriage. Thinking back, the best times we had together were when she was going to evening law school and we would spend most of our time together discussing the landmark cases she had to brief for class participation. We really had something in common then, a common ground we could share.

Most people think that the definition of 'intimacy' is having a 'sexual relationship,' but sex is only one part of it. It's sharing an interest, communicating, trust, and the freedom to say whatever's on your mind knowing that you'll get some support in return. Helping her study law started to get us closer to that, but never really got us all the way there. This evening's chitchat makes me think of our old conversations. Any verbal exchange between spouses that can go on for at least ten minutes without an argument starting is a good sign, almost as enjoyable as watching a long volley between professional tennis players.

To keep the conversation going I consider bringing up Stuart's adventures, but she never cared for him, so that topic is avoided. Several other topics are also being avoided and I get that old feeling like I'm walking on eggshells around her. If I say the wrong thing, she'll get mad again. This isn't fun anymore. Come to think of it, if we weren't discussing the law, it rarely was fun. I guess if you're not talking about something she's really into, you're just not a very interesting person. Maybe that's why she's so enamored with her boss and the job, because it's law, law, law, all day long. That reminds me of a line that William Shatner delivered in a *Saturday Nite Live* skit that featured him talking to a bunch of attendees at a Star Trek convention, all clad in Star Trek costumes - from crew members to Klingons. He looked down at them and said "people, get a life!" I think someone should say something like that to the people in her office.

At this point I'm already starting to sneak glances at the clock on the wall opposite where I'm sitting, hoping that this forced polite evening will end. I don't want to miss the eleven thirty P.M. Charlie Rose show on our local PBS station. He really knows how to ask questions. I'd like to see him cross-examine a witness in court.

After we've had another round of drinks or two and a couple of gourmet meals, the drinks are catching up on me so I excuse myself to make a pit stop. On the way to the men's room I notice that the local nine o'clock news is being broadcast, in English. With four screens in a relatively small restaurant, about the only time you can't watch one is when you're in a bathroom, but you can still hear it in there, and I did. The newsreader drones on. "Culver City Police have announced that they are zeroing in on a suspect for the parking lot murder that took place several months ago in Marina del Rey. This local department took over the investigation, so as not to cause a conflict between the Los Angeles Police Department and the local district attorney's office, currently finishing up jury selection on the same case, but with different defendants. We've never seen this happen before: another person being investigated for the same crime in which a trial with other defendants is taking place."

Almost breaking my zipper, I make a mad dash to finish up and get back to my table. Just as I exit the men's room, I see the newscaster wrapping up: "the police spokesman stated that most of their new information was provided to them by a private attorney who was formerly married to the deputy district attorney now prosecuting those other defendants in the downtown Los Angeles trial." When I get back to the table, Myra is gone, but our dinner check isn't, so it looks there really is 'no free lunch.' I can't help it. No matter how hard I try, everything I do winds up hurting her in some way.

I wonder what little girl could have been leaking information to the press. It looks like behind the scenes there were some people working for me that I didn't know about. Culver City Police had accountants going through Palmer's restaurant books, so it looks like he might also be a suspect soon. Another expected development is the phone call that I get from Stuart telling me that Maggie has been fired.

Her cases for sexual harassment and wrongful dismissal are temporarily being put on hold. She agrees that it would be best to wait until the criminal investigation ends. In the meantime, I have my other problem to worry about. After that disastrous dinner, Myra will probably do anything to get me back behind bars, so from this moment on I'd better act as if I was under a microscope, because I'm sure that the entire district attorney's staff, the LAPD, and the local press are watching my every move. And the moves they can't see might just get leaked to them anyway. At least one almost decent thing has happened: later this evening when I stop in at the Chinese restaurant to pick up a local throwaway magazine I see Maggie waiting on tables.

17

The television newscasters are having a field day with this new turn of events. Defense attorneys for the Asian gang members were successful in getting the trial continued until after the Culver City Police finish their investigation. District Attorney Bill Miller has suddenly become the *Invisible Man,* leaving poor Myra dangling in the wind, facing the news cameras and trying to explain away what is going on, and why two different police agencies are investigating the same case, with the focus of their interests going in different directions.

It was only a matter of time before Bill Miller finally would come out from under his rock. It only took him a few days to concoct some way to save his own face, so he scheduled a press conference. I see him on the early evening news while enjoying my guacamole at Pollo Meshuga, when he shows up on the TV screen. It looks like he's outside on the Criminal Court building steps and surrounded by alleged journalists, all shoving microphones into his face. After posing long enough for the still camera guys to get their shots, he starts his oratory. "This office has the highest regard for one of our finest trial deputy district attorneys, Mizzzz Myra Scot. It is therefore with deep regret that earlier today we have accepted her letter of resignation from our office. She has been under extreme stress for the past few months and wants to take some time off to consider pursuing other matters." Questions are being shouted out to him by the wolf pack of reporters.

"Mister Miller, is it true that she was fired for mishandling the Asian gang murder trial?"

"Mister district attorney, will the Asian gang trial continue soon?" It doesn't stop until Miller does exactly what I warned Myra he would do.

"This office is currently revisiting all of the preparation work that Mizz Scot did for this trial. If we find any inconsistencies, we will then re-think our trial strategy."

Damn, I'm sorry it had to happen this way, but it's just like I tried to warn her. He blames it all on her, and he just walks away. It hit the fan and not one piece landed on him. And the whole world, including Myra, believes that it was entirely my fault. I guess the police weren't about to admit that they're working with a pre-teen kid on a homicide case, so I get stuck with taking the credit.

The *RoadRunner* crushes the *Coyote* once again, without even trying. I wish there was some way I could explain that I never did anything to intentionally hurt her, but what's the use? She never believed me in the past, so why should she now? If she hadn't inherited so damned much money from her grand-father, I might actually feel sorry for her being out of work.

I may live to regret this, but an idea just came into my head that might solve all of my problems at the same time. If destroying Myra's career and doc's getting away with millions after killing his wife are the problems, why not invite Myra to help me give the doc enough rope to hang himself. That way her career can be restored, district attorney Miller will be shown to be the incompetent idiot he really is, and the doc gets nailed for whatever his crimes may be, including but not limited to the murder, conspiracy, fraud and poor choice in power boats.

A lot of ideas look good on paper, but the trick is to get people to go along with them. Myra and I differ in opinion most of the time, but there's one thing you can't take away from her: she's no dummy. Other than marrying me, she's done a good job of running her life. Her ambition gets in the way sometimes, but that's a normal error any human can make. My job now will be trying to gain her trust to join with me in the plan.

I call her at home. "Hi, it's me. Wait, please don't hang up, let me explain." Amazingly, she's very calm, probably under the influence of some Merlot.

"No Peter, I'm not hanging up. There's really not a helluva lot more you can do to me, so go ahead. What's the bullshit line de jour? Another burnt out boat to sell? How about some swampland near the Marina… I've always been interested in real estate." She's right about at least one thing; I've done so much to her already that things only have one way to go from here.

"Myra, I want you to know that when I took that sexual harassment case from Palmer's book-keeper, I never in a million years could have realized something like this would happen." Evidently, she knew nothing about Maggie's case. Miller, her idol, never told her how he got the information he had obtained. I could tell she was being kept in the dark.

"Sexual harassment, what are you talking about?"

The way to a male lawyer's heart is through his briefs. The way to a female lawyer's heart is through her curiosity. I explain to her that whatever the Culver City Police detectives found out and based

216

their case on came from statements my client made to me, overheard by the little Asian girl, who had already been doing some computer work for the Culver City cops.

After what seems like an hour of explaining, she finally starts to believe me. In all the years we were married she knew I was the ultimate screw-up, but she also realized that I never flat-out lied to her. Not once, unless you count those times she asked about looking fat in some dress. She even goes so far now as to admit that she believes that the boat burned without me knowing about it. This is it. I tell her my suspicions about the doc and ask her to join with me in getting his fraud exposed and maybe nail him for murder. To my surprise, she doesn't immediately turn me down. Instead, her concern is about our chances of success.

"That's a nice plan Pete, but me being on your dock would be like waving a cross in front of a vampire. Remember me? I'm the one who had your murdering doctor arrested and indicted last month."

"Yes, but when I explain how you were just following orders from your boss, he'll understand. And besides, if I can forgive you, then he should be able to."

"Aw, gee… I don't know about that. The 'just following orders' defense hasn't worked so well since the Nuremberg Trials…" I can't blame her for hesitating.

"Don't worry honey, I'll handle things with the doc. I'll tell him that I'm expanding my office staff and we want to go after his insurance company not only for the insurance policy amount, but for a huge punitive damage award on two separate grounds: first, after all the proper claim procedures were followed, they negotiated a settlement in bad faith. Second, they slandered doc by turning him in to your office. Both counts of the suit could total a multi-million dollar damage award that they'd surely like to settle without the publicity and going to court.

"We'll sign the doc up on only a twenty-five percent retainer. Being a doctor, he's cheap, so he'll jump at the bargain; they teach that at medical school. The lure of a multi-million dollar settlement and discount retainer amount will be too much for him to refuse. It wouldn't make any difference if I associated Osama bin Laden in on the case, he'd still jump at the bargain."

Silence. I go into my 'I'm not okay mode.' After the ten seconds that seems like an hour, she finally bites. "How do we spring the trap?" Good, now to reel her in.

"Simple. He's already convinced he's gotten away with it, so with an additional big bucks settlement as extra incentive, he'll open up like a sardine can, giving us all the info he'd normally never give the authorities in a million years."

"I know in my heart he's guilty Peter, but what finally convinced you?" This is the moment of truth. Either I trust her or I don't.

"Will you agree to work on this case with me or not, because anything I tell you has to stay strictly confidential. I don't want any of it to leak to your former boss."

"Oh, Peter, don't worry, I'm through with that louse Miller. I should have followed your advice about him a long time ago. Now let's hear what you've got." I have to trust her. There's no other choice, so I tell her about the second DNA sample that the kid sent in for analysis and how it established that who we thought was the nurse was actually the wife, who is not dead, but alive and in on the whole conspiracy. At first she balks, because if the wife is still alive, there's be no way to put him away for murder.

"Myra, you amaze me. I'm handing you a chance to get your career back on track, snooker your ex-boss and nail a bad guy, and all you can do is complain that it's not enough. Don't forget, there's an unknown victim in a grave on Catalina Island. Maybe you can get lucky with that case. If you don't want in on this, that's okay, I'll do it myself. Watch the evening news."

When I first started practicing criminal law, quite often a client would ask, "do we have a chance to win this case?" After a while I learned how to give the client an answer he could identify with. "You've got the question wrong, pal. It's not 'are we going to win,' it's 'are you going in or staying out?' It might take a little while, but soon it would sink into their thick heads, when explained a little more graphically. The clincher to my argument would probably be this question: "Listen Einstein, which would you rather do - plead guilty to a petty theft charge and do sixty days in county jail, or plead guilty to second degree murder and get out on probation?" That usually did the trick, and they'd finally catch on. It doesn't make a difference what the final outcome of the case is: it's the sentencing that counts, so it's not winning or losing, it's going in or staying out that makes the difference.

Myra must have realized the logic of my argument to her and she finally agrees, as long as she can show up Miller and put away a guy who he failed to convict.

"Okay, I'm in. What's next? Oh, and by the way Peter..."

"Yes my dear?"

"I don't satisfy the fantasies of lawyers any more."

"Neither do I, honey."

"Peter, you stopped doing that many years ago." I can always depend on her for a compliment.

We get together at her house and after mapping out some of our strategy, I call doc and make an appointment to meet with him and Rita on his boat.

The electricity in the air on doc's boat is intense. Rita and I look at each other like a lion tamer looks at his favorite big cat when he steps into the cage to start the circus show. There may be some mutual affection, but not enough nerve to get too close. I lay out the basic elements of the bad faith and slander cases to them, but they want to know why I want to go over the top with these new requests, including the one about exhuming his wife's body. I do my best to explain the strategy.

"Listen, there are a certain amount of people who still remember your being charged with your wife's murder years ago. Juries are usually populated with people who are old enough to remember things that happened ten years ago. And if you recall, the whole case was re-visited by the press during our recent indictment fiasco. If people didn't notice the two lines of news on the back page of the paper where our indictment was reported as having been quashed, they still think you're guilty of something. That means this case is more than just going in and proving up damages to a fair and impartial jury - it also mean proving that the murder case was bogus and that you're a completely innocent guy.

"You're the victim here, and we have to establish it, so that the judge, jury, courtroom spectators, reporters, and everyone watching the case on Court TV believe it. It's the only way we'll ever get serious money out of the jury. At one time or another, everyone has had a bad experience with an insurance company, and that includes the members of the jury. If we can convince them that you're really not a bad guy or someone who beat a murder charge on a technicality, then we might be able to give them a sub-conscious way of getting back at their own insurance companies. The other side knows this too, so if everything goes as planned, we'll probably get a generous settlement offer before the case gets to trial."

They look at each other and doc asks the sixty-four dollar question.

"Does Robin's body really have to be exhumed?" Oh boy, I was right. This must be his weak spot. He can't back out of allowing the exhumation, because that would almost amount to an admission of guilt. I've got him backed up against a wall, but I don't want him to feel cornered just yet.

"Yes doc, I'm afraid so, and just so you're not shocked with any surprises, I intend to have a camera crew shooting the whole thing. We want to get some sympathy out of the prospective jury pool, which is everyone watching the six o'clock news every night from now until the trial or the gag order, whichever comes first. And those viewers also include the judges and insurance company lawyers." After a couple of minutes of hand holding they both agree. I have carte blanche, and they will notify the alleged nurse Judy to be cooperative: not just politely cooperative, but one hundred and ten percent cooperative, because she'll be told that she's going to be cut in for a little taste of the damage award.

Now that we're all on the same page, I break the news to them about the identity of my new associate. Rita is not pleased by this announcement. "That horrible lady who had us arrested? Your ex-wife?"

"Yes, that's her, but she's seen the light and come over from the dark side to help us." They look at each other. "Please, let me handle this. I promise you that she agrees with me on this case, and having the former deputy district attorney who tried so hard to prosecute you now on your side can only help you. It may get the public to believe that your being prosecuted was wrong from the get-go. All that we both want is for you to get the justice you deserve." That last part is no lie. They finally agree to leave it in my hands and work with Myra.

First Myra joins the team, and then both the doc and Rita buy in. I love it when a plan comes together like this.

I call Jack Bibberman and tell him to get his video camera kit ready: we're going to Catalina Island. Myra insists that we fly over there. I know that her fear of seasickness is probably behind the suggestion, but it winds up being a good idea. Not only does it save us a lot of time, but any plane we hire can land at the airport on top of the island, which isn't too far from Nurse Judy's convalescent home and the burial grounds.

Also at Myra's suggestion, we bring with us a lady from the independent lab that did all the district attorney's DNA analyses. Her job is to get a sample from whoever is buried there in Robin Gault's grave, protect the legal chain of evidence custody, bring it back to the lab, and run every test on it known to mankind. She also took samples from doc and Rita before we left, so she'll have some fresh stuff for comparisons.

Doc and Rita decline to join us, which is just fine, because I want to avoid any awkwardness between them and their former persecutor. They agreed to work together, but I know in my heart that Myra still believes he is a murderer and doc believes she's on an unjust crusade, so the distance between them will work well for us.

Once on the island, our primary job is to document the exhumation and DNA extrac-tion. Behind the scenes, we want to get a look at the convalescent home's records to see who came in, when, who went out, when, and by what means. We're hoping to get a lead on who is buried in Robin Gault's grave.

I learned a good technique from Daniel Vincent, so on this trip I brought along a laptop computer and a portable scanning device. Those handy items worked well for his law practice and they will do just fine for mine. Any documents we find can be scanned into the computer and e-mailed back to Suzi at the office. No fuss, no waiting. The office will have them immediately and probably have a complete analysis and background check on everything and everyone involved before our plane returns to the Santa Monica Airport.

The plane we charter is a twin-engine Cessna Crusader, complete with leather interior, air conditioning, refreshment center, and other luxuries. It carries two crew and four passengers, with room left over for luggage, but not enough for an office manager and Saint Bernard. Other than me, our four-passenger list includes Myra, videographer Jack Bibberman, and the DNA technician, and we're all flying in first-class comfort. We don't care how much it costs, because part of the doc's retainer agreement includes my using his titanium American Express card to cover all expenses in getting the goods on the insurance company. Surprisingly, it isn't that much. The charter company sells $1/16^{th}$ timeshares, with monthly payments of less than two thousand dollars. By doing some Internet searching, our office manager found one of the participants who let us use it this week, so we got the trip for a really fair price, which is probably just a little bit more than we would have had to spend for all of us to come over on commercial flights… but on our own travel schedule.

If you've never flown to Catalina's mountaintop airport, make sure you're heart's in excellent condition before you try it. Approaching the landing strip, you're faced with a sheer vertical cliff. If for any reason there's a downdraft and the plane drops twenty feet or so, the plane doesn't go onto the runway, it slams into the face of the cliff. Fortunately, Myra and I are seated in the two seats that face to the rear of the plane, so we don't have a chance to see the death-defying airport approach that Jack and the DNA techie watch with eyes and mouths wide open. Surprisingly we make it. No crash, no airsickness, no problems of any type, until we all climb into the rented Volkswagen van that is hired to transport us to the convalescent home. It's a long winding road down the mountain, and our driver must have been trained as a Tijuana taxicab driver. By the time we get to nurse Judy's establishment, I'm ready to check in for an extended stay, but after remembering what happened to the unknown guest now buried in Robin Gault's grave, I change my mind.

The place isn't bad. It has a beautiful view of the California mainland, and on a clear day you can see the cloud of brown smog hanging over Los Angeles. You can also see down to Avalon Harbor, where boaters from all the Marinas in Southern California come to spend their weekends. The weather in this part of the country is ideal and perfect for all year boating, but there's just no place to go. People on the North East Coast only have about five good months to use their boats, but at least they've got some really nice destinations and ports to visit during their shortened season, plus the entire Intracoastal Waterway for a nice cruise up and down the whole eastern seaboard. All we've got here in our paradise is Catalina Island, so we try to make the best of it.

Down in Avalon Harbor, there are about 400 leased moorings, each privately painted with the name of the boat that has the right to tie up to it. When not being used by their lessees, the city of Avalon has the right to rent them out to visiting boaters on a first-come-first-serve basis for anywhere from twenty to eighty dollars per night, depending on the size boat that each mooring can accommodate. The moorings are leased to boaters by the city on a long-term basis for only a few hundred dollars a year, but having your name on one of those mooring cans means that you have first right to use it any time you want. All you have to do is call the harbormaster's office and tell them when you'll be here. I've heard rumors that to get an 'owner' to transfer the lease on a fifty-foot mooring can cost up to one hundred thousand dollars. I personally know of a nice fifty-foot Grand Banks that would really look good tied up to its own private 'can,' not far from the island's large round casino building where the island's only movie theater is located, along with the Catalina museum of its own history.

The phony Nurse Judy is extremely cooperative. She tells us we can see the books, copy what we want, snoop and pry to our hearts' content, and interview the other guests. Myra does the interviews. Some of the attendants do the digging, the DNA lab lady does all the tests, Jack Bibberman does the videography, while I concentrate on going through the records, scanning and e-mailing everything I can find back to the office by using a device that hooks the small laptop computer to my cell phone. Don Paige, our dock's Internet guru felt guilty about the misdelivered e-mails on his network, so he fixed us up with this device, hooked it up and showed me how to use it, all at no charge.

I have to hand it to Myra. She talked everyone at the home into giving up a DNA sample, including phony Nurse Judy and the attendants. I don't know what spiel she used, but whatever it was, it worked. Our lab tech's sample case is completely filled up by the time she's through. At over a thousand a test, I don't want to think of what it's going to cost the doc, but since he's sure that he'll recover his costs when we win the lawsuits, he doesn't seem to care about advancing the money for this dog-and-pony show.

I don't think we'll be finding anything remarkable while we're here, but I'm counting on our office to analyze the info we collect and spot whatever looks out of the ordinary or important to the case.

We finish up at the convalescent home, tip the two attendants generously for helping with the exhumation, thank Nurse Judy and depart the way we came, via VW van. All the way back to the airport and during the half-hour flight back to Santa Monica Airport, Myra says nothing. I can tell that something is going through her mind, there usually is, but this time I'm locked out of the loop. Just like during our marriage.

I'm glad it's a quiet trip, because I need some thinking time before reporting back to doc and Rita about how we dug up what was supposed to have been their mother's grave.

It'll be several weeks before DNA results from the island come back, so in the meantime I start looking into what can be done on Maggie's case. Criminal matters move a lot faster than civil ones do and I want to be able to nail Palmer for some of his money before it's all spent on a high priced criminal defense team. I call both Maggie and Stuart in for a briefing on Sexual Harassment law, and some possible strategy talk about her case.

When they arrive at the boat I think it best to give them a brief overview of the subject, so that we might all be on the same page while planning strategy. I hand Stuart a dollar bill. He's now considered on my staff as an investigator, so that in accordance with our state's evidence code, he's a person 'present to further the interest of the client,' and thereby doesn't endanger Maggie's right to assert the attorney-client privilege, should that be necessary at any time in the future.

In many previous cases the courts have held that the presence of a third person who was neither a party to the case nor associated with counsel has broken the expectation a client should have for enforcement of that privilege, but one dollar took care of that problem today. Suzi reminded me to get a receipt form Stuart.

It's now time to start my little lecture, and I can see why so many lawyers like to teach at local law schools for very little money: it's an ego trip.

"First of all, you should know that the federal law recognizes two different sets of legal grounds for claiming sexual harassment. The first is *quid pro quo*. Under that one, the plaintiff, that's you, Maggie, gets a demand from a person in authority, like a boss or supervisor, that you provide a sexual favor as condition for getting a job benefit, or keeping your job. So if someone where you worked tried to take advantage of you, that's one ground we might have to work with.

"The second category of the sexual harassment cases is called *hostile work environment*.

228

That's when some co-worker or supervisor of yours engages in any unwelcome and inappropriate sexually based behavior, and his hostile behavior creates an intimidating workplace environment that's so bad that it makes it difficult for you to do your job, and in some cases to even come to work at all.

"Does it have to be a federal case?"

"No Maggie, it doesn't. The plaintiff usually has a choice of whether to file in the federal court or locally in a state court." I'm glad to see her asking some questions, because it assures me that she's paying attention and getting involved.

"What's the difference?"

"Federal law sets minimum guidelines. Each state has the right to enact its own laws covering these situations, and many of the states go farther than the federal law does. This means that here in California we're much better off using the state court." She looks relieved. There's a remark people often make when they hear someone else trying to blow a situation out of proportion: "hey, don't make a federal case out of it." This has given proceedings in the federal courts a stigma of complication that they don't deserve. The Federal Rules of Procedure are so unfamiliar to the average attorneys that they try to avoid taking cases to the federal courts whenever possible.

"In most cases, the offender won't go so far as to create the quid pro quo situation. They won't actually threaten you with being fired or denied a promotion you might deserve, they'll just keep being abusive to you at work, often in a sexual way. Some examples of past cases included calling you offensive nicknames, writing obscenities on your work space or in your locker, directing degrading comments at you, propositioning you, touching you inappropriately anywhere on your body, covering the walls near your workspace with pornographic pictures and making rude references to it, and doing other cruel, stupid juvenile things that make it a horrible place for you to work.

"So first, we have to establish what conditions you were experiencing or subjected to. Second, we need some way to make your claim believable. That's done in a number of ways, like showing that you reported the behavior to your boss or told other people about it, finding others who have experienced the same things from the same people, finding someone who may have actually witnessed the bad behavior, stuff like that.

"Then we have to be able to put the blame on the company, by showing that they either knew or should have known that the bad behavior was taking place and did nothing to stop it. Once that's done, we go on to proving up fair damages, and the court looks at four main things to help out there: frequency of the events, severity of the conduct, whether or not it was physically threatening or humiliating, or mere offensive utterances, and lastly, if it unreasonably interfered with you doing your job properly.

"Got all that? Good. Now, keeping all those things in mind, let's talk about what happened to you, and maybe we can find a case somewhere in your facts." I see that Stuart is feverishly taking notes. When I finish my mini-lecture, I put his mind at ease by handing him the eleven pages I used as a reference. They were copied off of some university's website and they nicely sum up the subject. I know that Stuart wants to sound as lawyer-like as possible in the future. No doubt I'm inadvertently creating another Ricky Hansel. I'm beginning to feel like the Doctor Frankenstein of law clerks.

Maggie tells us that most of her problems were with just one guy, a fellow named Vito Renzi, the manager of Palmer's car parking valet service. He didn't bother her much in the daytime, because he only worked nights, but every evening she was waitressing at the restaurant, he would come in with customers' car keys and keep hitting on her to go out with him. She found him really offensive in the way he looked, talked, acted and smelled, and I sympathize with her, but so far I just don't see an actionable case here. One very prominent female local attorney would no doubt accuse me of being a sexist for not jumping on the bandwagon and starting some protest in front of the defendant's businesses, but I'd rather try to keep a cool head and let the facts do my marching for me.

Before going on to see if we can find anything to hang our hat on for her getting fired, I ask her how long the valet was bugging her. She says it started about six months ago and kept up right until that Tuesday. "What Tuesday was that, Maggie?"

"You know, the day that poor Chinese man got shot outside."

"You mean you saw the valet that afternoon? I thought he only worked nights."

"Yeah, but I was next door working on the books at the seafood place and he came running in the back door. I remember how strange it was, because when he saw me, he didn't even stop to ask me out or anything like that, so I knew that something else kinda heavy must've been on his mind."

I tell them I'll consider the facts and do some research, but the most amazing thing she told me was about the valet running in the back door that afternoon. If he wasn't working, what was he doing there that day? Maybe killing someone next door? This presents a new problem. Maggie told me about the guy running into the restaurant during our private meeting. She was telling it to me as her lawyer, so how can I then violate her expectation of privacy by reporting what I'd heard to any outside third person?

The solution appears out of nowhere. Suzi comes in to the saloon to say hello to Stuart. I take the opportunity to work it to our advantage. "Maggie, I wonder if you'd do me a favor. This has nothing to do with your case, but I wonder if you'd mind telling Suzi what you told me about that guy running into the restaurant the day of the murder. She's been following that case quite closely and would appreciate hearing any new bit of info that might concern it." Maggie complies by telling Suzi about the incident. I can't help but feel that the kid already knew. She hears everything that goes on in the boat, but at least this ruse succeeds in getting that little bit of information out of the privileged category and into the public domain.

The office has now started to work on a complaint to file on Maggie's behalf and a set of written interrogatories to serve on Palmer's restaurant company. The interrogs ask all the standard questions, like their policy for processing harassment complaints, names of employees who left their jobs in the past year and a lot other things.

18

The DNA results haven't come back on the island tests yet, but we did find out something about that convalescent home there: county records show title to the ten acres the home was built on is held by RGRET. Acronyms like that usually mean that it's a real estate trust. Our resident computer guru finally broke through the veils of secrecy and found out that RGRET is the Rita Gault Real Estate Trust. Hmmmn.

Bill Miller is seated at his desk going over budgets for the department's quarterly expenses when one of his flunkies comes into the office. "Chief, I've got some interesting news for you." Miller looks up, disturbed by the interruption. The flunky continues. "I got an invoice from the lab on the DNA tests we sent in for Gault's wife."

"So, what's interesting about that? It's old news. We've already used that."

"Yes chief, but this was from another test of the exact same DNA, sent in after our test was done."

"I'm still not interested. Sharp was probably re-testing the sample to firm up his civil case against the insurance company. If I remember correctly, we refused to release the original sample back to him, so he had to go get another one."

"That may be true, sir, and this test showed identical results as the one that we ran."

"Look young man, I'm a little busy right now. Is there some point you'd eventually like to get to?"

"Yes sir, the sample that the lab ran last week for attorney Sharp's office wasn't dried. It was done with fresh blood." Miller looks at him with a blank stare on his face. The stare lasts so long that the assistant starts to get uncomfortable. Miller finally stands up and gives him an order.

"Tell my secretary to call the grand jury foreman and let him know we're back in business. They finally made a mistake, and I'm going to shove it down their throats. And when it's over, Myra Scot Sharp and her conniving husband will be lucky if they can get a client who wants a simple name change. And if they do, hopefully it'll be a cellmate."

The local evening news features our famous district attorney Bill Miller making an announcement: "This office is pleased to announce the arrest of doctor Sherman Gault and his daughter Rita, as the result of indictments returned against both of them for attempted insurance fraud and investigation of murder. They submitted a false death certificate to their insurance company in a claim to collect life insurance on Robin Gault, the Doctor's wife, who is still alive. Furthermore, they may be involved in the murder of an innocent victim who we believe is buried in a grave that they wanted us to believe is Robin Gault's."

This was a turn of events that Myra wasn't planning on, and it was only by some stroke of fate that the DNA lab sent an invoice to the District Attorney's office. Nevertheless, she's involved now, and I convince her that we've got to see it through.

We draw straws and Myra gets stuck handling the arraignments. Bail is set at fifty thousand dollars each and with the help of Fradkin Bail Bonds, Doc and Rita are back on their boat later that same afternoon.

Rita gets notification that she is being suspended with pay by the airline, giving Stuart another case for him to 'look into.' The only good thing that comes from this unfortunate new experience is that the doc and Rita get a chance to see Myra go up against her former office, so they feel a little better about her working on the case. Myra doesn't feel too good about representing a guy she thinks is a murderer, but she's got the big picture in mind, hoping that he gets what he deserves in the end.

Doc has done some reading on the subject. "Peter, this was the second grand jury they convened for the exact same set of facts, returning an indictment for the same crime. Isn't that double jeopardy?"

"That's a really insightful question doc, but I'm sorry to tell you that it's not."

"Why not?"

"You read the papers, Doc. Even if you're not a political junkie you might remember what happened to a guy named Bill Clinton. In his case, special counsel Kenneth Starr convened a grand jury and tried to nail Clinton for lying under oath about his sexual relationship with Monica Lewinsky, and he was impeached by the House of Representatives. But, he was acquitted by the Senate, so he was allowed to serve out the rest of his term in office."

"I remember that, but what does it have to do with me?"

"Nothing at that point doc, but more than two years later, Starr's successor, special counsel Robert Ray convened another grand jury to determine whether or not Clinton lied about Lewinsky in his testimony in the Paula Jones case, and all the constitutional experts came up with the same conclusion, which applies to your case here: a grand jury doesn't convict or acquit people, it's the trial jury that handles that part of a criminal prosecution. The grand jury is looked upon as merely an investigative body, so that jeopardy doesn't attach when a grand jury is convened or an indictment is issued. That only happens when the case goes to trial and a jury is impaneled or the first witness is sworn in. So they can convene as many grand juries as they want and get as many indictments as they want, without it being barred by your Fifth Amendment protection from double jeopardy, because the first jeopardy never attaches at that stage of the investigation or proceeding."

They nod in understanding, but still don't know what basis of fact the grand jury could have been working with. "Peter, the DNA tests brought over from the island show that the body in the grave is my wife, so what the hell is the prosecution basing its case on?" I can't answer his question at this time, because I don't really know. The only way they could be going ahead with this much confidence is if they know about the second DNA test that Suzi had done on phony nurse Judy. A boat conference is in order.

Without an appointment, I knock on the forward stateroom door. The kid sticks her head out with an inquiring look. "Suzi, I hate to bother you, but did you happen to leak any information to your police friends about that DNA test on nurse Judy?" She nods in the negative. "Did you pay the bill that the lab sent us?" Another 'no' nod. Conference over. I call the lab to speak to their bookkeeping department, and found out what happened. Suzi told a little white lie to the lab when she sent in that sample, leading them to believe she was working with the district attorney's office. When they didn't receive payment for their invoice from Suzi, they sent a copy of the invoice to Miller's office. I'll bet Miller went ballistic with joy when he thought he finally had nailed us. Unfortunately, he was probably right.

Myra calls. "Peter, what the hell happened? How did Miller beat us to it? Did you or your office leak any information?" I tell her about the invoice and the telephone call to the lab.

"Listen, all this means is that if the doc is guilty, Miller beat you to the punch."

"Yeah, that's easy for you to say, but I've already appeared as his attorney of record. I'm going to have to try this losing case against Miller, and I'll be ruined again."

"Will you please relax? The DNA tests aren't back from our island trip yet. Maybe they'll reveal something we can use." She isn't impressed with my optimism. A dog-mail tells me that the DNA tests conducted on Catalina Island just came back, and they contain the truth about the entire matter. Suzi's message tells me that she now knows who the real Robin Gault is, who is guilty or innocent of all the crimes, and who is buried in that grave on Catalina Island.

19

The newspaper and television vultures are already congregating at the locked gate that leads down to our dock. From there down is private property and we have a guard posted to inform them that no trespassing will be allowed. I decide to use their presence to our advantage. Jack Bibberman and I walk up to the gate, go through it and try to reach my Hummer. The press mobs us and I stop them cold with "Ladies and Gentlemen, I'm now on my way to the district attorney's office, and we intend to be driving slow enough for you all to have a chance to call your offices and prepare for my press conference. I'll be making a statement on the steps outside District Attorney Bill Miller's office building." We have already made a call to his office and know that he will be in when I arrive."

The trip to his office looks like a celebrity's funeral procession My yellow Hummer is in the lead, with news vans following and a news helicopter overhead, no doubt broadcasting a block-by-block description of the trip. Riding in the back seat of the Hummer, I feel like O.J. Simpson during his famous slow-speed freeway chase.

When we reach the civic center office building, Jack drops me off and I strike a pose on the outdoor steps. The news people crowd around like sharks in a feeding frenzy, microphones and cameras ready. I hold up my new cell phone with the 'speaker' function on as I dial Miller's office. "I'm now dialing district attorney Bill Miller's office to let him know that I have right here in my briefcase, positive proof that the Gaults are not guilty of any crime." The phone rings and microphones are held up close to it. With the speakerphone function turned on, everyone outside with us can hear the conversation.

"District attorney's office."

"Hello, this is attorney Peter Sharp. I'm downstairs on the steps outside your office and I would like to come up and see Mister Miller, to give him conclusive evidence that will immediately clear my clients, Doctor Sherman Gault and his daughter Rita. Please tell Mister Miller that I am on a speakerphone and the public is waiting for his response." There's a murmur in the crowd as we wait a minute until Miller gets on the phone.

"Hello Sharp, I know what you're doing. We've got the television on in our office and it's all being taped."

"Good, then you won't mind if I come up and present you with some evidence."

"Yes, I would mind. You are persona non grata in this office. You've already had your one bite at the apple when you hoodwinked us into dropping the charges against you and your clients last time. Fool me once, shame on you. But fool me twice, shame on me. No, you cannot come up to this office. We are not interested in anything you have to say and are still investigating your involvement in the conspiracy." He hangs up and I make sure that their microphones pick up the dial tone that I'm left with. Now it's my turn again, so I turn to the cameras.

"That's it ladies and gentlemen, now you all know that we can clear our clients right now with this evidence [holding up my briefcase] but the district attorney isn't interested in the truth, he's only interested in railroading innocent people. That's the type of person who you've elected to office. After my clients have been cleared, keep this in mind, because the next election for District Attorney is rapidly approaching"

Right on cue, Jack pulls up with the Hummer and I get away without disclosing what our positive proof is. I only tell the press that we'd rather try the case in court than on the courthouse steps.

The doc's case has been set for trial and we're getting ready for it. Now that the Island's DNA results are back and we know that the doc didn't kill anyone, Myra's only option now is the destruction of District Attorney Bill Miller. She knows that the doctor won't be going to jail, so all that's left for her is revenge against her former boss, so the decision is made to let Myra take the case to trial. If everything goes according to plan, it will be a very short one. I rehearse her on the opening statement that she should treat with as much care as a President's State of the Union speech. She will memorize it and recite it word for word, so it coincides exactly with the advance copies that will be handed out to the press on the day of trial.

Miller blows a gasket when he hears that Myra will be handling the Gaults' defense. He files a motion with the court alleging that because she had recently been a deputy district attorney, her working for the defense on the same defendant who she had formerly tried to prosecute constitutes a conflict of interest that prevents her from handling the trial. As planned, Myra argues that this is a completely different case, charging a different crime. I've already done my grandstanding. My presence at the motion will only infuriate the prosecution, so we decide I should wait on the boat for everyone to return.

As expected, Myra wins the motion, and she'll be allowed to take the case to trial. While all this is going on, Maggie's complaint for sexual harassment is filed and served on Palmer at his penthouse in the Marina City Club. As soon as his lawyers file their answer, they get served with our set of interrogatories, and a week or so later their answers come in. Answering the written questions that are used during pre-trial discovery is an art form, because the answers must be truthful, but be as short as possible and provide little or no information that can help the other side. The trick is to hide your most important questions in what look like harmless ones, so most of the questions looked like we were playing softball: corporate info, dates of incorporation, statistics, company payroll info, and stuff like that.

Because none of the questions looked damaging, they were all answered to our satisfaction. This was turned over to our office staff, which pay great attention to the one question we asked that was answered with the information we needed to make the case. Jack Bibberman is given his assignments and off he goes.

20

Kate worked for Palmer in the seafood restaurant as a hostess, handling reservations and seating customers. Her only other job was fending off advances from Vito Renzi, manager of the car-parking valet service. He came into the restaurant to deliver car keys to late diners and get an occasional coffee, and every time he passed by Kate he managed to grope her as she stood behind the reservation counter. Kate complained several times to Palmer, and at first it looked like she'd be an excellent witness to establish a pattern of abuse in the restaurant, but upon further questioning Jack found out that Kate not only lived with Vito for several months, but also stayed over at Palmer's penthouse on many occasions. That raises the interesting question of whether or not a female who previously had consented to sexual advances can subsequently complain of them as harassment when they are neither consented to nor invited. A similar type of question is raised in some criminal cases when a wife accuses her husband of raping her during the marriage.

Instead of creating new cases for the Appellate Courts to consider, we advise Jack to go on to the next potential witness on the list that we subpoenaed from the restaurant's payroll service. All persons on the list who hadn't been paid in more than thirty days were assumed to be no longer working there, and therefore fair game for us to go after for 'pattern' evidence of an existing hostile work environment.

While Jack is getting witnesses lined up, I work with Myra, preparing her opening statement on the doc's case. She finally agrees to let me do most of the writing, as long as she's the one who gets to stand up and deliver it to the court and jury, humiliate Miller, and get all the press coverage.

In the great majority of criminal cases, time is the defense's ally. The longer a case gets stretched out, the more chance there is for witnesses to disappear or forget what happened. Quite often victims may lose interest in a case because of the frustration of numerous continuances and delays. In the doc's case, we want it over as soon as possible. The sooner the criminal matters are forever put to bed, the sooner the insurance money will be forthcoming, and the punitive awards, and the legal fees. No time is waived, so the district attorney is forced to follow California law and bring the defendants to trial within the statutory number of days. They usually expect defendants who are out on bail to 'waive' time, but there is no need for that here, because Myra wants to get in there and destroy Miller as soon as possible.

Our witness list is short and they are only expected to be in court for show, so the prosecution will realize that they are available to testify, if necessary. The list includes Nurse Judy, the two attendants who helped dig up Mrs. Gault's grave over on Catalina Island, Jack Bibberman, our cameraman, and the lab tech who took all the DNA samples. We have several confirmed copies of the required documentation and additional copies can be obtained from the nearby Hall of Records.

As a formality, all of our witnesses are served with the proper legal papers requiring them to appear at trial. Our opening statement is finished and almost committed to memory by Myra. I work with her every evening as she rehearses in front of our mock jury consisting of Suzi, Doc, Rita, Stuart, Jack, the dog and me. The cat usually sleeps through the rehearsals. It's going so well that one of our jurors can't stop drooling for her. After a while she really has it down pat.

We're ready to go to court. Extra copies of our opening statement are printed up for the press and packaged in envelopes, to be handed out on the courthouse steps the morning of the trial. This is the first time I've ever heard of a trial lawyer's opening statement being given to the press like this, and it has created media frenzy. All you have to do is wave something in the air that they can't reach and they go crazy jumping for it.

Calls are coming in every day from the high-powered journalists, begging for an advance peek. All they get is a promise that an interview can be arranged after the trial. Larry King isn't too happy with our answer, but he has no other choice. The National Enquirer's phone calls aren't accepted at all, because even if all you say is "hello" to them, they make up their own stuff and pretend like you said it. We avoid any contact with the press and instead decide to let Miller be the one making statements that he will have to eat.

As the trial date approaches, once again we're forced to put extra security on the gate leading down to the boats. Some so-called journalists even try to get to us by boat, but we have that covered too. The

Marina gave us permission to put up a temporary rope line across, between the rows of boats, so that no one can approach us by water. All the other boaters are being tremendously cooperative. It's a small boating community, and we all stick together. There's also no way that those vultures can pull up to the end tie and get off their little boats, because George C.'s boat completely covers that entire dock area, leaving no room for anyone or anything else. I start telling myself that George is helping us out on the case by keeping his boat there.

All of our efforts seem to be working. The news business is run like any other commercial enterprise. When the bean counters see that all their efforts are just wasting time and money, they smarten up and call off their dogs. A few independent paparazzi still hang around with their telephoto lenses, but after the sun goes down, every once in a while we shine the boat's spotlight towards the parking lot for their night-vision viewing pleasure.

The day of the trial we hire a huge stretched limo. The world loves a good show, and we intend to give them one. Our driver picks up the witnesses first and then comes to the Marina for Doc, Myra, Jack, Rita and me. Suzi is in her stateroom pouting because she isn't allowed to bring the dog with her to court. She decides to stay on the boat. We finally convince her that she'll actually get a better view by staying behind and watching Court TV.

It was no problem getting Miller to stipulate to letting the cameras in there. He's a big a ham, and the judge appears to be one too. Ever since the O.J. Simpson trial, judges have been aching for the chance to get famous. It helps their image when they decide to run for political office. Without a high-profile case being put on television, a judge can toil away for years in anonymity.

The judge is a white male. No need for them to pick and choose for this case. On high-profile cases like this, the judge might be selected for political correctness. You'll rarely see a black judge if the defendant is black, or a female judge if it's a rape case. That's why they chose an Asian non-athletic judge for the O.J. trial. The defendant was a black athlete, the victims were white and the lawyers were Jewish. What choice did they have other than that barely competent Asian who obviously hadn't the slightest idea how to control a courtroom?

It's a good thing the limo is almost thirty feet long, because there are plenty of us. All the way downtown Myra rehearses her opening statement, receiving our ovation when it's done, just as we pull up at the courthouse.

Jack has the press copies of Myra's opening statement, but we don't want them handed out before she gives it, so he keeps them in the limo, with instructions not to hand them out until he receives my call on his cell phone. The news people also know what the drill will be, so they just sit near the limo and wait. It might be an hour, or it might be several days. Everything depends on what happens up in the courtroom.

They mob us for statements, but all we do is point to the limo and remind them that copies of our opening statement will be available once it's being given in court.

There are other questions concerning our trial strategy, and to my surprise, Myra stops them cold with a statement: "We don't anticipate a trial in this matter. Our opening statement should convince the court and Mister Miller that a tremendous miscarriage of justice has taken place by the bringing of this case to trial. Mister Miller was offered evidence to that effect right on these very steps. Many of you were here that day covering Peter Sharp and saw how he was rejected by Mister Miller's office. Well, Miller can't stop the truth from coming out today."

I'm proud of her. She really nailed it. Along with her opening statement, she must have been secretly been rehearsing that announcement to the press. No matter. She did just fine.

The rest of the cast of characters is complete when Miller strides into the courtroom with his entourage. The light isn't that great in here because Court TV hasn't yet turned on those thousands of watts, but from where I sit, it looks like Miller is wearing makeup. Vanity roars its ugly head.

Miller's suit looked like they sewed it on him while he stood there. I haven't seen clothing fit like that since watching a concert at the Greek Theater in Los Angeles. It was Nat King Cole's final performance there and I was invited to watch the show from the band pit, courtesy of a good friend of mine who was playing in the orchestra. Being all the way on the right side of the pit next to the tympani, I had a good view of the left wings. Just before it came time for him to appear on stage, I saw Mister Cole coming from the direction of the dressing rooms. He looked great, but he wasn't wearing any pants! My mouth dropped open, but my friend told me to relax, because it was all under control. As Cole approached the stage, two assistants were waiting there with his freshly pressed pants. They helped him on with them while the announcer was going through his intro; he stepped into the pants, closed the fly and belt, and the assistants used a portable steamer on his outfit, to remove any wrinkle that would have the audacity to exist there! He was the neatest, greatest looking performer I've ever seen, and Miller almost comes close. I don't know how much that tailor-made suit he's wearing costs, but I'm sure it's not much less than Nat King Cole paid for that he wore that night.

Big courtrooms are saved for the big cases. Nobody likes to antagonize members of the press, so the reporters and sketch artists fill up most of the front row seats not being used by relatives of the victims or defendants. On the really big cases, remaining seats are usually given out on a lottery basis. This case isn't in the lottery category, but the tricks played by both sides in manipulating the media make it a big draw anyway.

Miller knows that his re-election may depend on the successful prosecution of this case, so he's decided to try it himself, instead of giving it to someone actually competent. We've both already stipulated to having the case heard without a jury. Judge Ronald Axelrod has a good reputation for fairness, so both sides feel good about having the case heard without a jury and we're all happy to save the time. Miller doesn't care that there's no jury present, because now he can prance and perform only for the television cameras, which will carry his image to a bigger crowd of potential voters than just twelve in a jury box and some alternates. He works the room like a celebrity in a nightclub, table-hopping from one reporter to the other.

Just like a Broadway show, a hush falls over the crowd when everyone hears the low double-buzz on the clerk's desk, signaling that the judge is going to take the bench. Court TV switches on the bright lights, little red lights start to blink on the front of each camera, and the uniformed bailiff addresses everyone in the courtroom.

"Remain seated and come to order. This Department of the Los Angeles Superior Court is now in session, the Honorable Ronald B. Axelrod presiding." Like a choreographed performance, the judge enters the courtroom through his private back door, just as the bailiff is saying his name. I always pictured judges and bailiffs rehearsing this dance routine in an empty courtroom when no one else is around. All that seems to be missing is an off-stage Las Vegas-style announcer shouting into a microphone with a drum roll in the background "Ladies and Gentlemen, the Superior Court of California proudly presents..."

No matter how many trials you take part in, those first few minutes when the case is called and each lawyer has to stand up, state his or her name and representation for the record and announce "Ready for the Defendant, your honor," it's always a rush. Fifteen minutes later when you're in the midst of arguing with opposing counsel or trying to get your objection sustained, you wouldn't notice it if the building was on fire, but those first few minutes are still always exciting.

Miller's opening statement is good. Most of what he wanted to say was blocked by our pre-trial motions that prevent him from using any facts about the doc's past trial for murder or previous indictment and arrest for insurance fraud. Nevertheless, he does it by the numbers, mentioning each piece of evidence he intends to introduce, to prove up each element of the crime charged in the current indictments.

This is the first time I've ever seen him perform where Court TV was broadcasting live, and he looks maahvalous. And, like a generous pro, he even gives the judge a chance to react for the camera, hopefully forming a bond between them as acting partners. His finale includes a promise to prove that not only is the defendant's wife not dead, but she is sitting in the courtroom, and he will call her to the stand, to prove beyond any reasonable doubt that the defendant is guilty of conspiracy to defraud the insurance company. I estimate no less than six cases of severe whiplash in the courtroom after that announcement as heads of the press spin around, trying to figure out where the reincarnated doctor's is seated.

By the time Miller finishes, he almost has me sold. If not for the fact that I know for sure that his case is going directly into the toilet in the next fifteen minutes, he would be assured of my vote next time he runs. Miller sits down and there is complete silence in the courtroom. You can hear the feverish note writing and sketch drawing being done by the press. Miller sits at the counsel table looking smug, no doubt feeling he has intimidated Myra into a state of fear. He glances over towards her with one of those 'you're in the big leagues now, kiddo' looks. Myra just sits there, ignoring his glance. She decides to let everyone wait while her silence builds up the tension. Finally, the judge becomes anxious. "Miss Scot, would you like to make an opening statement?" Myra slowly stands. She carries no note pad or notes. She's going to do this like we rehearsed it, from memory. I can hear the shuffle as everyone in the room starts to move to the edge of their seats.

"Yes, Your Honor, we would like to make an opening statement, and hopefully it will also be a closing statement, because when we have finished, we believe that you will have no other choice but to dismiss this case." This drives the press into a frenzy. I think I hear some pencils break. The judge bangs his gavel down with the usual warning that if the court doesn't come to order, he'll have the bailiffs clear it of all persons other than the litigants. I know in my heart he'll never do that, because no performer likes to clear a room before their act starts.

During our strategy conferences we discussed timing, because like any trapeze act, it is crucial. In a case that goes to trial with a jury, jeopardy attaches when the jury is sworn in. This case doesn't have a jury, so jeopardy won't attach until Miller's first witness is called to the stand and gets sworn in. If we give our entire presentation before that first witness was called, then the clients will be in a possible position of being re-tried, without the protection of the double-jeopardy rule. After a long and serious deliberation, it was unanimous between us all. Myra would do her opening statement immediately after Miller's. Not all attorneys make that choice, often reserving the right to make it at the beginning of their defense presentation, after the prosecution has rested its case.

Myra walks over to the lectern between the counsel tables. Forget what you've seen on television. There's no prancing around in front of those tables. The area between the counsel tables and the judge's bench is called the 'well,' and it's sacred territory in a courtroom. The only time you're allowed to go in front of those benches and set foot in the well is with the court's permission. That's why in a real case you'll hear lawyers ask the judge "sidebar, your honor?" or "may we approach, your honor?" or "permission to approach the witness?" Maybe Perry Mason or Matlock can get away with performing in the well or leaning his arm on the rail directly in front of the witness box, but try it in real life and you may be sharing a cell with your client later that afternoon.

As soon as Myra puts her hands on the lectern and clears her throat, I reach under some files that are piled up on the counsel table and press the speed-dial number on my cell phone that's programmed to call Jack in the limo parked outside. The caller ID on his phone displays my number. I can't talk on the phone now, but Jack knows that this is his signal to pass out copies of Myra's opening statement to the press. I wish I could be near a window to see what that scene looks like. Myra starts.

"Your Honor, if it please the court, we have laid out here on this display table several exhibits we intend to introduce into evidence. The prosecution has received copies of every item. It is their failure to analyze them properly that we will be concentrating on." Miller glances at his assistant with one of those smug 'yeah, fat chance' looks. Myra continues

"Defense Exhibit A is an affidavit executed by a person on our witness list, a lab technician employed as a DNA sample specialist with the D. Riddle Technical Company in Van Nuys, California. We would ask the court to take Judicial Notice of the fact that on at least four separate occasions during the past twelve months, Mister Miller's office has presented this person as an expert witness on the matter of DNA sample-taking and analysis. In each case, the court has accepted her credentials and she has been qualified as an expert witness. Each of those case names and numbers are included in the affidavit. When called to the stand, this witness will testify to the fact that she personally took DNA samples from the defendant's deceased wife, her attending nurse, the defendant, and the defendant's daughter. Furthermore, the witness will establish that the chain of custody of the samples was not broken. She personally delivered all samples to the laboratory, where she conducted the tests. Her initials appear on all test sample packaging.

"Next is Defense Exhibit B, a videotape of the exhumation of the defendant's wife. The videographer of said event is present in court, and on our witness list, and is prepared to testify as to the authenticity of the videotape, which when played on the set we have had brought into the courtroom will document the complete exhumation of the defendant's wife, and also the taking of a DNA sample from the remains by our expert witness, who as previously mentioned is also present in court." Just as rehearsed, she gracefully moves down the table pointing at each exhibit as it is being described to the judge.

"Defense Exhibit C is an affidavit of our expert DNA witness explaining the results of lab tests run on the aforementioned DNA samples, and Defense Exhibit D is a set of photographs showing comparisons of the samples that conclusively support every statement made in the witness' Affidavit."

Although it's not usually done during your opponent's opening statement, Miller stands up and objects. "Your honor, the mere fact that the defense has pieces of paper marked as exhibits doesn't really prove anything. Everyone's got exhibits. Having Affidavits does not an opening statement make." It looks like the judge wants to give Myra the benefit of the doubt, but he's getting a little impatient.

"Counsel, I'm inclined to agree with the prosecution. You've obviously got a nice display laid out there on the table, but sooner or later in your opening statement you've got to tell us what they will be showing. That's what an opening statement is you know, an opportunity to lay out your entire case by showing what you intend to prove, not just the fact that you've got exhibits."

This is what we wanted. Not only will she now stick her sword in with a 'thrust ho,' it will be done at the specific request of the stickee.

"Very well, your honor, we were just about to do exactly that, before being so rudely interrupted by Mister Miller. By using the previously mentioned Defense Exhibits A, B, C and D, we will finish our documentary evidence with Defense Exhibit E, and these exhibits, and the testimony of our witnesses, will prove the following three irrefutable facts: One, that the person buried in what we contend is the Defendant's wife's grave on Catalina Island is in fact the defendant's wife. Two, that the person who the district attorney mistakenly believes to be the defendant's wife and in this courtroom today is in fact his sister-in-law, the fraternal sister of the defendant's deceased wife, as shown by Defense Exhibit F, which is a copy of their birth certificates. And Thirdly, that the prosecution has absolutely no case at all against the defendant, all due to its failure to properly analyze the results which were provided in advance of trial. They were so intent on convicting this innocent doctor because their ineptitude prevented them from wrongly convicting him twice before, and we hope that by the court's dismissal of this case, the district attorney's personal vendetta against this doctor, the victim of Mister Miller's misdirected vengeance, will forever be brought to an end. Thank you, your honor."

Myra sits down and I swear I hear some muffled applause from the press in the gallery jumping up to run out to the hall, as they dial out on their cell phones. Several classic old black and white courtroom drama movies showed a bunch of character types wearing their vests in the courthouse pressroom. They would all have cigarettes in their mouths, making wisecracks and using their two-part dial telephones, yelling into the round, separate microphone part of the phone, "hold the presses!" Unfortunately, that doesn't happen any more. Now the reporters just go outside into the hallway and call their story in to a re-write person who has probably been watching the scene on Court TV and has most of the story written already. The lucky ones go downstairs to the waiting news vans and broadcast their stories directly to the television stations via those satellite dishes elevated up over each van on a satellite dish tower.

As the seats empty, the judge keeps banging his gavel, calling for order in the court. There is no need for him to threaten clearing the court, because Myra just did it for him. When she sits down, every reporter has already jumped up and run out. The judge calls for a conference with both counsel in chambers and asks his bailiff to bring all the exhibits in there. I have a feeling the case will end in there, because the judge signals to the court reporter that she should also join them in chambers.

I take this opportunity to call Jack and tell him what's going on. The reporters ran out so fast, they missed the judge calling for the chambers conference, and it was definitely a newsworthy item for them to mention in their stories.

During the twenty minutes of the chambers conference, the press has completely acquitted the defendants. When the conference is over, Miller uses the chambers hallway and takes the building's back elevator up to his office. When Myra comes back in, she has a strange look on her face, displaying a pained expression of success. She goes to doc first.

"Congratulations, doctor Gault, you've won. The case has been dismissed and you'll probably never hear from Mister Miller again." The Doctor and Rita shake our hands and everyone hugs. That is, everyone except Myra and I. She waits until Doc, Rita, and the witnesses all head for the exit, telling us that they'll be waiting in the limo. "Peter, I won't be riding back with you all of you in the limo."

"What's wrong? Don't you want to celebrate with us?"

"No, it's not that at all. It's because the judge did something in chambers that's going to make us part company for a while, professionally, I mean." I'm completely puzzled by this.

"What's going on, did he propose to you in there?"

"Not exactly, Pete. It seems that while we were conducting our brilliant performance here today, the police made an arrest in the Chinese restaurant owner's parking lot murder. They brought Vito Renzi in and charged him with the murder. I believe he's one of your potential defendant's in Maggie's sexual harassment suit."

This is certainly interesting news, but I still don't see why it would make Myra not want to ride back to the Marina in the limo with us and join our celebration, until she gives me the latest news: "Vito Renzi's case has been assigned to judge Axelrod, and because he was so impressed by my performance and handling of the district attorney, he asked me to stay behind after Miller left chambers. He then made me Court-appointed counsel, to defend Renzi on the murder charge... for killing Suzi's uncle."

21

I feel bad that Stuart couldn't join us in the limo, but even with his recent success at losing weight, there just wasn't enough room. He's already heard the news about our victory, and by the time we get back to the Marina, there he is on the boat, having a heated discussion with Suzi. He's another person she talks to, instead of me.

She is definitely not amused by Stuart's pointing out that while her best friend is a Saint Bernard, the people in her homeland are eating Saint Bernard meat. She admits to knowing about the Chinese practice, which infuriates the Swiss. The breed was named after Saint Bernard de Menthon, who founded his famous 'Hospice,' 8,000 feet up in the Swiss Alps back in 980 A.D. Although they were originally brought to the Hospice to serve as watchdogs, monks soon discovered that the breed was a great rescue animal, allegedly able to smell a human being up to two miles away, or buried under as much as ten feet of snow. They're also supposed to be able to predict an avalanche up to twenty minutes before it occurs. I don't know what that last talent is good for, unless they can talk too. I guess if you're in the Alps, and all of a sudden the dog takes off, it might be a good idea to follow it.

Suzi's dog is really a big one. A full-grown male of the species can weigh as much as two hundred pounds, and this one is probably very close to the limit. The most famous of all Saint Bernards was only half the size, weighing in at about one hundred pounds. "Barry," who lived for fourteen years back in the early 1800's, was one of the original compact, shorthaired types, born a good thirty years before the breed was crossed with the Newfoundland, creating today's longhaired variety. Over a period of twelve years, Barry was credited with saving forty people from death in the Saint Bernard Pass in Switzerland, including a half-frozen child who rode back into town on the dog's back.

Stuart was surprised to learn that Suzi is part of a volunteer organization that is trying to lobby the Chinese government to stop its practice of eating Saint Bernard meat. In response to their government's questioning what was wrong with eating that dog's meat, Suzi's organization suggested that the Swiss people inform the Chinese government that Switzerland is designating the Panda as their national food. Maybe that will help the Chinese to see the light.

The dog acts happy to see us all arrive at the boat. He couldn't have been too pleased with the subject matter of the conversation going on before we arrived. Stuart is also happy, because Maggie's tormenter is now behind bars, and with his credibility seriously damaged, it should be easier to prove up Maggie's case against Palmer's organization.

With the doc's criminal case now out of the way, I intend to give one hundred percent of my efforts to Maggie's case, and going after doc's insurance company. I've known lawyers who have hundreds of cases in their file cabinets. Even with a big staff to help out, how can a client really expect any degree of personal attention from a lawyer with that many cases going on? I guess I'm just old-fashioned, which is probably why I don't own my own large law building like so many of those other guys do.

When it gets to the point where you don't recognize the client's name or what the case is about when they call, then you're just too big for your britches. I suggest that whenever a client calls an attorney, they should time the minutes they're kept on hold. If it's more than three, it means the attorney forgot who they were and had to look at the file to re-familiarize himself with their case.

Having decided to concentrate all my efforts on just those two matters, I try to explain to Stuart why it will be impossible at this time for me to help him on his newest cause. He wants to bring a class action lawsuit against the fast food market, his contention being that like the tobacco industry, the fast food manufacturers knew the dangers of using their product as specified: the high fat, high calorie, high sugar, low nutritional value has damaged more people than cigarettes. Stuart quotes studies of wartime autopsies on servicemen, showing early signs of heart damage, even at their young ages, due mostly to poor nutrition and a diet of fast food. In further support of his contention he talks about the deaths of two people from heart disease who obviously didn't think that eating fat was dangerous to one's health: Doctor Atkins and the CEO of McDonald's.

He also cites the Saturday morning children's television shows with commercial ads featuring fast foods, violent toys and games. "Take a look at those frosted cereal boxes. All that junk food features cartoon characters, like the cigarette people used Joe Camel." He's obviously emotional about the matter and I personally agree with him only up to a certain extent, and that extent is the filing of a lawsuit. I've seen some of those commercials, and at times I would actually wince watching them try to convince young kids who don't know any better to eat that crap. You never see a vegetable commercial on Saturday morning, and we've even had past presidents who bragged how they either ate jellybeans or avoided eating broccoli.

A recent physical exam showed that my cholesterol was way too high, so the doctor enrolled me in a 'cholesterol class.' When the teaching dietician walked into the room for the first class, she greeted us with "good afternoon cheese and ice cream lovers." The entire class realized that she had our numbers, and so do all the commercial ad makers. I try to tell Stuart that perhaps the answer is to get the schools to try something new, like educating students about the four R's: Reading, 'Riting, 'Rithmetic and Reducing fat, cholesterol and calories.

Myra is busy preparing for Vito Renzi's murder trial, and I promised to stay out of her way with my sexual harassment case until her trial is over. I fax her the official police report I have on the murder, just in case she had received only a 'doctored' copy. The district attorney's been known to play that trick on defense attorneys in the past, and he'll surely be out for blood this time around, after what Myra did to him on the doc's case.

Suzi isn't too happy with my helping Myra on her murder defense. The kid was obviously quite attached to the victim. In one of her brief moments, she consented to listening to my explanation that until the triers of fact, whether they be judge or jury convict, the defendant is presumed to be innocent. It's the prosecution's burden to prove him guilty, not the defendant's job to prove his own innocence. This is all nice textbook stuff, but when it hits close to home and you personally know a victim, a lynch mob looks like a much better alternative. I sympathize with her. She doesn't know it at the time, but she really doesn't have much to worry about. The case looks like a slam-dunk for the prosecution. So easy in fact, that Miller has once again decided to try it himself. He wants his chance to humiliate Myra and make a last ditch effort to gain back the voters' confidence. Poll numbers show that his favorable rating is taking a nosedive. If he doesn't win this murder trial, he'd better start updating his résumé.

Part of any defense attorney's job is to also investigate the victim. I know that Myra will be doing this, so I give Suzi a heads-up and let her know (by e-mail) that if she knows anything about the victim that might affect the case, she'd better be completely honest about it and tell Myra.

I can tell that she's conflicted over my request. Over the weeks that we were working on the doc's case, it looked like she was getting quite friendly with Myra and certainly respects her as a trial lawyer. In some way she probably felt betrayed when someone she considered a friend wound up defending the guy accused of killing someone very close to her. I tried to explain to her that neither Myra nor I would normally go out of our way to represent that man, but this was different because it was a court-ordered appointment, and as a sworn member of the Bar and officer of the court, you can't turn it down just because you'd rather not do it. Myra even went so far as to notify the clerk that any fee she was to be awarded for her work on the case should be donated to a charity of the victim's family's choice.

Lawyers don't have the same luxury that doctors enjoy. When you're an MD on call in an emergency room and they wheel in two patients on gurneys, each one suffering gunshot wounds, the doctor doesn't have time to stop and inquire which one of them is the good guy. He just does his job and tries to save both of their lives. I don't remember ever seeing someone protesting about a doctor who saved some bad guy's life by performing an emergency procedure. To the contrary, it seems like the public would rather that the accused's life be saved on the operating table so that he could be put on trial, get convicted and serve eight years in prison, and then get paroled to continue his chosen career of crime. Even more confusing is when an execution is put on hold because the convict is ill.

The explanation to Suzi isn't sinking in. I try to build up my case with a logical series of questions. "Do you think that a person accused of a crime is entitled to a trial?" She gives me an affirmative nod. "Do you think that the accused should be entitled to have an attorney represent him at trial?" I take her silence as acceptance of the premise. "Do you think that the only type of lawyer allowed to defend a person accused of murder should be an attorney who believes that murder is appropriate behavior in our society?" More silence. I think I see the dog nod. "Okay, then if you agree he's entitled to a trial by an attorney who doesn't agree with the acts he's accused of, who should represent him? It's got to be someone, and since most criminals can't afford to hire a dream team, it's the court's job to appoint some lawyer to do the job.

"In most instances where there's only one defendant involved on a non-capital case, a deputy from the County's Public Defender's office handles it. If there's more than one defendant involved, the public defender can only handle one of them. It would be a conflict of interest for that office to handle more than one, because it would compromise one defendant's right to testify against the other. In cases like that the court usually chooses from a list of lawyers on the 'appointment' list. On high profile capital cases, the court can use its discretion to appoint anyone it wants to handle the case, usually someone the judge feels is competent and can give the accused good representation. So there you are. Myra is handling the defense. She doesn't have to like the guy or believe in his innocence, all she has to do is make sure that if he gets convicted, he's had an opportunity to have only admissible evidence properly presented against him, and that anything that could possibly be used in his defense is presented to the trier of fact, be it judge or jury. And if she fails to do that, then she's a failure as an attorney." They walk out of the room without making any comment. I don't think the dog was convinced either.

I don't know how she did it, but Myra convinced Renzi to cooperate with the civil case. Maybe she told him that showing he can be a stand-up citizen and cooperate with a court's discovery order might help him at time of sentencing if he loses the criminal case. It doesn't really matter what she said, the important thing is that with the approval of the County Jail, we are going to be allowed to take his deposition in one of the jail's attorney visiting rooms.

I've been in L.A.'s old County Jail many, many times, but never was very comfortable with the *Sally Port*. Before you can enter the area where the 'general population' is, you walk into a portion of the hallway that has a double set of sliding, barred doors. The first one opens and you walk in. Then that first door slams shut behind you and you're completely locked in between the two doors. After the first door slams shut the second one slides open, allowing you to continue walking down the corridor towards the visiting area. The system is designed so that at no time can both sliding doors are allowed to be open at the same time. It seems so nice that prisoners aren't allowed to casually stroll out like regular citizens; it fosters creativity so they can figure out other ways to escape, and they do. But Vito Renzi didn't, and the guards have him sitting in the lawyers' conference room waiting for us.

It's a small room but we all manage to squeeze in there, all six of us, including me, Myra, Vito, a guard, the court reporter and Palmer's insurance lawyer. Myra insists on being there to make sure that there won't be any mention of a fact that might possibly relate to the criminal case. I don't object: there's nothing like another friendly face around when you're in jail.

As expected, Renzi denies any abusive behavior towards Maggie. In his mind, all the acts he's accused of were invited by her and definitely

267

welcomed. She was just playing coy by pretending to be embarrassed by them. This is typical thinking for people who are accused of acts like this. In their own mind everything they do is justified. They're not doing anything wrong, it's everyone else's fault for misinterpreting it, and the alleged victim is only lying about her feelings by overacting and saying what her lawyers want her to say. It's all a conspiracy for greedy Jewish lawyers to make money.

After hearing the eloquent Mister Renzi give us his opinions about women and Jewish lawyers, I think I've heard about all I need to decide that I'd love to get him up in front of a jury. I thank Mister Renzi for cooperating and sharing his thoughts with us and end the deposition after only twenty minutes, instead of the planned two hours. During my questioning I wasn't interrupted once with an objection by either Myra or the insurance defense attorney. Everyone in the room but Renzi knew what type of personality we were dealing with. He's nothing but a racist sociopath and a sexual predator.

Maggie, Stuart, Jack and my office staff are all pleased with the results of the deposition. Armed with the printed transcript and the affidavits of several other former female employees of Palmer's restaurants, we have a pretty good chance to settle this case for a decent sum. Interrogatories answered by Palmer's attorneys show that they never followed the proper procedures as set forth by federal law. In 1991 Congress amended Title VII to permit victims of sexual harassment to recover damages, and in 1993 the U.S. Supreme Court broadened the reach of the law by making it easier to prove injury.

These developments caused most concerned businesses to put certain safeguards in place, both for the employees and the business itself. The courts will generally find an employer liable for hostile environment and sexual harassment by a supervisor or co-worker when the employer failed to establish an explicit *written* policy against sexual harassment, and did not have a reasonably available avenue by which victims of such conduct could complain to someone with authority to investigate and remedy the problem - someone other than the accused harasser.

The fact that Palmer was also rumored to consider himself quite a "lady's man" added to our complaint that he violated the law further by not providing an avenue of complaint to someone who is not involved in or condones that type of behavior. The insurance company said they'd consult with their client and get back to us. I only hope that the same defense attorney who attended Renzi's deposition in jail will have an opportunity to hear Palmer speak off the record. If so, he'll realize that they're both cut from the same bolt of cloth when it comes to lack of respect for women. These are two excellent witnesses for us to sicken a jury with. If they have a brain, they'll settle, especially because I elected to file Maggie's lawsuit in California state court instead of federal court. While each state must follow the federal guidelines, the states are also allowed to be more liberal towards victims, and California courts are. After all, this is the state where the 'casting couch' was invented.

There should be a law against most of the local news seen on television. It's so depressing. Due to Suzi's self-imposed cooking strike during the trial, I'm eating my thawed-out eight-ounce Trader Joe's Spinach & Mushroom Lasagna, as the blow-dried newsreader works from his teleprompter. "And now, here's an interesting development in the parking lot murder of that Chinese restaurant owner; this morning, Myra Scot, the former district attorney who recently beat her old boss in a high profile fraud case, informed the prosecutor's office and the court that she would be claiming her client acted in self defense when taking the life of that restaurant owner. We caught up with district attorney Miller later this afternoon and he made this statement."

There he is, in the flesh. The famous Bill Miller, looking like he just stepped out of a men's store window. The silk in his tie matches the silk in his exposed kerchief, and I'm sure that the leather of his shoes matches the leather of his watchband. It's too bad that he has to speak. It detracts from the fashion statement he makes.

"Mizzz Scot is showing us how desperate she is now. There's no way that the small, wiry victim could have threatened that husky defendant in any way, but we do have to thank his lawyer for saving us the trouble of proving that he shot the victim. You see, you've got to admit doing something before you can claim you did it in self-defense."

Fortunately the reporter is still awake, so he gets to ask one question.

"But Mister Miller, Miss Scot claims that the victim had a weapon, which he drew first. She claims her client shot the victim to save his own life."

"I want to say right here and now that the murder took place on a Tuesday afternoon, outside of

270

a restaurant that was hosting an inter-agency meeting of several local law enforcement organizations. Within a minute of the murder, the crime scene was crowded with over twenty professional, experienced law officers and a complete search took place. The victim was not armed. No weapon was found. I look forward to addressing that defense in the trial."

Suddenly this dinner doesn't taste as good as it did when I ate the first half of it last night. What is Myra doing? She would've stood a much better chance just admitting that her client was there that afternoon, but that the victim was alive when their brief meeting ended. They never found a murder weapon. I think she'd be better off denying the shooting and trying to establish probable cause that someone else killed the victim after her defendant left him; someone like maybe an Asian gang from the Gardena casinos. It couldn't hurt to blame the shooting on someone who the well-dressed district attorney was known to have made public statements about in the past, claiming his belief in their guilt. But who am I to tell her what to do? I never could do it during our marriage, and I'm certainly not going to try now. You'd think that Suzi would be happy to hear that an impossible defense was going to be raised. Now the killer of her 'uncle Charlie' would certainly be convicted. Every day she seems to sink even deeper into her blue mood. Maybe it's because she feels bad about how badly Myra will be embarrassed in court when she loses the trial. This is a lose-lose situation for the kid. Even if her uncle's killer is convicted, she'll still feel bad for her friend, the lawyer who lost the case.

Myra and I agreed not to communicate while she was handling this case. I want to honor my part of the agreement, so I don't call her at home to tell her my concerns and give her any strategy advice. She's a big girl now.

The doc's insurance claims are coming along fine. And it looks like we'll be able to get something in the neighborhood of fifty thousand for Maggie. The Doc will collect his two million policy benefit plus whatever punitive damages we can stick that company with, notwithstanding their clever tactic in suggesting we wait and settle the whole thing at one time. I let them know that we don't think waiting years for this matter to drag through the courts is such a good idea. My court motion is successful in having the matter severed, so that they have to pay the two million dollar policy amount immediately, and let the punitive damage portion take its normal course through the civil legal procedure.

Thinking that everything is under control never seems to work for me. It's like trying to sit down and get some reading done. Something always interrupts my solitude, and this time it's Stuart, who always manages to snatch defeat from the jaws of victory. He calls to let me know that he's being sued. I tell him not to worry, that we can stall any civil suit for at least two or three years. He can't wait for a meeting at the boat. He's too emotionally involved in it and insists on telling me over the phone, and there's no stopping him. According to Stuart, one of his weight loss supplement 'clients' has been taking that product he sells. After about six months on the stuff, she claims she's become a nymphomaniac. I have trouble trying to figure out how she'll go about proving up that claim at time of trial, but would sure like to see her try. This is definitely a new area of the law, one that I'm not really familiar with. From what Stuart says she's claiming that he negligently failed to have the product properly tested by a lab, and that his negligence has caused her condition. If I understand her contentions correctly, what she's proposing is that Stuart is liable to her on a theory of 'Negligent Nymphomania.'

This case is too interesting to pass up, so I start doing some preliminary research and can find only one case that even comes close to this one. It's an old case from back in the nineteen sixties. A woman was struck by a San Francisco cable car and she claimed that the trauma caused her the same problems: she became a nymphomaniac, and she got fifty thousand in a settlement. I tell Stuart that this is probably the best thing that could happen to him. If news of this case were to get out, he could make a fortune selling that potion to husbands and Lotharios all over the world as *"Stuart's Aphrodisiac"* and claiming that Sexual history has been made! Maybe he can make a deal with Pfizer and put together a 'his-and-hers' gift package containing a porno video, a thirty-day supply of his love potion, plus a batch of Viagra pills. Just what any fading relationship needs for a kick-start. I'll bet that Doctor Phil would endorse it on one of Oprah's shows.

Stuart is not amused. "Don't you understand? They want to drag me into court."

"What's the matter pal, when she struts into court looking slender, sexy, and all worn out, there won't be a guy in the country that'll vote against you. The jury will be all yours. It'll be a great victory for you and your product line." It's easy to give advice when you're not the one being sued. I tell him to try and relax and to bring any more legal papers he receives to my office. We'll handle his defense. Stuart follows my advice and a few days later he brings me the Summons & Complaint he was served with. I turn it over to my office staff for preparation of an answer and immediately notify the plaintiff's law firm that we want to take her deposition. I want to see this dame, mostly to find out what kind of whack job gets horny from taking the stuff that Stuart sells. Too bad I gave him that bottle back. I should have gotten Myra to try it.

Now that the doc has his first two million and is taking a round-the-world cruise on some big ocean liner, and Maggie's case will surely be settled soon, I have the time to devote to Stuart's case. He has plenty of money now, so he's obviously a target defendant. I let him know that if he weren't so successful, this case would never have been thought of to begin with. He agrees with me about the benefits that the publicity might bring him, so he givers me carte blanche for expenses in pre-trial discovery, motions and investigation. The game is afoot.

Our office schedules the plaintiff's deposition in the conference room of our court reporting agency's office and we're told to meet her outside the building at the downstairs newsstand, so that all of us can go upstairs together. This is another strange request from my office, but after a while I've gotten used to it so I just do as I'm told. Right on schedule the Plaintiff, Miss Nancy Cook shows up with a tall, distinguished man dressed in an expensive suit. I assume he's her attorney, so we shake hands like fighters do in the ring before the bell rings for the first round. We go upstairs together and are all seated in the conference room. The Defendant is also entitled to be present at all official proceedings, but after a lengthy discussion I convince Stuart to not be there. I want a clear crack at her without distractions or intimidating glares of contempt or disbelief being silently exchanged across the conference table.

The questioning begins as I read off of a prepared list. The people in the room look a little surprised that we're spending the money for this deposition just to simply ask Interrogatory questions, but I wanted the opportunity to see this plaintiff in person. My personal opinion of her is that she has always been a closet nymphomaniac, but finally latched onto a profitable way to 'come out.' She's an auburn-haired girl in her late thirties, with far too much makeup on. Not exactly in the Tammy Fay Baker category, but still too much for my liking. And you don't have to be a Saint Bernard to smell this human a mile away. It is definitely eau de cheape.

We go through the statistical stuff first: name, address, date of birth, occupation, driver's license number, job history, and on and on. She worked in several companies as a receptionist, and in between those jobs was a manicurist. My impression of her is that it wouldn't be too difficult to establish her as a party girl, but because she had never been engaged or married, it would be tough for us to establish a pattern of her sexual behavior. There's always a possibility that she might get away with proving up

275

an insatiable appetite for sex even if she didn't act on the urge. It's always a crapshoot when you get to court, so we have plenty of homework to do on this one. I hate to do it, but the questions have to be asked about her sex life, past boyfriends and all the steamy details. Strangely, she doesn't seem to mind. In a way, it's like she's exhibiting herself by parading the blow-by-blow description of her sex life for us would-be voyeurs. I've never handled a case like this before and have no idea of what a jury might think of her.

When it's prepared and delivered to the boat, I turn the transcript of the deposition over to the office so that they can give investigative assignments to Jack Bibberman. His results will either make or break the case. In the meantime, I decide to become one of the millions of couch potatoes who watch Court TV to see how the high-paid big shots do it.

My favorite local news program keeps me informed on the status of Vito Renzi's criminal case. After a week of jury selection, they finally have their people in the box and opening statements are supposed to start the following week. From what the news reports say about Myra using the self-defense tactic, I assume that her client will be taking the stand. Without any other witnesses to back him up, he'll have to tell the story in his own words with Myra trying to lead him along. I don't envy her position.

When the trial starts, Miller is in his glory. The newspaper printed his opening statement as if they were quoting from the scriptures. I hear from a friendly reporter that he took a lesson from my playbook and passed out copies of his opening to the press.

Not knowing for sure if Myra is trying to sandbag him into believing she'll use self-defense, he plays it safe with a regular opening statement, telling the jury that he'll be introducing evidence showing the defendant runs a car-parking valet service that competes with the victim's, and that the defendant had repeatedly accused the victim of 'hogging' the available parking spaces and had threatened him if the practice didn't stop. That's his show for motive. For opportunity, he promises to present witnesses that will place the defendant at the restaurant on the day of the crime, even though he usually only worked evenings.

He goes on to let them know that if Myra asserts self-defense, it is a common practice among guilty defendants who have no other way to go. Myra objects to that one and is sustained. The jury is given the customary instruction to 'unring that bell.'

Suzi follows reports of the trial and seems to be sinking deeper into her dark mood. I've given her several lectures on our judicial system, in contrast to how things work in other parts of the world, and that no matter what you think of our system, it's still the best. You can count on some uniformity from jurisdiction to jurisdiction. The laws are mostly set forth in the books, and no matter what most political protesters claim, the government and police don't have the time, money, talent, or motivation to create vast conspiracies against our citizens. I repeatedly tell her that without law there can't be any order. As usual, there's no response from the forward stateroom crowd.

I'm either the most ineffectual lecturer in the world, or she has a hearing problem. But what should I really expect from a person who comes from a part of the world where they developed 'burning in oil' as a form of punishment?

Next is Myra's turn for an opening statement. She did great when we were all working together on the doc's case, but that was the result of a prepared script and many nights of rehearsal in front of a mock jury. On this one she's on her own, and I'm a little nervous for her. The evening news sums it all up: she'll be presenting evidence to the effect that the Defendant did in fact meet with the victim in the parking lot, but during their conversation the victim lost his temper and pulled a gun. The Defendant had no other choice but to shoot to save his own life.

The first thing that the prosecution must prove in any murder case is that a murder did in fact take place, so Miller's first witness is from the medical examiner's office. The usual process goes on: establishing the credentials of the witness and then asking about cause of death, time of death and so on.

Having felt that the existence of a crime has been proved up, Miller calls a number of police officers to the stand. Each one testifies to the fact that they were inside the restaurant at the time of the murder, that they saw the victim exit the restaurant and that they heard the gun shot. They immediately ran out to the parking lot and after calling for the ambulance, they searched thoroughly. There was no weapon found on the victim or anywhere near where the crime took place. Then, just in case Myra might change her mind and not use self-defense, he brings in all the other witnesses from Palmer's restaurant, placing the defendant there and saying that he did in fact have a gun.

Maggie was one of those witnesses on the prosecution's list, but when I informed Miller's office about her sexual harassment suit against the defendant, he elected not to call her to testify. You never want a witness on the stand who has any other agenda going on with respect to the defendant. That's why any witness who has 'sold' their story to some tabloid magazine is viewed as not too credible on the witness stand. In a perfect world, a person like that would admit on the witness stand that they exaggerated their story because that's what the tabloid wanted, but their testimony in court now is really the truth. No way. Most tabloids have a clause in their contract that says if you sell them a story and then testify to something different, it destroys the value of what you've sold them and they'll want their money back. No one likes to give money back, so there's always the danger that greed will affect credibility.

The trial goes on like everyone expected. Miller is winning and Myra is losing. Her client doesn't make a very good witness. Having had the displeasure of taking his deposition at County Jail, I knew the jury wouldn't like him. He's an obnoxious jerk, and no amount of lawyer preparation can hide that from the jury.

After almost three full days of trial, both sides are getting ready to rest their respective cases. The judge tells them that the next day, if both sides are through, he expects closing arguments to begin.

This evening is no different than others. Suzi hasn't felt like cooking for the past week, so I'm boiling eight ounces of pasta, upon which will be poured a can of cream of mushroom soup, which is quite different than my other recipes which call for the dumping of a can of either vegetarian chili or Bush' nonfat baked beans on top. If it happens to be a holiday, a can of peas is added to the mix. This limited repertoire has served me quite nicely during my bachelor days. The only time that the Saint Bernard prefers being with me instead of its master is when I'm cooking. Not being the most graceful chef in the world, he can always count on some edible droppings. My concern isn't dropping stuff, it's tripping over him, because wherever he lies down he occupies quite a bit of floor space, and since he weighs more than I do, he's allowed to relax wherever he wants to. I don't want to accidentally step on him and cause a rerun of the nurse Judy affair.

I'm sitting down and eating out of my trough when there's a knock on the boat's hull. It never ceases to amaze me how my sitting down to eat or read can bring about an interruption with even greater certainty than a carwash can bring rain. The boat has fold-up boarding steps, so people can't just come aboard and 'drop in' when it's up, as it is that evening.

Looking out over the rail I see that it's Myra, asking permission to come aboard. This is a complete surprise and deserves an immediate lowering of the boarding steps. Maybe if she stays for a while I can get her to try some of Stuart's weight loss love potion. He brought me another bottle. She comes in, greets me, and upon seeing what tonight's blue plate special is comments with "the mushroom soup slop again?" After giving her the confession she wants I get right to it.

"I thought we had a deal. I won't bother you until your case is over, and you'll keep your distance too."

"You're right Peter, and I apologize, but Suzi called and asked me to come over here with an investigator from the D.A.'s office. He's down on the dock, waiting to be invited aboard."

"Well, there's no sense our being less that courteous. Please, tell him to come on up. What's the occasion? Here to arrest me again?" At this point, none of us know what's going on, but all of our questions are soon to be answered. After Myra and the investigator are seated in the saloon, I knock on Suzi's door to let her know that her guests have arrived. She comes out of the forward stateroom slowly, with her arms behind her.

Myra and I are concerned about her health. Myra asks her about it.

"Suzi honey, are you feeling okay?"

Silence. No reply. At this point the three adults are all confused. We have no idea what she called Myra to the boat for.

Myra tries again.

"Suzi, you know I'm always glad to see you, and I'm sorry about being appointed by the court to represent the man who was involved in the death of your uncle Charlie, but I'm right in the middle of a trial now, and if you won't tell us why you asked me to come over, I'm going to have to leave now and go back home to prepare for my court day tomorrow."

Suzi looks up at me. I look back at her with an expression that tells her I agree with Myra, and that if she wants to say something, it should be pretty quick, before she loses her audience.

Suzi still doesn't say anything, but she slowly brings her arms out from behind her back and we all see that she's holding a transparent plastic baggie. Through it we can see there's a gun inside. She walks over and hands it to the investigator with only three words "Uncle Charlie's gun."

22

I choke on a tablespoon of the gruel I just put in my mouth. Myra looks at her with a curious gaze. The investigator doesn't miss a beat. He takes the baggie, places his initials, date and time on the outside of it, and drops it into his briefcase.

All three of us are struck speechless. Myra breaks the silence. "Suzi, honey, can we talk?" They go out on the aft deck and have a private conversation for about ten minutes. When they return, Myra kisses Suzi, nods goodbye to me, and leaves with her investigator. I don't get any explanation. As Suzi and the dog pass by me on the way to her private domain I hear her mutter "you and your judicial system."

This is going to be too good a show to miss, so I'm going to court. Packed as it is, Myra arranges for the bailiff to save me a seat in the front row. The press has already received a leak as to what's going to happen, so there are plenty of cameras outside and in the halls. The bailiff does his usual bit of telling us to remain seated and come to order, and the judge takes the bench. The instant that the judge is seated and the case is called, Miller comes out of his seat like a jumping jack.

"Your Honor, we strongly object to what the defense is trying to do here today. She wants to re-open her case and admit new evidence. Every rule of courtroom procedure we can find says she can't do that, and we have had no advance knowledge of whatever trick she intends to pull. Furthermore…"

The judge stops him mid-sentence with a wave of his hand.

"Mister Miller, I think you've had a little too much coffee this morning. Officially, I haven't the slightest idea of what you're talking about. When we finished up yesterday, I said that if both sides were through, then I would be expecting closing arguments. At this point the defense hasn't tried any tricks yet, so let's give her a chance. Your objection in a vacuum is overruled. Now, does the prosecution rest?"

"It does, Your Honor."

"Miss Scot, do you have something you'd like to say to the court?"

"Yes I do, Your Honor, the defense would like to present a rebuttal witness."

Miller jumps up and starts to go ballistic again. The judge warns him to sit down and shut up for a moment. He then requests that both counsel meet with him in chambers. I catch Myra's attention and make a begging gesture, hoping she gets the message that I want to go into chambers with her. She thinks about it for an instant and then reluctantly gives me the signal to join her.

When we get into chambers, everyone is waiting for us. Miller shows his usual off-camera persona, pointing at me.

"What the hell is he doing in here? I want him out. He's got nothing to do with this case. He's a liar and I…" Myra interrupts him.

"Your honor, Attorney Peter Sharp has just associated in with me on this case. As soon as we get back out to the courtroom I intend to inform your clerk, so that she can make the proper notation on the court's file." The judge couldn't care less. All he wants to do is get in at least nine holes this afternoon.

"Welcome to the party, Mister Sharp, please make yourself comfortable and get a good seat. I have a feeling the show's about to begin."

Rather than let the attorneys create a battle scene, the Judge decides to calmly sum up the situation and then solicit some suggestions from both counsel. "It appears to me that we've got a sticky little situation here Mister Miller. Outside of the courtroom and not under oath, you made representations to the public at large, of which I am a member, that there was no weapon found anywhere near the crime scene. You have also made that representation here in my court, where it really counts, and I don't expect people to lie to me in here, especially elected officials like you. Then, Miss Scot here comes up with a weapon that is registered to the victim, has the victim's fingerprints on it, and reached her indirectly through a Culver City police officer that happened to be at the crime scene on the day of the murder. From what Ms. Scot has shown me, that officer has executed an affidavit to the effect that he saw one of your investigators find the weapon under a nearby parked vehicle, and when that investigator told you about it, you told him that he should wrap it up and bring it to your office. The police officer knew that what you were requesting was outside the official procedure for the handling of evidence, so when he got the opportunity, he 'borrowed' it from your investigator's automobile."

Miller is ready to explode. He doesn't say anything, but there's a strange vertical swelling down the middle of his forehead. I'm wearing my good

286

suit, so I step back, to avoid anything splashing on me if his head blows up. The judge calmly goes on "I couldn't help but notice that you never seemed to complain about the alleged theft of this gun, but by coincidence, that investigator is no longer working for your office. He is now working for Miss Scot, and was instrumental in bringing the existence of this weapon to the court's attention.

"Now, adding all these juicy little tidbits up, it appears to me that the Defendant very well may have been telling the truth, so I'll tell you what I'd like..." Miller's mouth opens, as if he wants to say something, but the Judge won't hear any of it. "Please, Mister Miller, don't say a word, sit back and listen. Among all the laws I've become familiar with, one of them is the Law of Holes, which simply states *when you're in one, stop digging*. Now that having been said, here's a humble suggestion I'd like to offer you. Why don't you just tell me that in the interest of justice you won't object to a defense motion for dismissal? I won't ask for any explanation, and then I'll go into the courtroom, thank and excuse the jury and let you use the judge's hallway and our private elevator to escape upstairs to your office, to contemplate your next move." He looks around the room. "How about it Mister Miller, am I playing golf this afternoon? They're waiting for me at Riviera, and Pacific Palisades is only about fifteen minutes away at this time of day."

As Miller walks out of chamber he mumbles: "watch out for the ninth hole, I hear it's a tough one."

Miller doesn't return to the courtroom. Instead, he sends one of his flunkies in. Myra makes the motion to dismiss and Miller's flunky doesn't object. It's all over. The reporters quickly make it out to the hallway or their news vans. Miller is the invisible man once again.

I have to hand it to Myra. She's got a lot of class. When the judge announced that the case was dismissed and excused the jury, the courtroom went crazy. The judge didn't even care. He just banged his gavel down once, got up, and made a hasty retreat to the clubhouse. Outside of the courtroom, and all the way to the car, we're completely surrounded by reporters. Myra only says that the district attorney had obviously found some weak points in his case that could only be remedied by the immediate dropping of all charges. And then one of the reporters drops the bombshell by asking a question that I didn't' think of.

"Miss Scot, since you've shown the public that you can run circles around our present district attorney, are you considering running against him in the next election?" Myra doesn't answer: she just smiles at the camera and says: "well, maybe it is time for a change in that office."

Jack, as dependable as ever, brings the Hummer around to the front of the courthouse and whisks us away from the press. Once in the car, she reminds me of something. "You know, I just remembered. My car is in the public parking lot." I tell her not to worry, Jack will drive her back for it after we've had a chance to unwind over a few margaritas at Pollo Meshuga. Neither one of us gave too much thought to Vito Renzi having been released directly from the courtroom; we figured he would find some way to get home without our help.

Back at the boat Suzi is not a happy camper, but we all know she did the right thing, so I'm confident that time will heal things for her. My main concern now is trying to save my friend Stuart's assets from this nymphomaniac. A phone call to her lawyer might help, but I can't find his card anywhere, and then remember that he didn't give me one. No problem, his identification should appear on the top left corner of the lawsuit, so I take a good look at it. His name isn't there. The caption lists Nancy Cook as the plaintiff, with her address given as being 'in care of' a legal workshop on Pico Boulevard in West Los Angeles. I drive over there and see it's one of those self-help places that provides unlicensed legal advice and typing services to "pro per" clients, meaning people filing lawsuits on their own behalf. This can go either way. Sometimes a court will bend over backwards to help a girl like this who tries to represent herself, probably out of pity for the poor person who can't afford an attorney. On the other hand, there's always an outside chance that it can work in our favor. I call our attorney service and give them an assignment, and then find out why we were told to meet Miss Cook outside on that day of the deposition. Jack was parked down the street with his telephoto lens, getting a few pictures of her.

Our next move is to set the case for trial as soon as possible and to also request a pre-trial settlement conference in chambers, at the court's earliest convenience.

The soonest available date that the judge can see us will be in a week, so it's time for me to get back to other things on my plate. I check on the parking lot situation to see how it's going and see that Vito Renzi is once again running the valet service for Palmer's restaurants and the Chinese restaurant is being as generous as it can be with the parking spaces. They now provide a 'drive-up' service, so that the take-out customers don't have to park. After calling in their Chinese food order and pre-paying by credit card, all they have to do is pull up in front of the restaurant and give their name and order number to the curbside guy, who goes inside the restaurant and then brings their order out to the car. Another problem solved.

Once the insurance defense firm had an opportunity to evaluate how their defendants would come across as witnesses, they realized how futile a trial would be, and Maggie's case settled easily for forty thousand dollars. I only took a twenty five percent fee, but with what was left over from Stuart's faith-healer case, the Peter Sharp bank account is looking good enough for me to hop over to Maui for a week or so.

There'll be nothing going on with doc's lawsuits against the insurance company for a while. Myra is busy building up a private civil law practice and contemplating running for district attorney, so I think I'll take some time off to get a little reading done under the Banyan tree. This trip is an extremely successful one. My completed reading list includes: on the flight there, *"In Her Defense,"* by Stephen Horn; under the tree, *"Hard Evidence"* by John Lescroart and *"The Judge"* by Steve Martini; in my room, *"Material Witness"* by Robert Tannenbaum, and on the flight back, *"Extreme Justice"* by Michael C. Eberhardt. This only leaves me with about thirty more to read by guys like Bernhardt, Freedman, Siegel, Turow and other guys who really know how to write and create characters I could use as roll models. I have a strange habit: every time I pass by the book section in Ralph's market, if there's a new legal thriller in paperback, I buy it. The actual reading might not take place for a year or so, but sooner or later I try to get around to most of them. To avoid buying the same one twice, I have a document in Microsoft Word saved as 'Books' that I update, print, and keep a copy with whenever I go shopping. After a book is read, I use a Sharpie to mark the completion date on the bottom, so I don't re-purchase it by mistake.

I really feel a sense of accomplishment when finishing a book. A friend of mine once suggested that I take a course in speed-reading, so I could get through my backlog of titles quicker. That thought revolted me. Not only do I *not* want to read these books faster, I wish I could read them slower. Very few things upset me more than reaching the end of a book I've enjoyed and being forced to say goodbye to those characters I've gotten to know. Where do they go when I finish the book? I want to know. I want to go with them.

The plane touches down at LAX, our Los Angeles International Airport, and I take the ten-mile taxi ride back to the Marina. I'd rather not fly at night because there's no sun shining in the window to read by, so arrangements are always made for me to get back home before dusk. When the cab drops me off at the gate to our dock, I look down and notice some activity going on. The Grand Banks is being towed away. When the taxi pulls out it has to stop by the underground parking exit to let a tow truck come up out the exit ramp. It's towing my yellow Hummer away. Leaving my luggage by the dock gate, I walk down to the now empty slip and am greeted by a throng of people that include Suzi and company, the Asian boat boys, Stuart, Jack Bibberman, and some guy with a clipboard in his hand. I hate people with clipboards; they never have good news for you and they always ask questions. They're all a bunch of little people who think those clipboards make them important. This particular twit is from a local organization known as the I.R.S. As he's leaving, Stuart is shouting out at him "you'll hear from my attorney."

People are too busy to explain anything to me. Suzi is acting like a drill sergeant, giving out orders in a foreign language. The Asian boys are running around carrying things. One runs up to the dock gate and fetches my luggage. Their spokesman comes up to me and gives me a line I've heard before. He points at doc's boat and says, "You live here now."

At this point, everything in my life is just a movie that I'm allowed to watch. My bills are paid, I have a place to sleep, there's always something to eat, and if I just stay out of the way of anyone who has a Saint Bernard, my life may go along just fine.

Doc's 42-foot Californian trawler is a nice boat, but nothing compared to the Grand Banks. I've had some experience in the aft stateroom, so it isn't a completely new environment to me.

Stuart finally confesses that he's been so busy for the past few years he never got around to filing either state or federal tax returns. He was also too busy to pay attention to their very nice invitations to join them at their office in the nearby Federal Building on Wilshire and Sepulveda. And, because of his deposits of the large settlement checks from his uncle's death and the faith-healing incident, some bells must have gone off at the I.R.S. center and they decided it was *their* turn to take a bite of the apple.

Unfortunately, the apple includes the Grand Banks that was still in Stuart's name, as well as the Hummer, which he bought for me after the faith-healing case settled, but put the title in his name to protect if from my ex-wife's lawyer. Well, as the Elvis song says, "Easy Come, Easy Go." I don't have either the energy or the knowledge to help him get his things back. To tell the truth, it's partly my fault that they were taken away from me. If I weren't trying to hide my assets from a then-angry wife, or trying to invent some way to avoid paying income tax on my earnings, I would have taken regular fees, paid my taxes and purchased the boat out of probate from L Martin's estate - and bought the Hummer on my own. Now, as a result of my own greed and stupidity, I'm off to the Hertz Rent-a-car re-sale lot to buy a one-year old rental return Mazda 626, and it'll have to do for a while.

Fortunately, Suzi was able to contact doc somewhere on a cruise ship and he graciously offered us his boat to stay on. It looks like he's not coming back for another year or two, and when his insurance case finally settles up, he'll be able to afford to buy George C.'s boat.

Not having a hell of a lot to do, I decide to turn full attention to clearing up Stuart's negligent nymphomania case. Maybe that way I can get him out of my life. He's really a nice guy and quite

293

harmless, but every time I get involved with him I wind up getting screwed one way or another.

Stuart's pre-trial settlement conference is scheduled later during the week, so I get together with Jack Bibberman to go over the results of his research assignments. If things line up the way I plan, I hope to be able to 'thrust ho' that nymphomaniac right out of court. Stuart complies with my request. When we all pile into my like-new Mazda, I see that he brought along the box I asked for.

This time there are no reporters on the courthouse steps. Nymphomaniacs aren't that important to them if it's not 'sweeps' week on television. During the rest of the year, strange sexual habits aren't big local new in Los Angeles.

The clerk leads Stuart and I into the judge's chambers, and at my request, the court reporter joins us. I notice that the tall well-dressed lawyer-like man has once again accompanied Nancy Cook, the nymphomaniac Plaintiff. Once we get into chambers and introduce ourselves to the judge, he signals the reporter to start the record, and then makes some remarks to indicate the name of the case and our purpose for being here. At this point, I make my first move "Your honor, for the record, we would request that all parties in the room identify themselves and state what their connection to this case is." I go on to set a good example by stating my full name and State Bar number, and then add that I represent the Defendant, saying that he is present, and spell his name out too. Then I look over to the well-dressed man. "Your turn, sport." He looks more like a judge than the judge does, so no one ever stopped to question his identity.

"My name is Duane Hendricks and I am with the new West Los Angeles Center For Justice." I can't resist this one. It's too good to let go by.

"Excuse me Mister Hendricks, but I didn't hear you say what your California State Bar card number is. Perhaps the judge would like to hear that; I know I would." The judge nods and looks at him.

"I don't need a license to practice law. I am a sovereign state citizen and we are not compelled to comply with any of your petty unconstitutional judicial rules. I am here to assist this injured woman and to see that she isn't brutalized by this corrupt system." With that, he sits down and glares at everyone in the room. The last time I was glared at like that was this morning by the cat.

I've got to hand it to the judge. He keeps his cool and picks up his phone: "no more calls please, we've got a winner." Shortly after the phone hits the hook, two large bailiffs appear and, to Mister Hendricks' dismay and objections, they rather strongly insist that he follow them back out to the courtroom. Just before he leaves the room, the judge gives him a break. "Mister Hendricks, I didn't see you practice any law in here, so I'm not turning this matter over to our City Attorney's office for misdemeanor prosecution, but let's leave it at my letting you know that I'm not looking forward to ever seeing you in my courtroom again unless you confine yourself to the peanut gallery. And if you don't believe in drivers' licenses either, please take a cab back to wherever you came from today.

"Now, Miss Cook, would you like a continuance of this settlement conference so that you can get a real attorney? Or would you like to continue representing yourself, keeping in mind the old adage about having a fool for a lawyer?" The judge's reference to representing one's self is obviously lost on her. She wants to get on with the case right here and now, probably feeling that the sooner it's over, the sooner she will be declared the victor, and get some money for a new trailer.

Unfortunately, I have something else in mind for her. As easy as it is going to be, it bothers me that I don't have a real opponent. It's like a professional baseball team playing the Cubs. Is it really a victory when you win? This dame's not unlike a lot of other people who are only interested in using our system of justice like a slot machine, not too unlike my own client. I smile at her. "Miss Cook, I have nothing against you personally, but I'd like to point out some things to the court and give you a chance to respond. First of all, the name you filed this suit under, Nancy Cook, is not the same name you've always used in the past, on other lawsuits. We have affidavits here from people who have identified you from your photograph as being Nanette Cook, Norma Cook and several other people, all having filed lawsuits in pro per, representing yourself, with the assistance of Mister Hendricks' make-believe factory. Due to the fact that you've acted as your own attorney in all of these matters, I'm going to invoke my client's rights under section 391b of the California Code of Civil Procedure, which provides that if a person has brought at least five actions other than small claims court suits within the past seven years that can be considered frivolous or unmeritorious by the court, that person can be declared to be a vexatious litigant and be barred from bringing further court actions without procuring the representation of a licensed attorney.

"Like the courts in general, I don't like to see matters bounced out without a proper hearing, but you push the limit. These copies of the cases you've filed were so far out of touch with reality, that you should be ashamed of yourself. The mere fact that you wound up with settlements as nuisance claims and don't have any defeats on your record doesn't really make that much of a difference. I resent the fraudulent way you kept changing your name on the cases, which were no doubt done for the sole purpose of avoiding what we've caught you doing. I suggest that you forget about this ridiculous claim of yours and head for the door, and just so there are no hard feelings, I've convinced my client to allow you to leave with a small gift." On cue, Stuart opens the box on his lap and displays a dozen bottles of his weight-loss-nymphomaniac juice. "This stuff must be doing a great job for your weight loss, because if you don't mind my saying, you really look nice, so why don't you just take this peace offering and let's call the matter closed." She looks at the judge, hoping for some help. None is forthcoming. He is even apologetic.

"I'm sorry Miss Cook, but there's nothing I can do for you this time. You've pushed your luck a little too far. I don't see anything criminal that you've done, but I sure don't appreciate you bringing that trained monkey in here with you. I was thinking he wasn't a real lawyer because his suit fit so well. Please, take the box of love juice and don't let the doorknob hit you in the rear as you leave."

She isn't too happy, but even as those shirtless guys on the "Cops" shows indicate, they can tell when it's over. They just lie down and wait to get handcuffed. She knew it was over for her when I exposed Mister Hendricks and had him thrown out of the room. The judge is happy, I'm happy, and Stuart is happy. On the way back to the Marina we stop at Pollo Meshuga for some vegetarian burritos and topless Patrón Margaritas.

I get back to the Marina while it 's still light and notice that Sally the sign painting girl is working on the back of doc's boat. She's doing some lettering. I walk back up to the street and down the next dock to see what she's painting. It's a new name for doc's boat. It has now become "the Suzi B." Just like I was trained, I don't say anything until a day or so later.

I casually mention to Suzi that it's not nice to paint your name on other people's boats without getting their permission. She has her argument all prepared. I feel like I've created a monster. She only asks one question: "Would you mind if I painted it on your boat?"

"That's a different story. Of course I wouldn't mind if it was my boat, because then it would be your boat too. But this isn't my boat, it's the doc's boat." At that point she does her own little 'thrust ho,' by handing me a note from the doc.

Peter, you've done a great job for us. My sister-in-law Judy and I have become really close and have decided to keep on going around the world on this cruise ship. Rita will be flying in from time to time to visit with us whenever we're at a place with an airport large enough for one of her planes to land. In the meantime, Suzi's e-mails make it look like you need a place to stay, so I've instructed my business manager to transfer title of my boat over to you and her. It's the least I can do, and you've certainly got it coming as a fee for helping us get the first part of the insurance company's money. Enjoy.

On the way to her stateroom she gives me a closing remark. "That Grand Banks you blew by not exercising your option to buy it from Stuart was our fee for settling the wrongful death case of his uncle, so it actually belonged to the firm." I couldn't argue with that. She is Melvin's only heir and entitled to his portion of that fee, and the other fees that may be due from Stuart. She's right again. I'll never win with this kid, but at least she talked to me again.

There's a new collection of locked-room mysteries I'm going to check out of the Marina Library, so I've decided to make it a long afternoon walk over there. I estimate that it's about a mile from the boat and a very scenic trip past the Marina City Club Towers, the Ritz Carlton, some restaurants and the fire station.

My cell phone is securely clipped onto my belt and I'm about half way to my destination and feel a vibration. I must have inadvertently activated the vibrator function on my cell phone, and it's a good thing that I did, because with the traffic passing by I probably wouldn't have heard it ringing.

Looking down at the screen I see that it signals a 'text message' has been received and can't help but marvel at this technology. The cell phone, just like the computer and satellite dish were some technical developments that I fought against availing myself of for as long as possible. But once purchased, became part of my existence and it's now hard to believe how I survived so long without them.

Checking the text message feature, a note from Suzi appears. I scroll through it.

An older grayish-haired man from the big boat on our end tie was here. He left something for you on your bed.

The end tie? That's where George Clooney's boat is docked. Is this possible? Could George have actually come to visit me on my boat? The famous George Clooney coming to see prominent attorney Peter Sharp? This is what I've been waiting for. Forget about the library, I'm jogging back to the boat. I knew it. He must have appreciated that DVD I left for him to watch and stopped by to thank me in person.

My breath is getting short now. It's been too long since my last jog. I see our dock now. Ah, here we are. I'm really out of breath, but I made it back and am now going to see what gift George left for me. There it is… a small package on my bed with a note attached. It's the DVD I left with his skipper. Stuck on the front of the package is a post-it note that says *please stay away from my boat. G.C.*

At least I got his autograph.

———◆———

The Peter Sharp Legal Mystery Series

#1: *Single Jeopardy*

Attorney Peter Sharp has been wrongfully suspended from the practice of law and thrown out of the house by his soon-to-be ex-wife, a newly appointed deputy district attorney. As a result of the eviction, he's forced to live in their back yard on an old, poorly wired, 40-foot Chris Craft cabin cruiser he's restoring, that is in danger of burning up at any time.

To make matters worse, as the result of trying to help someone fill out some claim forms, he gets arrested for conspiracy to defraud an insurance company. His alleged co-conspirator, a man charged with murdering his own wife to be with a beautiful flight attendant, is about to discover that Peter is also sleeping with her while the man is out of town. As Peter fights to get his law license reinstated, he discovers the secrets behind two murders, a fatal plane crash, and who framed him with the State Bar - all with the help of his legal ward Suzi, an adorable, quiet (at least to Peter) ten-year-old Chinese girl and her huge Saint Bernard.

Peter also gets involved in matters concerning sexual harassment, vexatious litigation, double jeopardy, and a groundbreaking case of *Negligent Nymphomania.*

#2: *...By Reason of Sanity*

In his second Adventure, Attorney Peter Sharp gets retained to defend a man accused of capital murder. The only things making this case a little harder to defend than most others are that the client's acts were captured on videotape, he confessed to the police, and he wants to plead guilty. To make matters worse, the District Attorney's office has brought in a special prosecutor for the trial: Peter's ex-wife Myra.

While he's preparing for trial on the murder case, Peter is also hired to represent an insurance company, to defend it against a man who slipped and fell while inside a bank that was coincidentally robbed later that same day. Peter thinks the case would have died when the claimant was murdered, but at usual, he's wrong.

In this adventure, while Peter is involved representing Vinnie, the prolific, peeing pornographer, he also helps solve several bank robberies by catching the entire gang, and makes the acquaintance of a new friend who runs an autopsy store - all with the help of his legal ward, the adorable ten-year-old Suzi and her huge Saint Bernard.

#3: *A Class Action*

In his third Adventure, Attorney Peter Sharp is retained to represent a man accused of murder, by the planting of bombs in vehicles. The client is also suspected of being part of a conspiracy to assassinate the President of the United States in an upcoming Fourth of July parade.

With the assistance of his legal ward Suzi, Peter cracks the case, identifies the real murderer, and at the same time solves the mystery of a dead body found in his friend Stuart's automobile trunk... all while falling for a lesbian lawyer, winning a Will contest, breaking up a stolen car ring 4,000 miles away, and battling with his ex-wife, who has been elected to the office of District Attorney.

In the adventure's finale, Suzi miraculously manages to get 'Bernie,' her huge Saint Bernard into a courtroom, where she makes her first official court appearance, holds her first press conference, and becomes a local television hero.

#4: *Conspiracy of Innocence*

Suzi once again saves Peter's case by finding the connection between two crimes that allegedly took place in different parts of the State, one of which Peter was arrested for. And once again, Peter falls for a woman who he thinks could really 'be the one' this time.

Peter's ex-wife Myra must make the decision as to whether or not she should resign from prosecution of a case in which she may have a conflict of interest – Peter's murder charge.

Everyone including Peter is sitting on the edge of their chairs as this double murder mystery comes to a shocking conclusion that involves a mafia hit man, revengeful drug dealers, a local police chief, and the ever-popular FBI.

#5: *...Until Proven Innocent*

Tony Edwards, A dock neighbor of Peter's, is charged with murder. Unfortunately, he is a suspended police officer with a known dislike for people who are the color of his alleged victim. He's also the subject of many citizen complaints for using excessive force in the minority community.

At Suzi's request, Tony has taught her how to help him re-load his target practice ammunition, also giving the little girl a basic course in ballistics.

When a local black movie producer who Tony was working for gets killed, Suzi and talks Peter into handling Tony's defense... which doesn't look too good because he was arrested at the scene of the murder with his gun still smoking.

Along the way, Peter once again gets involved with who he thinks might be 'Miss Right,' represents a 500-pound woman who is being discriminated against, uncovers a white supremist militant organization, and also stumbles onto a group of people who are pirating DVD copies of recently released major motion pictures.

Peter's ex-wife, District Attorney Myra Scot, makes a mistake when she subpoenas little Suzi to come and testify as a prosecution witness against the defendant, Suzi's friend Tony.
After what Suzi does to solve the mystery and destroy Myra's case in court, everyone knows that the District Attorney's office will never subpoena Suzi again.

#6: *The Common Law*

Peter Sharp encounters a client with amnesia, who not only can't tell Peter what his own name is, but who also has absolutely no recollection of the crime he is charged with committing. In lieu of his memory, Peter's obtains video surveillance footage that establishes his client's guilt beyond a reasonable doubt.

The usual crew also gets involved, including Peter's close friend Stuart, Jack Bibberman the investigator, Laverne the 'amorous houseboat lady', and Stuart's employees Vinnie and Olive – who are having some disagreement as to whether or not they're legally married; and last but not least, little Suzi B. and her big Saint Bernard.

The law firm is still operating from their 50-foot Grand Banks trawler yacht in Marina del Rey, California... the vessel that Peter still doesn't know how to drive. As in past adventures, all involved continue to visit the local haunts.

One way or another each of Peter's cases winds up being a conflict with his ex-wife Myra, who is the county's chief prosecutor. He also may be more closely involved with FBI Special Agent in Charge Bob Snell than before, as they share a dangerous high-speed situation on a winding road.   Suzi's new friend Lotus and her mother also play an interesting part in this adventure as Peter finds that he is fighting a ring of credit-card fraud experts.

#7: *The Magician's Legacy*

Suzi has decided that she wants to study magic in this eighth legal adventure she participates in. Unfortunately, her teacher is the main suspect in what appears to be an 'impossible' crime... the shooting of a man in his completely locked 'safe room.'

In order for Suzi to clear her magic teacher of liability for this crime, she must convince Peter to handle the case, which he does under one condition: Suzi must help him by solving the mystery of this locked-room murder.

Her task is made difficult because all events took place in a secure 'panic room,' with steel doors in place, and no windows. Somehow, the alleged murderer is believed to have committed the crime and successfully escaped from a room that could only later be opened by a crew using blowtorches.

Suzi is especially motivated to solve this enigma when she learns that an attorney who she dislikes may be involved.

#8: *The Reluctant Jurist*

There's a mini flu epidemic going around in Los Angeles and it has especially taken its toll among Superior Court Judges in Santa Monica, who all seem to have been infected at the same conference they attended.

Peter has been 'drafted' to fill in as a temporary judge for some civil matters, but winds up getting stuck hearing a big criminal trial involving a devious attorney as the defendant... the same attorney who Peter crossed swords with in a previous situation.

Suspense enters the picture when Peter's legal ward Suzi fails to appear as guest of honor at her own birthday party, and every local state and Federal peace officer in California wants to locate her.

This is the second adventure that Peter and Suzi B. have been involved where Suzi's Saint Bernard may be partly responsible for a successful conclusion.

#9: *The Final Case*

Suzi dislikes a certain devious attorney who Peter keeps coming up against.

When Peter's new romantic interest invites him to a cocktail party, Suzi and the other guests are shocked by a loud noise down the hall, coming from their host's study.

Other guests at the party include the chief of police, mayor, and district attorney, who unanimously conclude that the dead body they discover is the result of a suicide.

Even Suzi is inclined to go along with their conclusion... until she learns that the devious attorney she dislikes may be involved in handling some legal matters for the deceased.
Suzi won't let go of this one. Against everyone's advice, she keeps working to prove her suspicions about that devious attorney and his connections to what Suzi believes must have been murder.

#10: *an Element of Peril*

In this tenth and newest Peter Sharp Legal Mystery, Peter faces a double task: defending a person who is charged with murder, and also trying to locate the missing victim, who was allegedly killed in a completely locked room.

Somewhere behind the tangled mess of a down-ward-spiraling celebrity starlet, a battling married couple, a missing currency trader and a disappearing corpse, attorney Peter Sharp and his legal ward Suzi must find where the truth lies.

As in the past, while Peter's client's trial nears, Suzi has failed to come up with any workable solution that can save Peter from certain defeat and humiliation in court.

You'll be sitting on the edge of your chair as you see the courtroom drama that takes place during the last few minutes of the trial.

#11: *A Good Alibi*

In Latin, the word "alibi" literally means "somewhere else," and to any person charged with a crime, it is an extremely valuable asset to have because it can mean the difference between an acquittal and a conviction.

However, just having an alibi isn't enough: it has to stand up to scrutiny, because any good prosecutor knows that breaking an alibi and proving it was fraudulently concocted can lead a sure-thing conviction.

In this eleventh adventure of the Peter Sharp Legal Mysteries, Peter is drawn into a role he never thought he'd be playing – that of a prosecutor, being brought in as for the singular purpose of trying to break a defendant's apparently 'airtight' alibi.

#12: *Legally Dead*

Nobody likes a killer, but sometimes you have to put your personal feelings on hold when you're a trained professional called upon to do a job.

When attorney Peter Sharp's former wife Myra calls to ask a favor, he finds it difficult to refuse her, because any occasion to work with her is always a pleasure for him.

The favor that District Attorney Myra asks is for Peter to represent a client in court who wants to plead guilty to a crime. A plea bargain the defendant agreed to is already in place.

Peter agrees to the contemplated one-hour of work as a court-appointed defense attorney and makes the court appearance. But when the case is called, the surprises start, and don't stop until the unexpected end of this twelfth of the Legal Mystery series, during which time Peter gets his first opportunity to defend a dead person charged with murder.

All twelve of the Peter Sharp Legal Mysteries are now available at bookstores and can easily be ordered from Ingram Book Group or Baker & Taylor book distributors. They are also available online from Amazon.com.

To order at your local bookseller or online, simply provide the title's ISBN (International Standard Book Number), or insert it into Amazon's search block.

The Series is also now available in eBook form:
see **www.legalmystery.com**

Editor's note:

If you happen to notice any blatant typographical errors in the text of this book, we suggest you bring them to the attention of the author, who was the last person to sign off on the manuscript. We feel quite comfortable shifting the blame onto him for any errors he may have missed.

He can be reached at: gene_grossman@yahoo.com

About the Author

Gene Grossman worked his way through high school, college, and law school as a shoe salesman, welder, process server, bail bondsman, tire changer, saloon piano player and 'extra,' appearing in seven motion pictures. He then spent 20 years as a trial lawyer, during which time he served as Dean of a small local law school, and taught several classes.

The film and video company he started while working in the motion picture industry produced over fifty special interest DVD titles on everything from boating, to bankruptcy. Now retired from the practice of law, Gene writes aboard his yacht in Marina del Rey, California.

You can see pictures of attorney Peter Sharp's boats, yellow Hummer, Suzi's e-cart, and Laverne's houseboat at **www.petersharpbooks.com**

Pictures on the next page are of the author, working on his next novel – in his dinghy in Marina del Rey, California, and in Avalon, over at Catalina Island.

C.S. Champe